The
Marmot Drive
John Hersey

*This low-priced Bantam Book
has been completely reset in a type face
designed for easy reading, and was printed
from new plates. It contains the complete
text of the original hard-cover edition.*
NOT ONE WORD HAS BEEN OMITTED.

RLI: $\dfrac{\text{VLM 8 (VLR 5–9)}}{\text{IL 9–adult}}$

THE MARMOT DRIVE

*A Bantam Book / published by arrangement with
Alfred A. Knopf, Inc.*

PRINTING HISTORY

*Knopf edition published August 1953
2nd printing ..... November 1953
3rd printing .... February 1968
Bantam edition / June 1976*

*All rights reserved.
Copyright 1953 by John Hersey.
This book may not be reproduced in whole or in part, by
mimeograph or any other means, without permission.
For information address: Alfred A. Knopf, Inc.,
201 East 50th Street, New York, N.Y. 10022.*

ISBN 0-553-07468-7

Published simultaneously in the United States and Canada

*Bantam Books are published by Bantam Books, Inc. Its trade-
mark, consisting of the words "Bantam Books" and the por-
trayal of a bantam, is registered in the United States Patent
Office and in other countries. Marca Registrada. Bantam
Books, Inc., 666 Fifth Avenue, New York, New York 10019.*

PRINTED IN THE UNITED STATES OF AMERICA

THE POLITICS OF
LOVE AND EVIL

Two young lovers, an obsessed and powerful man,
and a town driven by anger and ignorance
into a cruel and treacherous pursuit.

"[John Hersey] has written *The Marmot Drive*
very well . . . The narrative moves at an accel-
erating pace."

—*Washington Star*

"The style is concise, it is sometimes beautiful . . .
The Marmot Drive will occasion a good deal of
critical controversy."

—*Saturday Review*

Bantam Books by John Hersey
Ask your bookseller for the books you have missed

   A BELL FOR ADANO
   THE CHILD BUYER
   HIROSHIMA
   THE MARMOT DRIVE
   MY PETITION FOR MORE SPACE
   A SINGLE PEBBLE
   THE WALL
   WHITE LOTUS

One

ONE FOG-LIDDED DAWN in summertime a city girl, whose name was Hester, stood near the whipping post on the Tunxis village green with half a hundred strangers waiting to round up woodchucks. It was but five o'clock in the morning, and though Hester was of the sort that is always looking for something new and for someone other than who is at hand, nevertheless this early start was something almost too novel for even such as she. Self-conscious in brand-new rough clothes, she knew she was standing gracelessly, for her whole body was gelid with damp summer-cold and sleepiness and embarrassment; she was obliged to be glad that the mist hid her urban awkwardness from the villagers around her. Most of the volunteers had convened here in front of the Grange Hall. Her friend Eben had been called off on some errand and had left her alone in the crowd of murmuring strangers, his townspeople of Tunxis, in whose early morning commonplaces she could hear truculence, humor, and half-wakened malice.

"Goin' to rain?"

"Nope. This'll burn off."

1

"Positive?"

"Ayeh."

"Never knew yourself to be wrong yet, did you?"

"Nope."

"Never in your born days fired into the wrong flock, did you?"

"Nope."

"What makes you so sure?"

"My knuckle joints."

"Praise God from whom all blessin's flow!"

"This'll burn off."

A huge form, the shape of a gigantic man, loomed and went shivering past Hester, drawing eddies of fog behind it.

Hester pulled back, startled, but then she remembered the enormous citizen with the woodwind voice at the caucus the night before, and she almost laughed out loud. What a confusion that meeting had been!—these outwardly dry Connecticut people standing up, in turn and out, stirring the ancient dust on the rafters of the Grange Hall with their angry shouts and sudden laughs, their protests, cheers, and challenges; townspeople arguing about a local woodchuck drive as if it were going to be as memorable in Tunxis history as the Revolutionary skirmish on Johnnycake Meadow that Eben was always talking about. Eben's famous battle! With what funny, vainglorious ruefulness had Eben, who was at any rate a sorry antiquarian, often spoken to her in the city about that small old action! There had been trifling bravery spent in it, he had confessed; there had been only one casualty; a single embattled farmer had been given a musket ball in one of the hassocks of his seat, which he had put before the enemy during an impulsive resignation from the lists of human freedom. Yet the episode had been purified and formalized in the annals of the town, and every year during

Eben's boyhood on Training Day the townspeople had re-enacted the Engagement on the Meadow, he had told her, simulating the ill-clad Tunxismen in noble ambush of the hated, dandy Lobsterbacks, and oh, the memory of those Training Days seemed to figure grandly in Eben's view of happiness: happiness to him still seemed to be a kind of grab barrel full of gingerbread, costumes, Chinee firecrackers, dedications, maple sugar chunks, flags, blank cartridges, and callithumpian orgies on the Legion drum.

Then, with a vividness that caught her by surprise, Hester saw again in recollection the figure of the Selectman the night before, moderating and controlling the wild palaver of the caucus, quiet, dignified, firm, yet strangely a target of much hard feeling—the Selectman, Eben's father, who might become her father-in-law, or might not. Thinking of the Selectman's easy presidency of the caucus, Hester remembered, without knowing why she did, that once Eben had said to her, "Father would rather climb a tree and tell a lie than stand on the ground and tell the truth."

Why did Eben say such things? When would Eben come back from his errand? When would these people get started?

Hester could barely see, to her right, the outline of the white Grange Hall, whose miniature Palladian façade, with its blistered and off-curling paint, Eben had called to her attention before the caucus the previous evening, for her to laugh at. She had obliged; she had laughed—the Hall was comically pretentious against its simple setting of elms and maples on the new-mown triangle of the town common, as out of place, she had thought, as a cameo pinned on the flank of a moo-cow.

Near her, now, on her left at the highwayside, a boy seemed to be climbing and gymnasticating on the platform before the town notice board. This bulletin board was bolted, the Selectman had told her while they had waited for the caucus, to a perdurable cypress log that had been brought from the Carolinas by Captain Thankful Pitkin, Puritan ancestor to the present Town Counsel, and had been used "until later than one would think," Eben's father had said, as a whipping post. The boy on the whipping platform was whistling, off key, *Onward, Christian Soldiers.* Hester merely sensed the whipping post and platform and the notice board, for she could not clearly see them in the fog; having seen them at sundown the day before, she fabricated them now from the sibilant phantom on her left. She shivered. A few more volunteers were straggling onto the common. She guessed there were by this time three score or more of groundhog hunters on the edge of the green between the post and the Hall.

A young fellow in the crowd suddenly cackled over some joke with indecent hilarity, like a concupiscent rooster who feels his loins stir as the earth rolls to morning.

Hester was embarrassed. She had not realized that Eben was bringing her out from the city for this weekend with such formal intent—to show his family his serious girl, as doubtless he thought of her, and as his blunt father had made her see herself during the drive home from the railway station the day before. Besides, she had not known, nor had Eben, that the woodchuck drive was to be held this weekend; and now, in her new blue jeans and white shirt, she worried because she wouldn't know how to behave, she wouldn't know how to walk like a native in the woods. She felt childishly shy, and again something like a chill shook her.

Someone bumped into her in the darkness.

"Who's this? Belle?" a man's voice asked, and she saw a head float through the vapor toward hers, apparently peering, but in the murk it had no face; it was like a coin worn out by a million thumbs. She supposed she was blank, too, and this made her a little bold.

"You don't know me," she said. "I'm visiting the Avereds."

"Oh," the voice said. "Ayeh. We heard Eben was be-twattled after a girl from where he moved to. They say"—the voice seemed emboldened, too; it was as if Hester and this man had had a chance encounter on an ocean voyage and were not inhibited by a fixed and reminding landscape—"they say you're ripe enough to rattle." Then, hastily, a decorous withdrawal: "Thought you were Belle Sessions."

"Are we going to start soon?"

"Just waitin' for the Selectman to blow his nose, I guess. Well, young lady, what do you think of all this to-do?"

"I don't know when I've gotten up so early," Hester cautiously answered.

"Groundhogs are up and about with the sun, they don't keep city hours, I guess you know that." Then the voice was unctuous, evidently in atonement for the mild rebuke: "Whose division you in, if you don't mind my askin'?"

"The captain's a woman. I've forgotten her name."

"You in Mrs. Tuller's division? She drives to kill, that old girl, she'll keep you rustlin'. She teaches school, I had her in school some while back. I was al-ways late in the tide—on the hind end of nothin', you might say, as far as arithmetic went, and b-r-r-r, I can still feel her ferule on my hand."

"Her which on your hand?"

"She uses one to this day, you know, it's a little slap-per thing." The voice had a pleading tone. "She don't believe in all this new mollycoddlin'. She says Connect-icut's made of ledge and glacier stones and hardpan, she can't see the sense of bringing in a lot of slush at this late date."

Then suddenly, without Godspeed, the head and the voice were gone. Hester wished she had asked the man for his name; his voice had been perhaps a little too ingratiating. She considered for a moment the contemptuous phrase it had uttered: "... waiting for the Selectman to blow his nose." A qualm stirred in her as she thought of the ugly scene at the caucus the night before, when such ill will and spite toward Eben's father had been shown by the townspeople. Perhaps the Selectman's intelligence made them want to destroy him, she thought, perhaps they resented his always seeming to be talking "afore folks," with citified grammar, or perhaps his apparent goodness made them feel inwardly sick, perhaps they envied or feared him, or perhaps there was something she had not been able to discern in him that his neighbors and his son had found out. Surely their bitterness toward him was hard to understand.

■

THE TRAIN had stopped with a squeal and a shudder as the dry brakes had seized.

"Tunxis!" the conductor, standing at the open door, cried, "Tunxis!", pronouncing the name each time as if the n might become lodged in his nose forever.

Eben was all alight. Walking along the aisle of the car stooped forward, peering out the windows to find his mother and father, he bumped the suitcases against the seat arms again and again. Hester felt her face flush and wondered whether she had too much make-up on. At last she clattered down the car steps, and happy Eben came down after her, ungainly as the Jabberwock.

Hester saw a dull little station of gray clapboard, hooded by magnificent elms, and across the way she got a glimpse of a row of half a dozen store backs, cheaply built structures crowded together with a squalid, tenemental look far out of key with the clean landscapes of tilled valleys and traprock cliffs through which the train had come for the second of the two hours the trip from the city had taken; out of key, too, with the image of Tunxis that Eben had induced in her mind, of white houses and a white church breasting a quiet common. The center of Tunxis, she thought with disappointment, was to be after all just another montage of soft-drink signs, tar-paper shingles, gas-station pennants, and grinning billboards; somewhere beyond the stores she supposed she would find a rank growth of television masts, new bulrushes in a dark swamp.

Here came Eben's father walking along the platform. It was clearly Eben's father—the nose bigger than the son's, the jaw set a little more aggressively, the brown eyes brimming with the same warmth; Eben's father, no mistaking. There was a mole on the side of his chin, a small black badge as impossible to hide or forget as grief. He was wearing gray flannel trousers badly in need of a pressing and a walnut-colored coat garnished with buttons that were surely pewter. His hair was black and gray, and not fussily brushed; and he said to Eben, "Mother's in the car. So this is our Hester." Eben's mother was sitting in an old green Pontiac, a woman with a face that seemed to be compounded of skim milk and strained virtue—round, barriered with rimless glasses, not the least like Eben's in looks. She was noncommittal in her greetings, even to her own son. Hester saw in the first instant that Eben's city pretensions, his manners and "style," were, like those of so many young people they knew, erected on plain footings. On the train Eben had tolerantly analyzed his parents.

Eben got into the front seat with his father, Hester with Mrs. Avered in the back.

"Well, boy," Eben's father said, "how's the great marketplace?"

"O.K.," Eben said impatiently, and Hester imagined that his father must always ask about the city with some such ironical formula, always presumably knowing as he asked that the city was still the city, immutable.

All four were silent for a few moments. The car swung around onto a macadam road past the fronts of the stores Hester had seen from the platform; from the street they looked clean and charmingly awkward, good country stores with gambrel roofs and a brick-veneered post office. The faces of these buildings showed a fine character indigenous to their place, while the parts that were supposed to be hidden were cheap and foul in the universal way. The whole tone of the town was a pleasant surprise from this side of the tracks. The car took a right fork, moved around a curve, and rolled past the town green.

"This is Tunxis for you, Hester," Eben's father said. "We hope you're going to like it—and we hope we're going to like you."

So, with a bluntness Eben had not inherited, his father had faced the fact, as she and Eben had openly not, that she had been brought to Tunxis for inspection.

Hester's response to this frankness was delayed, because, as Eben's father spoke, she was looking at the lovely village common, which was all that Eben had helped her to picture and more. She had not conceived the sense of community such a plot of ground, necklaced with inward-facing central-hall houses, could give. The homes were built with deference to neighbors; the church and the Grange, she could see, were for the use of all, the prosperous and the hard-pressed, the educated and the benighted, the wise and the foolish, who could walk with an illusion of equality on the common grass. Then, having quickly pondered this Tunxis, Hester understood, with a lurch of feeling, what Eben's father had said and meant. She wanted to blurt out that she didn't know whether she loved Eben and certainly hadn't decided to marry him and that it was unfair to treat her like an extravagant purchase being brought home for a few days on approval; but instead she said, weakly, of the village, "It's better than Eben described it."

"He never was much at describing," Mr. Avered said. "I recollect once when Eben was just a little spicket, he came home with a gash on his forehead that needed a seamstress to fix, not a doctor, and we asked him what had happened. He said Roswell Coit had done it, and that's all he'd say. Had Roswell pitched a rock? No, Ros just did it, according to Eben. Well, had Ros tunked open his head with a tomahawk? Unh-unh, just did it. It took us a week o' Sundays to find out what Eben's 'just did it' was, but we found out. This Coit boy—he's still around here, you'll see him tomorrow—he'd asked Eben on a Saturday if he wanted to have some fun with the teeter board in the school yard, and he sat Eben on one end while he rolled over a barrel from the Booges' place, other side the road, and up-ended it opposite the free end of the teeter board, and climbed up—talking a blue streak the whole time like a sleight-of-hand artist keeping his audience fuddled—and then took a flying leap off the barrel onto the stick-up end of the teeter board, and Eben, who was a lot smaller anyway, shot up into the heavens like the frog of Calaveras County, and of course landed kerflummox on his head. Do you think 'just did it' covers that case?"

Hester hardly knew how to answer; at last she said, "So that's what the scar's from."

"It's a blessing he didn't have a concussion," Mrs. Avered serenely said.

"Rubber head," Eben said, and Hester saw that he was trying to make the best of something he had not liked.

"Son," the Selectman said, not bothering to pick up loose ends, "we're finally going to clean the woodchucks out of Thighbone Hollow."

"Who's 'we'?"

"Volunteers from the town."

"Is this another of your crackpot ideas?" Eben asked with sudden, overblown, resigned weariness.

"This young runnygade," Mr. Avered said over his shoulder to Hester in quick, strong mimicry of New England accents, "considers everythin' out-a-line that ain't done *his* way." Then, in his own tones: "Mite arrogant, don't you think? Matter of fact, he's just ignorant. What he doesn't know is that in the old days around here, when there was need or danger, we all did our jag of work together. We had house raisings, fence mendings, church daubings, bush stubbings on the roads, and all of that. We didn't like the work or each other very much, but we got a lot done. As you know, Mr. Eben," the father said mock-formally and rather severely to his son, "we're long overdue to clean out Thighbone Hollow. Those creatures are about ready to move into our front parlors, they're so full of gall."

"I saw one walking right along Sodom Street the other day," Mrs. Avered said, speaking gently to Eben, "that looked like he thought he was the Pinneys' dog—just so pleased with himself!"

"We're going to have a caucus tonight at the

Grange," Mr. Avered said, "to tell folks how the drive'll be run off."

"How can it be a caucus?" Eben asked. "A caucus is a political meeting."

"It can be a caucus because I decided to call it a caucus, and I'm the Selectman, that's how it can be a caucus."

"Now don't be high and mighty, Matthew," Mrs. Avered said.

"I don't like this young aristocrat telling me what I can say and what I can't say," the father answered.

"I'm sorry, Dad."

Mr. Avered neither accepted nor rejected the apology; he seemed not to notice it. He drove as if dreaming through the village streets at a very slow rate of speed. Now he said, "Expect to have some people raising high-tantrabogus at the caucus tonight"; and he explained to his son that since Eben's last visit home, the town had split itself down the middle over the location of a new school; half the town wanted to place it down by the Leaming property, he said, near the state fish hatchery, and the other half wanted it on Johnnycake Meadow—both fair enough situations for schools, but people had grown obstinately set on one or the other site, for all sorts of meaningless reasons. "They've lost all their neighborliness," he said. "I tell you, Hester, these folks in Tunxis can be real Yankees when they put a mind to it."

Hester, still dismayed by the realization that she was on trial, and for a moment hoping that active curiosity might be thought to equate with good breeding, or with whatever the Avereds esteemed, asked lamely, "What is a Yankee, anyhow? I have some cousins in South Carolina, you see, and they seem to feel ..."

Mr. Avered waited a few moments, after Hester's voice trailed off, and then said, "Being a Yankee doesn't have much to do with what I was just saying; cantankerousness is just a side issue. A Yankee, a real Yankee—well, that's a person who's an idealist even after he's come to see how hopeless life is. The folks here in Tunxis know the whole situation is rotten right to the core. They know their private dreams'll fail, sure as night follows day; they have a sneaking idea God's mostly a hailstone-thrower. They hate each other, they feel good when somebody goes to pot. And yet they go on living with straight backs and high hopes as if they could make everything better. Of course where they run into trouble is trying to make each other better. . . . They know how bad things are, but at least they keep trying to be decent people."

The phrase "decent people" caught in Hester's mind, and she thought of a time in the city when Eben had . . . The sudden flashing memory made her think how much she loved the city . . . Something, something in what Eben's father had said was disturbing. . . . It was in a tiny nightclub they had wandered into after seeing a musical; they had been glowing with the sentimental wish-dream into which they had for a few hours been transported. The place was just a small dark room with a bar and a piano. A waitress led Eben and Hester to a table near the piano. The piano player was a woman whose features were handsome but whose skin was evil with pockmarks—a livid battlefield, some indefinite time ago, of adolescence. There were several rather noisy, perhaps drunken, young men at the bar, revolving around one they called Duncan. After a while, Duncan went into the ladies' room, and in a few minutes he came back out with paper towels on his head, arranged in careful overlapping scallops, with water poured over them so they would stay plastered in place, and he went out on the dance floor and did a dance by himself. He was very funny. He was obviously trying to attract the piano player's attention; several of the young men tried to persuade Duncan to stop dancing and go back to the bar, but he waved them off and shouted at them, "Get away from me, all you phonies." Hester and Eben laughed at his antics, and Eben said, "I bet I can get him over here," and he walked out on the floor and invited Duncan to join them for a drink, and Duncan did. Perhaps Duncan accepted because there was a girl at the table; Eben seemed to feel grand. All the time Duncan continued to eye the piano player. He still had the towels on his head. He was really very tight. He fell out of his chair, finally, in a graceful, sprawling spill; his head hit the floor hard, and Hester thought he would have to be carried out. But he stood up. The piano player was laughing at him. Duncan began to shout that his watch had been stolen, and that he was going to get the police into the place. Before long a policeman did appear from somewhere and showed Duncan quietly out onto the street. "He was just mad because I laughed at him," the piano player, still smiling, said to Hester across the piano. The waitress serving Hester and Eben seemed upset, and after the piano player had moved to the bar to take a rest, she told them that this little nightbox had used to be doing fine, but that now the managers were going crazy, because they had booked this piano player "and they billed her 'Straight from the Tin Halo,' you know," she said, "you know, that place on Ransom Street, and the minute she walked in the door, they started coming in here. By the dozens. Drunks. You heard what he said: 'Phonies.' They hate daylight. Nothing to live for except staying up nights trying to forget the days. Look at their faces!" And then Eben, who had been laughing hard not long before, asked the waitress, evidently trying to keep his question light, "Where do we find the decent people in this town, anyway?" . . . Eben had already lived in the city for at least three years at that time, Hester realized . . . and now she was struck by this echo across the Avered generations, their vague and separate, though shared, quest for something they unclearly called decency.

"Whatever can they find to fight about tonight?" Mrs. Avered asked, leaning forward in the back seat.

"Some of these hardmouthed people can't see any purpose in cleaning out the hollow," the Selectman answered.

"They must be the ones who don't grow any vegetables," Mrs. Avered said. "If they'd had those creatures in their dooryards, they'd see some purpose."

"No, I expect they do have gardens. They're the ones who don't want Tunxis to collect any taxes to speak of, but also get deathstruck with rage if the town doesn't plow them out half an hour after a blizzard or if it leaves a puny frostheave on a back road where they have to drive."

"Well, I'm sure you'll shame them, Matthew," Mrs. Avered said placidly, sitting back again.

Soon after that, they reached the homestead—a former farm just outside the settled area of the village. The house was red, with white trim. The Avereds led Hester around to the front door, though it was obvious, from where the car was parked, that familiars usually entered through the kitchen. Inside, the house was fairly clean and smelled of cooked bacon. In the small front hall, Eben's father said sharply, "I declare, Uncle Jonathan's stopped again." He was quite angry. He opened the door of a grandfather clock and began to rattle the works. Hester remembered Eben's accounts of his father's four tall clocks, named for men who had owned them: Uncle Jonathan in the hall, after Eben's grand-uncle; Ardon (Eben's maternal grandfather) in the living room; Sam Jones, bought at an auction, in the kitchen; and, upstairs, Himself, which Eben's father had made with his own hands. All four, including the one Mr. Avered had built, had wooden movements and brass chimes, and they tolled the hours, when all ran properly, not exactly together but one by one, in order of seniority, Ardon speaking deeply first, then Uncle Jonathan, one of whose brass pipes was cracked, Sam Jones next with a whang and a whine from beside the breadbox, and finally Himself at the head of the stairs with a slightly tipsy authority. Eben had said that his father had had the patience to spend the nights of four winters carving the cogwheels of cherry for Himself, the pinions of laurel, the case of maple, and the white-wood face with its warty, tuberous numbers, and time then had seemed the least of his worries; but nowadays if Ardon ran a minute slow or if Sam Jones slipped his chime a quarter hour, it apparently drove the Select-man into furies. It seemed that Uncle Jonathan was being troublesome this season. Eben's father straightened up, turned with glowing cheeks and desperate eyes to his wife, and said, "That damned clock'll be the death of me."

■

THE BOY on the whipping platform abruptly stopped whistling in mid-hymn and began to make the noises of a rifle fired down onto a stony desert—percussion, the flight of bullet, whining ricochet; he was, it appeared, a Good Guy crouching in his eyrie, from whom all Bad Guys were getting their comeuppance as the mist thinned on the mesa. It was growing a bit lighter. An open truck drove up and parked behind another that had already been standing not far from the whipping post. Hester overheard two townspeople reviewing the caucus of the night before. "Didn't you get the goose-pimples," one voice, a woman's, asked, "the way old man Leaming threatened to spit in his face?" And the reply, from a jolly-sounding man: "It was just as good as the Selectman hittin' him in the potroast, the soft answer he gave him! You could most hear old Leaming groan." There was a duet of merry, sadistic laughter.

Eben came back. Hester could tell even before he spoke that he was angry. "They're gone and switched me to another division," he said.

"What does that mean?"

"It means I won't see you all day. I came up here to have a weekend with you, not to go thrashing around in the brush with these fogies. I knew it would be like this."

"If you knew it would be like this. . . . Can't you speak to someone?"

"Already complained to the Selectman," Eben said. "He was a great help! He said to do as the Romans do. He thinks Tunxis is Rome."

"Couldn't you ask Mrs. Tuller?"

"I tell you I spoke to my father," Eben said, as if there were no higher, no other appeal. Then he added petulantly, "I wanted to be with you."

"Me, too," Hester lied, recognizing as she said the words that she was, to the contrary, perversely relieved—perhaps because she was so self-conscious about how she would conduct herself in woods and swamps that she was glad she would not have Eben's disapproving supervision of her every footfall. "I'm sure I'll make a fool of myself," she said.

"Don't be anxious," Eben said with quick concern, his anger and distress all gone. "It'll be easy." Hester was aware of his eager warmth, but for some reason she did not feel properly touched by it.

Someone called out from the steps of the Grange

through a megaphone, telling the divisions to assemble
at various points on the green. Division Four, Mrs.
Tuller's, was told to go to the big elm at the left end of
the building. With the sound, now, of an urgent fire engine, the Good Guy hurried down from the whipping
platform and howled off across the green to his rendez-
vous.

"What division did they move you into?" Hester
asked hastily. "Where'll I ever find you?"

"I'm in Three," Eben said. "We'll be next to yours,
at least. I'll try to find you when we rest—or at
lunchtime, anyway."

The two young infatuates were pulled apart by the
mill of hurrying volunteers, and Hester made her way
reluctantly to the big tree.

About a dozen people gathered there gradually. A
short woman with a very big head, evidently Mrs. Tuller, began to speak in what seemed to Hester a gentle,
kindly tone; Hester had expected gravel to come spit-
ting out of the teacher's mouth, after what that half-
seen man's pleading voice had told her in the fog. Mrs.
Tuller reviewed the part Division Four was to play in
the drive: It was to advance across the low ground of
Thighbone Hollow, along the canal, on the right-hand
end of the whole picket line. At first, she said, the division would echelon out to the right, each person about
a hundred feet from the next, on a line of bearing that
would connect the right flank of Division Three with
the bend in the canal, which would be somewhat forward of the rest of the line at the start. Mrs. Tuller said
that her group would have to wait, holding that diago-
nal line, about half an hour while the gang of advance
men drove the woodchucks out of their burrows; this
period would require patience and diligence, she said,
since it was possible that the animals would be in a
panic and might try to break backwards through the

line, in a swarm. She reviewed the instructions on stamping, shouting, and especially whistling, and warned against rushing at the beasts. When the signal would come down the hill from Division One, up against the traprock ledge on the left flank, which was to move first, Division Four would slowly pivot forward on its fulcrum at the canal, keeping in contact with Three on its left, until it would be in a straight line with the rest of the drive, perpendicular to the axis of the hollow. Then it would move forward with the canal on its right, crowding a bit toward the canal, since the animals were liable to double back at the water's edge. "We shall move forward in order and tranquillity," Mrs. Tuller said, belying Hester's anticipation of the event. And Mrs. Tuller said, "Don't plunge too valorously into the cat brier. We want to catch the marmots in this drive, not ourselves. But hold your spacin' if you possibly can. Keep track of each other by your whistlin'." She said that to get to the starting place, the division would ride to the Spruce Gate on the Cherevoy farm in the second of the two trucks parked by the notice board, and would walk from there up Manross Lane through the woods to the mouth of Thighbone Hollow. Mrs. Tuller was done.

"Why don't we have two lines, one in front the other?" a man's husky voice behind Hester asked. "If the groundhogs form up in a tight patrol and bust through us when we're in a single line, we'll never in a dog's age round 'em up again."

"That's a good question," Mrs. Tuller said, dropping into the encouragingly patient manner of a school-teacher speaking to a slow boy in class; "but as you know, it's not up to us to think up ways of collarin' these creatures that don't fit in with the rest of the drive. The Selectman and his committee decided how we're to proceed."

"What in the name of Sam Hill does the Selectman know 'bout tactics? I don't see why our division couldn't try to do it right."

Suddenly Mrs. Tuller's voice, though it kept its warm timbre, was imperious and not lightly to be disregarded. "You'll obey orders, Roswell. I guess even in the Rangers they expected you to obey orders, didn't they?"

"I know one thing for a fact," the young fellow grumbled in acquiescence. "We never would've used ice-age tactics in the Rangers." He turned to whoever was beside him and loudly asked, "Where'd our great Selectman ever go to school to study tactics?"

This would be Roswell Coit, Hester realized, the one who had catapulted Eben from the seesaw, and she turned to look at him and could just see against the white Grange Hall a fine torso of a bully, a man as thick as his voice. Suddenly she thought of Eben as a habitual victim, dodging out of the way of arguments and fights, apt to whine under pressure, yet like a worried gamecock forever encountering, if not actually seeking out, adversaries—wits and brutes. She thought of a story of revenge he had once told her, and guessed that Roswell Coit might have been the one on whom the tables had been turned. A certain boy, Eben had said, who could "flax out any kid in school," had stretched himself one day on a slope between a big, half-rotted sawmill log and a brook and had casually told the three smaller boys before whom he'd been showing off that they could, if they wished, roll the log down the hill over him and kill him—never dreaming, of course, that they could budge it. But with a united spasm of strength nourished on resentment, Eben and the others had managed to start the log, and before the big boy could scramble out of the way, it had struck him, rolled over him, and gone on into the brook.

Hester remembered vividly Eben's delighted description of the big boy standing up, his mouth full of dry rot, his nose bleeding, his eyes streaming tears, as he spewed out, in a hoarse Yankee drawl—yes, that huskily mimicked voice must have been Roswell Coit's—his incredulous protest: "Gaul durn you boys! What on earth did you do *that* fur?"

Hester stood alone, at first, when the discussion was over, but soon Mrs. Tuller came over to her and said, "You're Eben Avered's friend, aren't you? Mrs. Sessions told me about you."

"Yes, I'm staying at the Avereds'," Hester said.

"Eben always had a remarkable head of hair," the teacher said. "There might be times when I'd use that expression to mean there wasn't much to speak of underneath the hairline," she added cryptically—giving Hester an impression, but scarcely a certainty, that this was not her intention in Eben's case.

A middle-aged man with monstrously short and bowed legs rolled up to Mrs. Tuller and, in a suppliant voice that Hester recognized as belonging to the one who had bumped into her near the whipping post (how grotesque that brief fogbound intimacy seemed now that she could see the creature who housed the voice!), he said, "The Selectman's given us the high sign to start, Mrs. Tuller. If you'd ask your people to load into the second truck—that's the one Rulof Pitkin'll be drivin'—we'll get away in five minutes. 'Preciate it."

"Thank you, Mr. Challenge," Mrs. Tuller said. "You're goin' to fall in with our division later on, we hope?" The teacher spoke as graciously, Hester thought, as if she were inviting the oddly shaped man to some lawn party or open house.

"Pleasure," Mr. Challenge said, reciprocating her formality, "—just as soon's we stink the little boogers out their burrows. I'll scamper back in your line quick's I can. Believe Anak Welch is goin' to do the same."

"Fine and dandy," Mrs. Tuller said.

Mr. Challenge half bowed to Hester, without seeming to recognize her, and then moved away on his cabriole legs, a self-important courier, to the next clump of people on the green.

"Mr. Challenge—he's our local political genius," Mrs. Tuller murmured to Hester, on a note of cautious contempt. "He pulls the wires of the Republican Party hereabouts. You can always count on fair dealin's from Mr. Challenge—as long as you're face to face with him." Then, caution predominating, she added, "We all respect him. He wouldn't lame a titmouse—though I calculate he could get a titmouse elected to office here in Tunxis, if he put his talents to it."

Hester wondered if that last remark reflected on the Selectman but, suspecting that it did, held her tongue.

Mrs. Tuller rounded up her volunteers and ushered them to the hinder truck. As she passed its cab, she stopped at the window and spoke to the shadow within: "This your conveyance, Rulof?"

"Ayeh, this is me, ma'am," the man at the wheel answered. "Would you folks like me to pull up to the whippin' platform so's you could load yourselves more convenient?"

"Oh, we're all spry as pullets in this division, I guess," Mrs. Tuller said, looking round at her flock. "We'll just clamber on right here, Rulof."

With that Mrs. Tuller moved from the cab to the rear wheel, put a foot up from the embankment of the green onto the tire, and, with an agility that was startling in a white-haired lady, moved like a spider up the web of the truck's wooden side-racks. Hester did not know whether she herself could get up at all, and she hung back.

Roswell Coit was the third or fourth to go up, and as he climbed he grumbled, "What is this—a God damned obstacle course?"

"Mind your hairy tongue, Roswell," Mrs. Tuller said with dreadful firmness.

"Sorry, ma'am," the young man said. "I dreamt I was back at Camp Whisnant."

Soon Hester, pushed by something half way between fear and vexation that was probably courage, moved forward and took her turn at the unsteady ladder. She was surprised at how easily she rose up, and at the top, where she knew she needed no help, Roswell Coit took her elbow and gave her an awkward boost that nearly upset her. Without thanking him, she edged away from him toward the tail-rack of the truck and watched in the dim morning for Eben or Eben's father, but neither one came near the truck, which was soon packed full.

A tall, fair man of indefinite age, next to Hester, with enormous eyebrows over eyes so deepset that the dawn had not yet reached them, said to her in an accented voice, "Permit me. I am Friedrich Tuller. You are young Mr. Avered's—um—houseguest, yes?"

Not sure that she liked being so widely famous in Tunxis, or perhaps notorious, Hester repeated the shaggy-browed man's last word, "Yes." Then, with a mischievous mockingbird fidelity of tone, she said, "You're our captain's—um—husband, yes?"

"Yes," Tuller said, cheerfully playing the game, mimicking Hester's treble in one syllable better than she had managed his tenor in a sentence. Then he added with ludicrous irony, "My rôle is camp follower, my wife is my captain! my captain!" Then, elaborately sociable: "How long do you honor Tunxis?"

"Just for the weekend."

"I'm so sorry," Tuller said, succeeding with his overstressed speech in sounding as if he were. "I hoped you were here on vacation and you'd come to my class. Mrs. Tuller teaches dunces, I teach the dance." And he added, with a covetousness that had no danger in it, "You have nice long legs."

"How do you know, when it's hardly even daylight?"

"I scaled the walls of the citadel after you," he said, nodding toward the side-racks. "I saw. You are ever so little knock-kneed—that helps for the dance, you know, makes you graceful." He threw his big eyebrows up and murmured with facetious passion, "I want you." For his class, he harmlessly meant, Hester understood.

"I'm sorry," she said, laughing, "but you can't have me. A metal desk on the seventeenth floor of a steel and concrete building in the midtown area has me, forever and ever."

"What about Avered?" the dancing master simply asked.

"Oh, well," Hester equivocated.

Then Hester realized that if the dancing teacher knew about her, she also knew at least one thing about him. At supper the night before, she remembered, Eben, picking up currency about various people in the town, had asked about the Tullers, and Eben's father, after remarking that Mrs. Tuller still held the seventh grade in a state of cornered terror, had said, "As for Herr Tuller, he's in his crystal-spangle phase"; and the Selectman had told how the dancing master had hired local workmen to dig up stumps from the bed of a stream and from the swamp near Johnnycake Meadow, and had dried the roots of the stumps, had cleaned certain gnarled forms, and then had suspended from the ugly pieces of water-grayed wood tiny glass spangles and droplets he had taken from an old chandelier, as if they were clear water dripping from the dead and rotten roots—"purity falling away from corruption," the

Selectman had said. Hester, wondering how this rare-fied German dancing teacher had drifted to Tunxis and into the substantial arms, the loglike arms, of the el-derly schoolteacher, decided she was beginning to feel something like awe for this town—this backwater, as she had condescendingly thought of it the day before.

Tunxis, Eben's father had said to her during that same supper, was deep enough in Connecticut to be, as he put it, "apart." It was too far from the metropolis to have been settled by a swarm of undesirable com-muters, and was just far enough from the state capital, too, to be outside the easy range of those of its well-to-do who wanted the pretense of being simple country-men. Tunxis had a scattering of summer people, the Se-lectman had said, dangerous drunken drivers who came to town meetings in city department-store blue jeans to vote in favor of local school appropriations. "I guess they do it," he said, "because they think it's charitable to pour a few mills of taxes into a poor little eddy in the stream like Tunxis, and gracious me! they are kind-hearted"—except, he had added, when a native trespasses on their precious land or when they get it in their heads that a Tunxis handyman or grass-cutter or plumber has been cheating them in his prices; "that's when you feel like a manure-spreader's just been hauled across you." Then with a strange, fierce glitter in his eye the Selectman had said to his wife, "Our Eben'll be taking a summer place up here one of these first years." He had turned to his son. "Don't forget to come to town meeting in a nice loud check shirt and brand spang new overhauls, son," he had said. Hearing this bitterness of the Selectman's against outsiders, Hes-ter had recalled Eben's telling her on the train coming to Tunxis that ever since his father had gone away to college—only twenty-three miles southwestward to a state normal school—and had come back with a certificate and a tranquil face and "a suitcase full of books and 'doesn'ts' and 'isn'ts,' " he had walked through the village as one estranged, a magician, a clown, an Oriental wise man, respected, often called upon, rarely loved—really an outsider himself. That was what Eben had said.

The truck started up. "Wait till you see the incredible valley where we go today," the dancing teacher said through teeth that chattered with the truck's motion. Then motion and changing sights relieved Hester of the obligation to converse, and she was glad to be alone among the unknown creatures who pressed against her, as lonely as on a teeming subway car. Pulling away from the village green, the truck passed through the Tunxis that was "apart," past modest porched houses standing free and away from each other, connected formally by sidewalks of huge, slanting, frost-thrown fieldstone slabs that glistened like wet steel, and informally by dark lawns lying back under great trees that still dammed back a large measure of the new day. The houses were gathered together in townhood, but they seemed to insist upon their separateness, their privacy; yew, hemlock, forsythia, and privet set up their definite screens and fortifications. The much-patched asphalt street had a steep-humping crown, which the truck seemed to have to keep struggling to surmount. Very soon the settled area of the village was behind them, and the road, after running beside a river for a short distance, turned away from it and began to oblige a series of farms. In time the truck swerved and entered one of them, bounced on a dirt road past its barns and through some of its fields, and fetched up, behind its companion, the other truck, at the edge of a meadow near a clump of evergreens, still black and mysterious in the half-morning. In the east a thin veil of sky-gauze had begun to glow with the softest of colors. "The sunup looks good on you," the dancing master said to Hester, nodding his head, as they waited for their turns to disembark.

A few minutes later Mrs. Tuller took her division—the first to start, because its right flank would have the farthest to go of any unit to get into position for the drive—through a gap in the dark conifers, evidently the Spruce Gate, and along a path set between high, casual rows of wild laurel. The path ran through hip-deep grass that was covered with dew, and Hester's blue jeans were quickly soaked. The lane climbed upward toward a kind of saddle.

The party soon reached the top of the divide, and Hester saw stretched out ahead of her the scoop of Thighbone Hollow. Up to the left was high ground, capped by a forbidding rampart of traprock, which, reaching away to the northward, set against the sky a dark, ragged limit to that side of the valley, while down to the right, running parallel to the ledge, could be seen a rigid, architectural stream of water, a gay ribbon of reflected cloudtints, the canal. Between the parallels lay that part of Thighbone Hollow through which the drive was to go, a long, melancholy stretch of woods and stone-walled fields, sloping down to low ground, some distance away, then up again at the opposite end to another saddle like this one—a shape like a lengthwise half of a spoon's bowl. At the lowest part of the scoop the fog still lay over the black terrain in pale, frayed heaps, and off to one side a sharp gray spike jutted up through the mist, a steeple with its belfry, which was, it seemed to Hester, askew, quite far from straight-standing.

Mrs. Tuller took her division diagonally across a wet meadow and through some gate bars at the far corner into a field beyond, where she stopped and said, "This is where our left flank is anchored. Roswell, will you keep the left pivot? Keep touch with Mr. Sessions' division up above there. Then, dear," Mrs. Tuller said, speaking to Hester and leading her along the stone wall, "you'd better be next here, let's see, about a hundred feet. Just mull along easy, straight ahead, whistlin' and shoutin', when the time comes, and keep track of Roswell up there and of my dear decrepit husband on your right, I'm goin' to put him next.... Now, Friedrich," she said sharply, "you're next and—let me think—we'll slip Anak Welch next to him when he gets back. . . ." Hester found herself alone at her starting point beside the wall.

She sat down on the stones, looking down into the somber hollow, shivering and waiting alone. Soon she heard, then saw, more people emerging from the laurel lane, another division taking its place; its drivers moved uphill to the leftward away from Hester, except for one man who came across the field toward Mrs. Tuller's line. She saw that it was the Selectman, who had told her that he was eventually to be in the advance party that would drive the woodchucks from their burrows. He stopped for a moment and spoke to Coit, then turned and walked to her.

"Came to see how you're making out," he said, "while we wait."

"I'm sopping," she said. "Is that steeple in the distance cockeyed, or am I?"

"That's the abandoned church," Mr. Avered said. "The spire took a twist in the hurricane of 'thirty-eight."

He sat down on the wall beside Hester and glanced at her. The sky had begun to glow more gaudily now, and the sunrise looked cheaper than Art, and Hester wondered whether the new, brighter downcast pinks were still becoming to her—if, indeed, the dancing master had not simply been flattering her when he had said she wore the first of the morning nicely.

"You look kind of streaked. Are you scared of something?" the Selectman asked.

"Yes, I guess I am," Hester said.

"What of?"

She thought she was afraid of the woodchucks' teeth. She remembered how, at the caucus the night before, the town dentist had talked about the marmots' teeth. "Incisors like chisels," he had said; and he had said the enamel is only on the fronts of the teeth, so the backs wear away and keep the chisels sharp. And she remembered he had said the jaws are hinged in such a way that they have no sidewise motion, only up and down and backwards and forwards. She was afraid of those rotating chisels. "I'm afraid of the woodchucks' teeth," she said.

"That's silly."

She was afraid of the thick skulls that woodchucks have, and what was it that the college boy with the glasses had said?—that their hides get to be a quarter of an inch thick! "They've got such thick skulls and thick skins," she said, "how could you do anything to them?"

"It's silly to be afraid of woodchucks."

"I can believe you; I guess I can. But that doesn't stop me from being afraid."

"Being a little scared can't harm you—just stirs you up. There's a woman you'll meet tonight, old Dorcas Thrall, you ought to know about her if you're timid. She's ninety-one. She was always very stout of wind and limb. To begin with, she had a queer family. There's an old well that's covered over now with a big flag of bluestone in the turnaround of the driveway on the Thrall place; they say it used to be eighty-five feet deep. One day Dorcas's Uncle George went down that well head first, and no one ever knew whether he meant to go down or was just peering down there look- ing for something and lost his equilibrium. They never got him out; spoiled the drinking water. Her father was avaricious and tight-fisted. Once he harvested a whole barnful of onions when the price of onions was on the rise, and he decided he'd hold the crop till the top of the market came, but before he knew it spring came in- stead, and the price fell kerplunk, and pretty soon the onions began to sprout and the shoots began to stick out between the boards; Evits Thrall's hairy barn was famous all over the county. Oh, they were a queer lot. Now, about Dorcas being afraid. She was always physi- cally powerful, as I say, but she had one weakness— she couldn't abide birds. Sometimes in the evening she would be out on the lawn, and the swifts would begin to dart and dip, and Dorcas's hands would flutter up around her head, and then she'd pick up her petticoats and run for safety. Birds abound in these hills, and especially around the Thrall place—it has so many chokeberries and crabapples—beautiful birds in May and June: you can hear the chestnut-sided warbler and the black-and-white warbler all day long, and wrens seem to love that house; and brown thrashers shouting their heads off! Dorcas was constantly in a panic in all the leafy seasons, as you can imagine, and the winters, with swarms of juncos and chickadees, weren't much better. Once she went to the Tullers' for tea, and the Tullers had a pine siskin they set great store by, no great shakes as a singer but a friendly codger, and the siskin got out of the cage in the room where Dorcas was, and for a few minutes everyone thought that Dor- cas was crazy for good and all. She's been fearful all her days, yet look at her: ninety-one years old, strong as a post of locust wood, and everyone says, 'What a good and happy life old Dorcas Thrall has had.' "

"I don't want to live till I'm ninety-one, and I'm still scared of woodchucks."

"I'm kind of wary myself a lot of the time—but never of groundhogs! Jehosephat! Your trouble is, you don't know enough about them."

"What are you afraid of, then?"

"My friends and neighbors: these folks are so almighty censorious."

"Don't you know enough about them?"

"Too much! It may not be the same for you, but as for me, I'm as brave as the front of a bank building till it comes to two kinds of things—those I can't see for the dark, and those I can see as clear as the pores on the back of my own hand. Half-knowledge makes me fierce and self-reliant. If I could know just a little but not too much about everything and everyone in this world, I'd never tremble or wake up in a drench in the night."

He stood up. "I'd better get back up with my crowd," he said. "About time for us to start." He looked down over the hollow with a vague, abstracted look in his eyes that Hester had seen several times since her arrival, a look of awful, absent-minded involution, as if he were a helpless voyager in a searing, epic daydream that could only be interrupted for a few minutes at a time; he ran his tongue around his mouth over his lower teeth. "Be a hot day," he finally said, coming part way back from his reverie. Then he turned and faced Hester and said straight to her, "I arranged to have Eben moved into Manly Sessions' division, because I want to get to know something about you today and tomorrow without the boy around making cow eyes at you and forever shutting me up. Also want to tell you a little about him and us, if I'm able." He looked back up toward the saddle where the laurel alley debouched and where a few townspeople were now moving to and fro; from this distance their scurryings seemed both urgent and aimless—insectile. "I don't mean to be a busybody," Mr. Avered said, "but by and large, the way two young people get themselves into a trance and get married ..." Then, looking in Hester's eyes again, so openly and cleanly returned from his daydream that she felt for a moment on the verge of true communication with another human being, he said, "I don't want to try to manage anybody's life"; whereupon she realized, with an inward shudder, that he was after all thinking mainly about himself, not about her or even about his son, and the ribbons that she had fancied about to run from his mind to hers and from her heart to his were suddenly frayed at the ends and now blew altogether away over the stone wall. Then the man himself was gone.

Even with the palpable landscape before her, its folds and recesses coming into view under the lightening sky and giving her, by the exposition at last of clear details, a testimony of reality, nevertheless she had for a moment after Mr. Avered left an uneasy feeling that perhaps she was daydreaming. Perhaps she was at her desk in the city daydreaming. Her situation—sitting on a New England stone wall waiting to take part in what the biologist at the caucus had called a "marmot drive"—was too unfamiliar, up to now too frightening and too marvelously beautiful, to partake of any reality she had previously experienced. To keep hold of the conviction that she was awake and reasonable, she tried to think what she actually knew and believed about what she was doing.

■

THERE WERE folding wooden double seats in the "speechin' room" of the Grange for about two hundred people, and not only were all of the chairs filled; people were standing around the walls and in the doorway to the hall. The outdoor night was warm; here blood and breath and village envy increased the heat. There was a pitcher of icewater on the felted table on the platform, but the six glistening people in straight chairs behind the table looked to Hester as if they thirsted for more than water—for recognition, for lenity, for something they could call love. In the hot light of high bare bulbs their faces looked hard—hard yet painfully yearning; even the Selectman's face looked oaken and awful. What a setting for "pure democracy"!—for that was how Eben had once characterized the regular town meetings of Tunxis. Here the governed villagers sat face to face with others of themselves, their own begrudgingly chosen governors, in a glaring clarity of overhead light.

The Selectman opened the meeting, speaking gravely and anxiously. "We all know why we're here," he said. "The creatures over in Thighbone Hollow are getting too forward and destructive, and we've come to a situation where we've plain got to clean them out. I don't know how many of you folks have actually run across one of the groundhogs from the hollow lately, but if you have, you know they're uncommon big and ferocious. I hefted one, about a fortnight since, and he was somewhere around the weight of the Swanson baby, which as you know is a healthy boy child more than a year old."

For a few moments Hester entertained a picture of this unknown Swanson baby as a malevolent beast of the forest, and she lost the thread of the chairman's remarks.

"... In June this summer," he was saying when she rejoined him, "groundhogs took every leaf off of Alenam Rust's acreage—that was beets and early lettuce transplants, wasn't it, Alenam?—which is three miles from the hollow and hasn't a burrow anywhere around it; Alenam's looked into that. So you can see they're bold and don't mind a hike. We used to think they were lazy—ha! Anyhow, tonight we want to let some who've studied this thing tell you what we're up against, and then we'll have a discussion, and then tomorrow morning we'll get after them."

The first expert put forward by the Selectman, to tell how the problem had come up, was Anak Welch, a huge man, appreciably more than six and a half feet tall, whose forehead seemed incandescent, so close was it to a lightbulb hanging over him; a giant who looked as if parts of him were still growing and burl-like would never stop: his prognathous jaw, his hands like the beginnings of wings, his great ears that lent much, along with his persistent stoop, to his air of monstrous humility—for who, Hester thought, is as humble as a hearer? His voice was even, courteous, and low, and it commanded closer attention in the crowded, stifling hall than had the sharper note of the Selectman's.

The huge man mildly said that the trouble had begun, in his opinion, during the last century, when the railroad had been put in, by-passing Tunxis and running round through Whigtown and Treehampstead. When the canal had come through in 'twenty-two, the village had thought it was "goin' to turn into a little star or a wheel on the map of the state"—be a real center. It was just after that, he said, when the potash works, the two tanneries, the clock factory, the spoke works, the carding mill, and the mincing-knife factory had settled in Tunxis. "We were goin' places! Yes, sirree!" But then in 'forty-seven, because of the way Beggar's Mountain up north of town lined up with Thighbone Ledge, the railroad people decided they had to go round to the west and miss Tunxis. "Our biggest 'numeration was in 'fifty-two; we lost twenty-three men in the Civil War, and that was a terrible loss for a little hamlet; and we've been dyin' on the bush ever since. D'you know the way sweet honeysuckle gets on a tree that's let itself get weak and overwhelms it and kills it by-and-by? That's what's beginning, in my opinion, with these woodchucks. They calculate that Tunxis is on the wane, that's the way I see it, and they're movin' in on us, they'd be glad to nudge us out altogether. We've got to tend to 'em early in the game and show 'em we have a mind to stay here, if we do. I, for one, do.

"We humans think we're pretty high-soarin', with our combustion engines and electric radios and now jimmyin' open the almighty secret itself, splittin' God to make explosions, but what we forget is that we're still part of the woodlot where it grows rank and wild. We're in it just as much as the volunteer hemlocks on the edge of Johnnycake Meadow and the black snakes on the lip of the Sessions quarry. We can't afford to get absent-minded and forget *that*."

"Stick to the subject, Anak!" a bass voice called out, and a gust of soft, refreshing laughter ran across the hall like a brief puff of northerly breeze in a hay meadow on a cloudless summer day.

The giant grinned. "You folks know me too well," he said. It had been about seventeen years ago, he went on, just before Parson Churnstick died and the First Church was abandoned, when the men who worked the fields up toward Thighbone Ledge—old Mr. Manross, Romeo Bacon, and Frank Cherevoy were three he named—had begun to have bad trouble with ground-hogs. They would put poison in all the burrows they could find and fill the mouths of the holes and set traps and shoot the creatures and do everything within their gifts, yet still they would lose their crops. They could grow nothing but sour weeds, and that was no way to farm. There was a bay in one of Romeo Bacon's meadows, the big man said, with woodlots of chestnut, hemlock, and hickory on three sides of it, and the animals seemed to be gathering in that area— "buildin' a village 'cross from ours, you might say. You remember Romeo got to be a case, about that time, and I think maybe the woodchucks had some- thin' to do with it, and old Mr. Manross died, and Frank Cherevoy moved away to the other side of Hartford—maybe he wanted to get those big insur- ance companies between him and Tunxis." So for the next ten years, and all through the war, nothing was done about the woodchucks in the hollow. The Bacon meadows come up strongly in clover, and that just made the situation worse.

"By the time young John Leaming bought his track of land up there four years ago—without walkin' over it careful enough, if you'll pardon me sayin' so, John—they'd really got themselves dug in, both in the old bay on Romeo's acreage and in the woods and right up to the ledge itself. These weren't fat old field chuck- ies. These were forest groundhogs, lean creatures, ac- tive as squirrels. They were pretty fierce, and some were tougher'n a hair halter, as George Challenge's German police dog found out to its sorrow and doom. Some of 'em were turning black—young Pliny For- ward'll tell you about the scientific side of all this; I'm no intellectual, as you folks know, and the only college I ever studied at was Doin' It College. All I know is that these creatures were an everlastin' bother. They were on the increase, too, faster'n the hordes in India. Nobody's ever counted 'em, of course, but that time Mrs. Tuller went up there for an experiment and gave 'em a concert on the bull fiddle, the folks who were with her said at least two hundred groundhogs stood up on their mounds and listened to the music. Never heard nothin' about none of the creatures clappin' when the pieces were over and done, but that's neither here nor there, is it, Mrs. Tuller?

"We first talked here in the town about tryin' to control those creatures I'd say ten years ago, but we'd learned from Exodus not to covet our neighbor's ox nor his ass—nor his troubles neither. So let old Romeo and Mr. Manross and Frank Cherevoy holler till their gills broke open, nobody'd listen—except Matthew Avered, I'll say that for him, even if he's a Republican and I ain't. By and by-large, over the years, the colony of groundhogs was just a curiosity for professors and a dandy excuse for young folks who were sparkin' to get 'emselves up into the woodlots. It wasn't but three years ago, when the creatures begun to wayfare such great distances, that the town got in a fever about them. It's too bad about Frank Cherevoy's beanrows, but when they get into mine! That's different! Well, the next thing we knew, we'd put Matthew Avered in the Selectman's office on a split vote, and he'd been cogitatin' about those creatures all along, and so here we are on a hot night, and that's about all the history I can give you at the present sittin'.' "

There was a brief rattle of applause, and as it died down, the voice of a man who had stood up near the back of the hall shouted, "Mr. Selectman!"

"Mr. Sessions has the floor," Mr. Avered said.

"I just wanted to ask," the man named Sessions said, "what the Selectman is tryin' to pull off here. Looks to me like he's advocatin' the use of taxpayers' money to help an individual property owner—to help young Leaming clear the pests out of his lots. Is that it, Mr. Selectman?"

For some reason, this question, which had been earnestly uttered, was greeted with laughter all around.

This gust was different from the earlier easy laughter during the big man's speech. This puff had force in it; this wind was harnessed to a storm.

Probably because of the laughter, the Selectman did (in retrospect it seemed) the wrong thing—he ignored the question and left Mr. Sessions dawdling on his feet, to sit down, eventually, turning his head from side to side, angrily scrutinizing his fellow citizens' attitudes. "Our next speaker," Mr. Avered blandly announced, "is a young man this town is rightly proud of, Mr. Pliny Forward. As you know, he walked off with all the brass-plated honors at Harvard College this last graduation. His strong point is biology, and because he got interested in this situation up in Thighbone Hollow some years back, he did his thesis on the groundhog, about which there'd previously been very little understanding in Cambridge, Massachusetts, where this particular college is seated. So you see he knows what's what! He's helped us no end with the planning for the cleanout, and we thought it would be time well spent if he told us a little about the animals we're contending with. Mr. Forward, come forward!"

A pale young man wearing green plastic-rimmed glasses stepped to the podium and said in a shaking and startlingly cultured baritone, "Let us, to begin with, be accurate. The animal under consideration is a member of the marmot family. Our activity tomorrow and Sunday will be a marmot drive. Let us be exact." For a moment Pliny Forward seemed to sag under the weight of his knowledge; he appeared to be fainting. Then he straightened up as if he had been watered just in time.

"Arctomys monax," he managed to say. " 'The bear-mouse monk,' the fellow's called. And what more do we need in the way of description?"

The young biologist paused again, drooped again;

Hester had for a moment the idea that since no more description was needed, he would give no more, but would subside and perhaps even expire then and there, he looked so feeble. She suffered a short panic for him; but again he revived.

"What we do need," he said tremorously, "is to understand how the marmots in Thighbone Hollow differ from the ordinary field marmots in this part of the world. I'll try to express the difference by ringing a change on the common names we use. We call the species woodchucks. Some think this may come from an Indian word, others think it comes from combining 'wood' with the diminutive once used for pigs in some farming districts in England, in Devonshire, for instance: woodland 'chuckies'—forest piggies. We also call field marmots by another name, groundhogs. Now, to see the difference between our animals in Thighbone Hollow and other Connecticut marmots, we must think of the local animals, not as being like little piggies or fat, idle hogs, but as the counterparts of wild boars."

Paler than ever, pouring off sweat, Pliny Forward nevertheless looked and sounded stronger now, for he was obviously on known and loved ground, forgetful of his environment and audience. "Let me cite you some actual differences between our local marmots and the common run in New England. To begin with, ours are bigger than their neighbors. Common woodchucks in Connecticut grow to about two feet in length, counting their tails, while the full-grown animals in Thighbone Hollow average twenty-eight or thirty inches. The ordinary ones become ludicrously fat, especially in the fall just before they crawl away to hibernate. Ours sleep less of the winter away, and they're leaner and stronger; after all, they go several miles to eat. Ours have unusually thick skins and heavy skulls. I've skinned some and tanning the hides with hickory bark made leather a quarter inch thick. Their crowns are practically petrified.

"And take the matter of color. We biologists are taught that the standard 'characters' of the marmot are these: 'Supra fusco cinereus' "—the young man chanted like a priest—" 'subtus subrufus, capite, cauda, pedibusque fuscis, naso et . . .' "

Someone in the hall let out a two-note whistle of admiration-derision.

Pliny Forward's head turned slowly in the direction of the sound. "Whoever made that noise," he said, the color of life suffusing his cheeks for the first time, "will be useful tomorrow and the next day. We usually hear that noise used as the mating call of the not yet fully adult male of the North American Homo sap., but its second note will be extremely useful in our pursuit of Arctomys monax, and I'll tell you why in a moment. But to get back to color: The coat of the normal groundhog is a grizzly or yellowish gray, blackish-brownish on the back, crown, and tail, and rusty on the underbelly, whereas—this is eerie to me—a very large proportion of our animals in Thighbone Hollow are in what we call 'the melanistic phase,' which occurs only now and then among common eastern marmots. This means they are black or blackish all over.

"Now, about that whistle. Most of you probably think woodchucks are silent, but they're not. When they're terrified or furious, they'll do one of two things—chatter their teeth together, so they sound like dangerous little chopping machines, or else give out intermittent, high, shrill whistles, warning their fellows. Connecticut marmots don't have many occasions to use their alert call, but our local ones seem to have developed these shrieks to an unusual degree. In this, as in other ways, our woodchucks tend to be close to the Rocky Mountain marmots. We've found that by imitating the marmots' whistle, we can alarm them and drive them along overground; and a little later we'll demonstrate the sound.

"Why did this pack of abnormally wild marmots pick on Tunxis? From what I hear, some of our ancestors—not so far back, either: Parson Churnstick would be one—would have said we were being punished for horrible things we townspeople had done or even thought in our heads. On the other hand, we've got some people right here in this hall who think we're all good and they—the marmots—are all bad, and that they are after us, as the evil always hunger to cannibalize the good. I try to be a scientist. I can only say that Mr. Welch must have been partly right when he put the beginnings of this thing a great many years ago—perhaps, as he said, about when the railroad came through the county. For one thing, most of the natural enemies of these creatures were stamped out about then—wildcats, foxes, eagles, big serpents, and even weasels. And I think Mr. Welch may have been right about the animals sensing the sapping of the vitality of our village, its gradual decadence. Marmots can see, they have eyes: the church in the hollow has been empty a long, long time, the mills on the canal smoke no more, the meadows up near the ledge haven't been tended for more than ten years. But even that's too simple. Why did clover come up so richly in the hollow? There must be complicated reasons for this visitation that I, in spite of all my education you people like to laugh at, don't understand. Maybe some of you older people are wiser and know the real reasons. I leave them to you."

Pliny Forward, who in these last sentences had grown rather bold and forceful in manner, sat down, and at first the mysteries he had webbed in his clumsy, callow way, and in his urbane university accent, lay like a shroud over a spiritless audience; then the people stirred and a few clapped rather angrily.

The Selectman stepped to the podium and said, "Dr. James Fantigh, our dentist, who has plugged up holes in most of our heads, has kindly agreed to highlight the main point of interest of these wicked animals we have heard about—their chinchoppers." (In the early morning, on the stone wall under the pink sky, thinking back, Hester remembered the way the Selectman had gleaned that one small word, "wicked," from young Forward's speech. She wondered vaguely whether Mr. Avered's unnecessarily pulling that word out had any meaning: whether it helped account for the Selectman's longstanding interest in the woodchucks in the hollow; whether, in key with Pliny Forward's blacks and whites, he saw evil in the beasts but not in himself—or the other way round; whether the light of this small word, in some refracted way, could illumine those long, staring abstractions of his.)

"My report," Dr. Fantigh, a tidy man with hair parted in the middle, read verbatim from a filing card, "will be brief. The animal in question has upper and lower pairs of incisors, no canines, ten upper molars, and eight lowers. I have examined specimens brought to my office by Mr. Forward. The jaws are articulated in the vertical plane and have no sidewise motion. The incisors are like chisels, strong, narrow, and wedge-shaped, with enamel on the anterior surfaces only, so that by a constant wearing away of the posterior surfaces the teeth are kept filed to a very sharp edge. No caries was observed. If my patients"—the dentist looked up for the first time—"had teeth as sound as these, I'd be a poorer but happier man than at the present time." He returned to his written words. "In summary, these teeth are dangerous. My professional advice is—keep away from them."

The brevity, concreteness, and intensity of the dentist's speech was in such sharp contrast to the troublesome, unanswerable, still overarching why? of Pliny Forward's last sentences that the crowd now suddenly burst into a racket of clapping and happy laughing, as if Dr. Fantigh had brought much-desired good news from afar.

■

THE MEMORY of the rest of the caucus was confused in Hester's mind. The rapid give and take of discussion, the intermittent instructions and warnings, the many mentions of names and places new to her, the swiftly mounting emotions of the crowd—all were blended in her recall with sensations of her own confusion and despair. She kept thinking that the facts she had heard about marmots, as the young biologist had called them, had fascinated her in exactly the same way as had Eben's confidential and condescending lectures to her, back in the city, on new inventions in aviation, on the bowels of new instruments of war. It could have been, for all she knew, that the self-sharpening principle of the woodchucks' dangerous incisors had only recently been contrived by ingenious scientists in secret laboratories of New England. She realized, with disappointment and then fear, the reach of her separation from natural things.

Hester did remember, all too clearly, the final scene of recrimination, spite, and comic bad manners, just before the caucus ended; most of what led up to it was hazy in her recollection. She remembered passages of the intervening time, but she could not piece together the logic of the crescendo of anger against the Selectman, if logic there had been. She sensed that there must have been some background of feeling in the town about which she had still to know, something beyond the division of the citizenry over the location of a new school—though that, too, was an explicit factor in the ruction.

After the dentist's short report, Mr. Avered had spoken at some length about the tactics to be used in the drive. He had propped up on an easel a map of the hollow, and had described how the picket line of volunteers would, on the first day, dislodge the woodchucks from their homes and drive them along between the ledge and the canal until they had crossed Job's Creek—a stream transecting the hollow, running down from springs on Thighbone Ledge to the canal. Plank bridges had been placed across this stream in recent days, and they would be withdrawn as soon as the animals were herded to the other side. Since the water-fearing woodchucks had never been known to cross either Job's Creek or the canal, and because Thighbone Ledge beyond Job's Creek was impossibly sheer for them to climb, there was virtually no likelihood of their trying to return to their community in the Bacon Meadows, once driven across the creek. They would probably burrow underground during that night and would have to be surfaced again the second morning. Then the picket line would drive the creatures forward into a long funnel of "rabbit-proof fence," sunk under the ground as well as raised over it, at the constriction of the hollow four miles beyond Job's Creek, known as the Lantern Flue. At its narrow end the funnel led into a corral of the same fencing, built, as the funnel had been, for this drive, on the edge of Judge Pitkin's land. There the woodchucks would be destroyed; he did not say how.

The Selectman had continued in detail, explaining the system of divisions, naming the captains, assigning known volunteers, and outlining the duties of each division at each stage of the drive. Here Hester's attention had wandered, as it had used to wander when she had been taken, much too young, week after week, to the church on the wide avenue. The pew-backs there had been hard, like the seats here in the Grange; she had used to lean sideways against her mother, who on Sundays had always borne the ineffable scent of a nameless flower. She was aware now of Eben beside her, breathing a little hard: poor Eben!—embarrassed by his father's absorption in the minutiae of his beloved project.

How different Eben seemed in the city from here in Tunxis! Hester remembered how, when Mr. Avered had pointed out to her the previous afternoon a slender mourning dove in the high branches of a white pine near the homestead, she had suddenly thought of peanut-surfeited pigeons on befouled cornices above the sun-parched street across from the park in the city. Eben in the city was always congenial, and acquaintances took to him quickly, yet he was always, at last, alone like one of those birds on some high corner of sun-soaked, ordure-striped stone. She did not blame the city for that; on the contrary, she thought perhaps he had become practiced in loneliness as a child in this Tunxisful of defiant and separate identities. He had no intimacies but hers, and she was not sure that she was his friend. She remembered a conversation one evening when she and Eben were dining in a crowded restaurant in the far west side with the McCleods. Sam McCleod had gone to the same small New England college as Eben, and that night they began to talk about another classmate who lived in the city and whom all four of them knew, envied, and disliked.

"Wonder who'll go to Cramp's funeral when he dies," McCleod had said. "D'you suppose enough people'll show up to make it a proper funeral? D'you think they'll be able to scrape up six pallbearers?"

"When I die," Hester had said, "I don't want any pallbearers. I haven't asked my friends to carry me while I'm alive, and I'm not going to ask them to when I'm dead."

"I don't have six friends," Peggy McCleod had said. "Who does?"

"Cramp does," McCleod had said.

Peggy had answered, "Nonsense, he doesn't have any friends. All he has is useful acquaintances. He has a system of mutual advantages, but no friends. Nobody has six real friends."

At last Eben had spoken. "It won't take six people to carry me," he had said. "I'm going to be cremated. So it doesn't matter whether I have six friends or not."

But it did matter; that was what had made his utterance not mildly reckless and sophisticated, as he had seemed to mean it to be, but only mildly pathetic. The city was a frustrating place for Eben—and for Hester, too, since she was so much with him—because their life there consisted of a continuous search for intimacies, which had the maddening repetitive structure of a rondo, over and over and over: a series of explorations of a series of newly met acquaintances, ending almost always in disappointment on one side or the other, as "attractiveness" was fragmented by familiarity into its too clearly seen elements; or ending, at any rate, in just happening not to meet again. In Tunxis there would almost never be new faces, there could almost never be new acquaintances; there must be a kind of stability of separateness and loneliness here, she thought, an atmosphere in which deep friendship might paradoxically be possible; though she was not at all sure—did the Selectman have any friends who were close and true?

"You've all probably seen the paths woodchucks beat across the meadows to their feeding places," the Selectman was saying. "Follow those paths whenever you can and wherever they run along the general direction of our drive...." Hester heard him warn that groundhogs would turn and fight fiercely against attackers far bigger than themselves, if pressed too closely; so they shouldn't be rushed. The drivers should take their time, stand back and whistle and stamp, and maybe shout, until the animals moved of their own free wills. Baby chuckies, "in their innocent valor," he said, were the meanest and quickest fighters of all, though of course they couldn't inflict such severe bites as their parents. It was expected that the animals would take refuge stubbornly in stone walls, where there might be big enough cavities to house them, or under the vaulting roots of partly washed-out hemlocks in the hanging wood below Thighbone Ledge, and if they did, they could be driven out with the same insect-spray bombs that were to be used to dislodge them from their burrows in the first place. Experiments had been run with DDT bombs, he said, and it had been found that the animals hated the smell of the insecticide vapor and would invariably move away from it. . . .

The Selectman said the meeting was open for discussion.

From the very first the questions addressed to the chair showed a rancor that was puzzling to Hester, who thought the townspeople should be grateful to the Selectman and the others for the careful planning they had obviously done.

"I'd like to ask the Selectman," one man declared, "why in heaven's name he picked this particular time of year for his piece of funnin', if that's what 'tis. He knows this stretch of summertime is one of the very wust times of the hull year—for folks that have to work outdoors, that is, and there's still some of 'em, you know."

Polite as a basket of chips, the Selectman said, "Pliny, I think you're the best one to answer that."

(Later Hester thought perhaps Mr. Avered's passing this first question on to Pliny Forward was a disastrous mistake, since the young biologist had already roused the resentment of the crowd with his superior accent and his unsettling why?)

"There are two reasons," the pale young man said. "One is that in midsummer the marmots are widest awake and spryest; we can move them faster then than at any other time. The second is the more important reason. Marmots belong to the order of rodents, and almost all rodents have a very queer trait that shows up now and again: When they gather in close-packed communities that are perhaps a little too big—rodent cities, almost—there comes a time when they get restless, a mob feeling of the fidgets spread through the whole city, the rodents want to get out and go somewhere else. In some cases, all of them do move; in others, part of the colony moves; and in still others—and this is often true of marmots—they just seem to go through the heebie-jeebies and stay where they are. You've all heard how lemmings migrate, sometimes with such hysterical impetus that the whole pack walks straight into the sea and drowns. Rat towns move this way, and sometimes end up in locations less favorable than the ones they have left, so far as food and comfort are concerned. I personally think it was because of this trait of rodents that the Pied Piper of Hamelin had the success he did. At any rate, a number of us who appreciate this phenomenon have been watching the marmot colony in Thighbone Hollow very closely for several seasons. You've heard how they started wandering three years ago. Real fidgets set in last summer, and came back even stronger this spring. We're convinced that now is the time to push the marmots, as their own instincts might never be quite strong enough to do, out of a situation that gives them the willies." The young man paused, then added, "As a matter of fact, this trait isn't confined to marmots: don't we see it sometimes in ourselves? Haven't you ever had the feeling we all ought to clear out?"

"Got it right now!" a woman cried from the audience. Her shout was arched, it was a joke; the humor was nasty, and the crowd emitted the storm-laugh again.

Apparently the guffaws roused the man named Sessions, who had been laugh-tossed earlier in the evening, and now he was up again, saying, "I want to repeat what I asked before: Are you proposin', Mr. Selectman, that we use taxpayers' money to help an individual property owner?"

This time an intense silence followed the question, for now people seemed to want an answer to the question they had ridiculed before.

"The taxpayers' money isn't being used for this," Mr. Avered said, a note of querulousness barely audible in his voice. "All we've asked for is volunteers."

"What about those plank bridges? What about all that fencin'?"

"Mr. Leaming, Senior, contributed the fence posts and planks, and I paid for the wire mesh myself, as it happens, because I've been wanting for ten years to see this chore done with. There are about a dozen young men who helped plant the fence, and I've already thanked them in writing."

"What's old man Leaming up to, lettin' loose all that lumber?" asked a man who did not choose to stand. "Tryin' to influence the Selectman's office when it comes to locatin' the school?"

"I resent that," shouted a white-haired, crimson-faced man, evidently Mr. Leaming, Senior, who stood up to cry out his three heartfelt words and then sat down again.

"Why'n't you just trap the creatures?" asked a sober-faced man in a black suit, with a strong tone of resentment. "Trappin' seemed to suit our forefathers. My father and his father kept our land spandy clean with traps, and so should I, if I'd've tended to the fields and hadn't a-gone into my present occupation."

"Traps won't work with so many, Enos," the Selectman said. "We couldn't buy and service that many traps. Leave a groundhog in a trap for half an hour and he'll gnaw his foot off. I'll tell you one thing, too, Enos, though maybe you know it already: A groundhog is a lot more economical about such things than other animals, muskrats, for instance; where a muskrat'll leave two or three inches of his leg above the jaws of the trap, your groundhog'll trim himself off right at the steel, neat as a burnt-out candle."

"Trappin' was good enough for our forefathers," the man named Enos said in heavy reproach as he sat down.

"There's a modern way!" exclaimed an excited young man who had been on his feet raising his hand school-fashion for some time. "You back a car up at midday, when woodchucks are always to home, then run a hose down from the exhaust into the burrow, block off both ends of the burrow, and start your motor—that's all! It's a gas chamber! That ought to do the job thorough and easy."

"Are you going to back your beautiful Chevvy with the fenders taken off it up into the bay on Romeo's acres, Eustace Thrall?" the Selectman asked. "You ever been up there? And what about the ones in the woods?"

The excited young man flushed and sat down.

Then, from somewhere outside the hall and close to

it, through the windows at Hester's right, came a shrill and penetrating whistle.

Pliny Forward struggled to his feet on the platform as if the sound had dizzied him. "Did you hear that?" he said tensely to the crowd. "That was a marmot's shriek, that was the alarm I was talking about. But it's strange! I never heard one at night before."

"Mebbe none never hearn you at night afore," shouted the woman who had had a success with her previous quip, now vulgarizing her speech, but this time no one laughed, no one at all.

"Do you suppose they know what we're doing?" the Selectman asked Pliny Forward. A smile showed that he, too, meant to be humorous, but his eyes were not enlivened by his joke; he seemed wan.

There was a long silence in the hall; the crowd was appalled. Finally the Selectman faced the audience and said, "Now that we've heard from the opposition ..."

A sudden, surprising roar of laughter arose, as the crowd's ridiculous tensions—its fear, its fear of fear, its hatred of fear, the understanding it must have had that fear had been, in those moments, unwarranted but ineluctably epidemic in the hall—were suddenly released. It was possible, too, Hester thought later, that the crowd was unconsciously laughing over the ambiguity, perhaps itself unconscious, in what the Selectman had said, for his "opposition" could be understood as of either woodchucks or townspeople. For a few minutes, at any rate, the latter sort was abated by the whistling episode, and perfunctory talk of tactics ensued.

But anger, like a hungry dog coming back to the scene of an unforgotten feast, soon returned. Hester, who had been daydreaming again, could not be sure what smell of a new repast attracted it back to the hall. She had picked up a note of cruelty in what Eben's father had said about trapped animals gnawing themselves free, and that had made her think of a time when she had been driving with Eben in Florida, during the vacation they had shared there, and they had passed a runover cat on the road, and Eben had said, "Once in 'forty-seven I drove to Springfield and I killed twelve cats on the road," and she had said, flaring up, "Pleased every time, I'll bet," and he had said, with comic-book finality, "Pow! Pow! Pow!"

By the time a sense of renewed tension brought her interest back into the Grange Hall, Hester gathered that the school issue had come into play.

"When are we going to have a decision?" Mr. Sessions asked.

"We're here to talk about Thighbone Hollow," the Selectman said. "Can't we dispose of one problem at a time?"

"With due respect," Mr. Sessions said, in a voice raucous with a want of respect, "I don't see how we can. All our problems in this town are tied in together. My attitude on Thighbone Hollow depends on your attitude on the school—specially since the Leaming boy is mixed up in this groundhog business. No, you can't take things one by one here in Tunxis, Mr. Selectman."

Several people stood at once and poured out their cross-purposed sentences without waiting for recognition by the Selectman: a woman do-gooder saying in hectic presidential tones that the school was badly needed, there would be double sessions in another year, the hot-lunch program was imperiled; Mr. Leaming, Senior, tempting apoplexy with his still outraged protests that his son had nothing to do with the school issue, "in fact he's dead set against me on the whereabouts of the schoolhouse"; the man named Enos, saying that when he was a boy, he'd walked four miles to school in the snowdrifts, and he couldn't see why we needed all these buses and moving-picture machines and frills nowadays; and others and still others, in a compulsive outpouring of anger that frightened Hester. There seemed to be continuity, no progression; yet steadily there was built up a triangle of heat and hate—the Leaming faction against the Johnnycake Meadow crowd, and both, with bitterest force, against the symbol of authority, the Selectman. By a round-about course, amid the fury, Mr. Leaming, Senior, who had seemed to be closely co-operative with the Select-man on Thighbone Hollow, came to be abusive toward him on the school issue. The Selectman gave him firm answers. Mr. Leaming blushed dangerously between shouts. The Selectman offered the worst provocation: He kept his temper. Mr. Leaming, who seemed to have mislaid his temper several seasons back, occasion-ally stammered, as if he were rooting around in the cor-ners of his mind in search of his lost self-control.

Finally, apparently beyond caring what people thought of him, Mr. Leaming cried out, "If I was only close enough to that plat-plat-platform, Mr. Selectman, I'd spi-spit in your face."

Quietly, with a humility so profound that it seemed insane, the Selectman answered, "Why don't you step up here and do it, Mr. Leaming, if it would make you feel any better? I could wipe it off easy as pie."

The crowd sat aghast. Mr. Leaming looked sick at his stomach. People who had been clamoring for a chance to talk sat down. As if nothing had happened (except that he seemed ever so slightly short of breath as he spoke), the Selectman said he thought most of the points on the woodchuck drive had been covered—but would the gang of advance men, who were going to gas the groundhogs out of their burrows, mind staying a few minutes to talk over their program? Then, if there was no further business, he said, the caucus would stand adjourned. Murmuring, the crowd arose and broke. Hester had a feeling that its anger, though checked, was far from sated. Mr. Leaming was still rocking on his feet.

Two

THE SUN WAS UP. Across the meadow from Hester's right Mrs. Tuller came, and as she strode through the tall grass the teacher swung her right arm back and forth across her body, gracefully snapping her wrist at the end of each swing so her hand seemed to be weightless and followed her forearm like a flag waved to and fro; and Hester, still sitting on the stone wall, realized soon that Mrs. Tuller's right hand was manipulating a nonexistent musical bow, and then Hester saw that the fingers of Mrs. Tuller's left hand, which had seemed to be scratching her left shoulder, were instead drumming out on the throat-strings of a phantom instrument the stops of a passage of music that must have been, to judge by the transported expression on the teacher's massive face, cause for ecstasy on a summer morning. As Mrs. Tuller came closer, Hester heard her humming in time with her shadow-playing. The teacher sat on the wall beside Hester, spread her knees to grip the imagined violoncello, and played a final passage, a desperate trilling run up the fingerboard of air, her outsized head bent over the work and wagging slightly in counterweight to her flying bow arm, her left hand trembling a vibrato when her little finger at last hovered over the final ghost-tone.

"Practicing?" Hester foolishly asked when the teacher finally dropped her arms.

"Wish I played the piccolo," Mrs. Tuller said; "something you could just slip in your pocket and take wherever you went. There ain't time enough in a day in the summer."

"What were you playing?"

"Brahms's violin and 'cello concerto, opus one hundred and two; doubt if you know it."

"Oh, yes, I've heard records of it," Hester pretentiously lied.

"Isaac Stern was on the violin part with me there, and the Boston Symphony was carryin' the background. Koussevitzky—only he's dead. Wish you could've heard us!"

"So do I."

"That's the trouble," the teacher sighed. "It sounds so much better in my head than when the blighted instrument is right there in my embrace."

"I used to play the piano," Hester said. "I gave it up when I went away to college."

"There's more music nowadays," Mrs. Tuller said, "more music everywhere. When I was a girl, nobody'd ever heard of Johannes Brahms up here. On the Sabbath the only musical instruments they allowed in this village were churchbells, the trumpet, and the jew's harp. No one ever got sent to the whippin' post in my lifetime for breakin' that rule, but they did in my great-grandfather's time—my father told me that."

When Mrs. Tuller spoke of the whipping post, a light came into her eyes, a kind of fervency, a gleam of allegiance to a fearful and wonderful past. Mrs. Tuller seemed to have an abnormally large head, but Hester realized that this was at least partly illusion, for the teacher wore her voluminous gray hair in a vast system of cranial bunting, a large turban of braids and loops and buns that made her quite topheavy. Still, the head was big; her face was broad, her eyes wideset, her lips generous, her earlobes redly drooping. Her mouth and eyes were sweet and warm, but they held between them, as if a hostile and scarcely manageable captive, a mean, sharp, Puritanical nose which seemed, now and then, to infect its neighbors with its own bleakness, so that the lips would suddenly seem thin and blue, the eyes metallic and cold; these moments were brief, however, mere glints as of ice, sun, and cloud on a winter's day of open-and-shut. Such was the glint when she spoke of the whipping post. Mrs. Tuller's shoulders were narrow and sloping, her torso compact, her hips and legs sturdy and thick, and she wore a delicate light blue blouse and a cotton skirt made bold with large checks of black and white.

"Last night they mentioned a concert you gave the woodchucks once," Hester said. "Did that really happen?"

"Sure it did. Best attended recital I ever gave. Young Forward had noticed the woodchucks perked up whenever he sang to 'em, so he asked me to go up to Romeo Bacon's lots and play to 'em one sundown, and I did. I sat on a foldin' chair right in the feedgrass in the middle of their mounds, and they came out there by the score and set up as quizzical's could be, turnin' their heads back and forth and settin' there more patient, if you ask me, than humans. I think they liked Sindbad's music from Scheherazade best of all. They just hated Mozart, and that's one reason I hate them."

"You must dislike a lot of human beings on that count."

"I do, child."

"Why were people so angry at Mr. Avered last night?" Hester asked.

"Some people in the town think he's a little too stuffed with brains. You know the expression, 'Missin' a few buttons'? Well, these people think the Selectman has a few too many buttons, and that they're sewed on peculiar. There was a whisperin' campaign goin' round durin' the election that his father and grandfather were both very meanderin' in their declinin' years, due to excess brains, and that our Matthew was about ready to follow in their footsteps. They think he just imagines the threat of these groundhogs."

"But he doesn't, does he? They came to your recital, didn't they?"

"Yes, there're groundhogs up here, all right. Maybe not so many nor so serious as the Selectman thinks. I do believe his imagination's a shade too sprightly."

Pushing down an impulse to make a remark about Mrs. Tuller's just-completed performance with Stern and the Boston Symphony, the applause for which must scarce have died down in the teacher's ears, Hester asked instead, "But what about all the evidence that young biologist had?"

"Pliny Forward? Gracious me, he is addled. They said at Harvard College that he's a genius, but I taught him, I know better. There's an old sayin' that fits him: 'He's too bright to be right.' "

"Do you mean you think there's no reason to hold this marmot drive?"

"I can't say as to that. May be and may not be."

"But you're a captain of a division. You must believe in it."

"I believe in holdin' with my fellow townsfolk."

"Should I marry Eben?" Hester blurted out.

"Gracious, child, what a question!" Mrs. Tuller said. "I can't answer that. Do you want to?"

"Oh, yes; at least I think so. But you ... you frighten me, with the things you say."

"Don't misunderstand me," Mrs. Tuller said. "Matnight and made an awful noise through the whole thew Avered's a kind-hearted man. Barrin' Anak Welch, who's so tall he's obliged to be mild-mannered, there's no more gentlemanlike person in Tunxis than our Selectman. More than that, he loves us all! That's his weakness! You're old enough to know, child, there's somethin' terrible troublesome to plain mortals about saints and near-saints. Bein' a saint is gettin' awful close to the edge.... By the bye, they say the only witch we ever had in Tunxis in the old days was an Avered. She was the daughter of Philemon Avered—he was a famous doctor here that tended people durin' the spotted fever in the seventeen fifties. As they tell it, this girl, Nell Avered, was terrible saucy, and she married a blacksmith, name of Pinney, and bore him a son. Right after a new wild-eyed preacher came down from Massachusetts and started frenzyin' the village, Nell bust out with a temper like a tomcat—it came out mostly at neighborhood. She began to lay spells on Pinney, so that if he shod a horse when she'd put the wrath onto him, no matter how careful he was, no matter how sound the hoof and how strong the nails, the shoe would loosen and the horse would throw it in a matter of minutes, after the animal was led away from Pinney's smithy. Before long Nell's ways got so scandalous she was branded a witch, and the blacksmith was forced to turn her out or else be considered by the parson and the congregation to be in league with Old Harry. Nell took her son and went up to Zion Hill and built a shack o' poles and boards, with filthy straw on the floor, and she supported herself and her boy by beggin' from door to door. No one dared refuse her. Once she asked a Pitkin housewife for pork ribs; the Pitkin denied her them; and afterwards the family's hogs all failed—they became like the lean kine of Genesis, and nothin', not even fresh oats and whole milk, could fatten 'em. If she'd come in on a housewife spinnin', the band of the wheel'd fly off. If she visited a churnin', no butter'd form. They tell how once a man whose wife couldn't get a churnin' to cease remembered that Nell had dropped in to see her while she worked, so the man heated a poker to burn the witch out of the cream and stuck it in the churn—and the butter formed right off. One day a party of girls, includin' one of Nell's younger sisters, went up near her cabin to pick grapes. They moved secret and posted a sentinel between the vines and the cabin, and after a while the sentinel warned the others that Nell was comin', and though they ran across lots so's Nell never saw 'em direct, all the same the grapes proved spoilt and unfit and no good. Nell and her son both died from exposure durin' their first winter in the cabin, so the village was spared havin' to take steps.... But that was all near two hundred years ago, child."

Hester, conscious that her sickly looks must have brought that final assuaging protest, remained silent; she had begun to understand what the pleading voice in the half-dark had meant when it had talked about Mrs. Tuller's ferule.

"I wonder," Mrs. Tuller said pleasantly, surveying the hollow, "what's holdin' us up. Can't imagine what they're waitin' for, unless it's the Earl of Chatham."

"The Earl of Chatham?" Hester asked, on the verge of tears.

"The Earl of Chatham, sword all drawn,
Was waitin' for Sir Richard Strachan;

Sir Richard, eager to be at 'em,
Was waitin' for the Earl of Chatham."

■

DIMLY on the left Hester heard whistling and shouting.
Nearly half an hour had passed since Mrs. Tuller's
brief visit, the sun was well up, the world's oven was
getting warm; and Hester had begun to wonder
whether discord among the leaders of this adventure, or
stubbornness among the hunted in their burrows, had
caused a delay that would never be overcome. She half
hoped so; she was not sure she wanted to go into the
dark woods ahead. Then the noise of the suddenly
stirred-up drivers drifted down to her from the woodland toward the ledge, and she stood up; Coit waved
to her, and she waved back with a sudden festive
thrill. They waited for the group on their immediate
left to start moving. She considered what Eben, in that
group, might be thinking just then. He was so boyishly
ambitious, she thought, and his ambition was so vague
and objectless.

"What do you want in life?" she had asked him during one of their very first conversations, when they had
been eagerly discovering each other.

"Something *big!*" he had said, his eyes a-smoke.

She could see him, in her imagination, standing
alone in the untended, half-overgrown meadows up to
the left, rather tense, determined to excel, to make himself famous with some heroic exploit, in this drive that
he thought ridiculous; intent upon himself, as was his
fixed habit of being, and only incidentally ringing in his
relationship to the objective world—to woodchucks,
now, to his father, and to her. He was in a kind of lingering hobbledehoyhood. He was forever looking in a
mirror and seeing an untrue image; he and his real self

were bare acquaintances. He wanted to be big; she had a fear that he might some day prove merely swollen, inflated, pompous, lighter than the summer air—yet see himself as big. Sweetly she ached; motherly pity, wearing a mask, so that she thought she recognized it as love, warmed her, and she suddenly hurt all over for him, as if feverish, and a feeling of incipient power flowed into her; she would help him to be full and big, whatever true bigness he might strive for or drift toward. Ah, Eben, she thought, I love you and I'll manage you.

She saw Roswell Coit put his fingers to his lips and then she heard a piercing whistle that would make woodchucks prick up their ears all the way to New Hampshire; she decided she would shout, not whistle, during the drive, for she couldn't compete with that metallic mouth of Coit's. But shout what? Suddenly she was overwhelmed with the absurdity of what she was doing. She saw Coit cup his hands and heard him call to her, "Move forward slowly!"

Caught in a team, she made her own delicate megaphone and shrilled to the dancing master on her right, "Move forward slowly!"

"O.K., dearie," Friedrich Tuller called back to her; and then he passed the message down the line.

Hester stepped into the jeweled meadow before her. Unlike the adjacent fields up toward the ledge, this one had been kept up for hay, and its good-shafted grass, just coming into seed, bent slightly now in the shallow sunlight under a treasure of sparkling dew. Moving at last, wading through better-than-diamonds, Hester felt giddily happy. The field sloped fairly steeply forward and somewhat to the right, and beyond it began a stretch of second-growth woods. Hester's legs grew soaking wet again. On both sides of her along the picket line, now near, now distant, she heard the sharp-pointed whistling of young men who knew how to make their breath scream through fingers and lips, while down to the right Friedrich Tuller hallooed as if to nearby, visible creatures that needed his persuasion, "Hi! Hi on, now! Go on, woodchucks! Go on, now! Hi on, there! Aha! Move along, my friends!" Timidly Hester began to mimic him; she heard other cries up and down the line, and soon she felt less self-conscious and quite recklessly shouted. She thought of the image someone had used at the caucus of a fence of noise, and as she walked and called she began to feel that she was part of a substantial moving barrier that would surely contain its quarry. The pace of the line was very slow; it was hard to picture this leisurely amble as a serious hunt. Nevertheless it seemed soon, too soon, that Hester approached the hedgerow at the beginning of the woods, into which she was loath to go. The sun, coming from the right and from beyond the woods, touched only the elegant crowns of the trees; below, from where she came near, could be seen only darkness, dampness, impenetrability. She walked into the shadow; her cries grew anguished, as if she were the threatened, not the threatener. On her right, since the line of the division was echeloned that way, the dancing master had already been engulfed by the thicket, and from within it she could hear him shouting, "Hi on, there, you woodchucks! Get on!" Coit to her left was still out in the sunlight in the precious meadow. She hesitated. She saw a wall covered with vines that she recognized as honeysuckle (for Eben had, the previous afternoon, showed her the shape of poison ivy and cat brier leaves—"the only things you really need to know for this damn-fool drive of Father's"—and, in passing, of those of honeysuckle, too). Low along the wall, on both sides of it, there was a screen of young trees and shrubs, honeysuckle-heavy;

she parted it, climbed the wall, and broke through into the woods themselves. She had gone forward only about twenty feet when she heard Coit's voice bellowing, "Hold up, Avered's girl! Pass the word to hold up!"

"They say to hold up!" she called to Tuller, and she heard the dancing master's rather merry call to his next neighbor.

Hester looked around her. She was twenty-four years old; she had never been in woods like these before—wild, undisciplined woods like these. She had been in city parks; she had been in thin groups of man-subservient trees on the edges of the Massachusetts town where she had gone to college; and she had been in clean pine woods in the South. But here the honeysuckle fighting the trees for light made an equatorial jungle in New England. It climbed trunks and hummocked triumphantly over underbrush it had long since choked. The gloomy, embattled green was islanded with patches of in-sneaking sunlight. Now that the line of the hunters was silent, Hester suddenly heard the sweet clamor of hundreds of startled birds, themselves drawn back somewhat from the fence of human noise and apparently trying to raise a stockade of sounds of their own. Hester felt exhilarated by the woods; to her surprise, she felt relieved of fear and entranced.

Then her fear returned, as down to the left, ahead in the falling-off forest, she heard a noise that moved: limbs and twigs were being broken, there was a swish of continuous motion toward herself, or at any rate toward the line. She had to be in the open where she could see; she scrambled back to the wall and out into the field and ran part way to Coit and called to him, "Something's coming up through the woods! Do you hear it?"

"Don't wet your pants, baby doll," Coit said. "I

heard it. Ain't naught but some of the advance men comin' back to the line. You better hold your position."

Hester, furious at her panic and Coit's contempt, said, "My panties are no dewier than yours, my friend," and felt badly unsatisfied with her retort.

She went chagrined back into the woods.

In a few minutes three men—the Selectman, Anak Welch, and George Challenge—showed themselves approaching the line half way between her post and Coit's. Because she was in the woods on their side of the hedgerow, they saw her first.

"Where's your captain?" the Selectman called, as if Hester were no one he knew.

"Mrs. Tuller's down by the canal," Hester answered. "Roswell Coit's anchoring this end of the division, right back there in the field."

"Here I am," Coit, evidently overhearing, called; and he pushed into the woods toward the three men. Hester moved over to them, too. Their faces were red with exertion and excitement. The Selectman's two companions each carried a pair of insect bombs.

"They're up ahead," the Selectman exultantly said. "They flushed easily. So many you couldn't count 'em."

"You ought to've seen 'em, Ros," George Challenge said to Coit.

"At least four hundred. Four to five hundred, I'd calculate," Mr. Avered said, pounding a fist into an open palm.

"Less, I'd say," the huge Mr. Welch softly disagreed. "I'd say around two hundred."

"Oh, Anak, there were twice that many!" the Selectman vehemently urged.

"Two hundred at the outside," the big man insisted.

"What does it matter? What does it matter?" the Selectman said, childishly joyful, verbally capering. "We've got 'em on the run."

"They could hear the line back here—it made 'em move," said George Challenge.

"We've got to tell everybody," the Selectman said. He commanded Challenge to go down and find Mrs. Tuller and Coit to run up to the pivot of the next division; word should be passed along the whole line that a very large number of woodchucks had been successfully surfaced and were moving northward along the hollow; that a small party of advance men were deployed beyond the burrows to keep the animals from coming back to ground; and that the line should move forward firmly and vigilantly now. Hester was surprised at the peremptoriness of the Selectman's orders, and, seeing the others stiffen at his lack of tact, she was visited by a disquieting reminder of the anger that had not been wholly laid to rest at the caucus the night before.

Coit said Mrs. Tuller had wanted Mr. Welch just beyond her husband in the line; he didn't know where she wanted Mr. Challenge. Hester noticed with interest and satisfaction the thickset bully, the dauntless Ranger, using respectful "misters" after hearing harsh commands.

"I'll walk with this young lady for now," the Selectman said, falling in with Hester.

"Never saw it to fail," Coit grumbled loud enough to be heard, in another kind of response to heavy authority. "The brass gettin' itself a setup."

"There were hundreds of them," the Selectman said to Hester, acting as if he had not heard Coit's impudence. "Almost all black, Pliny was right. Oh, what a sight!"

The others moved away.

"This means a lot to you, doesn't it?" Hester said, slowly leading Mr. Avered back toward her place in the line.

"It means I can look these Tunxis people straight in

the eye," the Selectman said. "Last night took the gimp all out of me—I believe some of the folks at the caucus thought these groundhogs were just some kind of nightmare I'd had, and I swan, I began to think so myself."

"It's a good thing you have witnesses."

"You ought to see those dark creatures moving in a herd," the Selectman exclaimed.

How like one of Eben's mild raptures, Hester thought. The capacity for excitement and happiness, for being lifted toward ecstasy by commonplace surprises—this was one of the qualities she liked and admired in Eben, though she could wish it augmented a hundredfold, for in truth his joys were somewhat pale. What she did not yet know was whether Eben could be exalted by extraordinary surprises beyond the verge, right over into the realm of shattering delight she sometimes experienced, into such a state of rapture as that into which she had been momentarily dissolved when she had stepped out into the dew-spangled meadow a few minutes ago, giving her an instant, as insubstantial as the fast-drying magical droplets that had inspired it, worth a whole month of bickering, grubbing, moping lazy and alone in a city. Could Eben, could the Selectman, transact such delight? They were both articulate men, they used their tongues readily enough—but seldom, it seemed, to speak of deep emotions. Hester wondered whether, keeping too long their Puritanical silence on all such feelings, they might, in the end, cease altogether to feel.

"I'll tell you what made things so bad last night: These people didn't really want me for Selectman in the first place," Mr. Avered said. "It was all very chancy, my getting this job, and now I don't know if I want it."

"Mr. Welch—is that the giant's name?—said something about a split vote," Hester said, trying to be sympathetic; disappointed to see Eben's father's near-bliss aborted by self-pity.

"It was because of the school fight," he said. "People weren't going to vote regular, they couldn't agree on a candidate. I was a compromise—and now it curdles 'em to see that I won't compromise. I just refuse to whop over from this side to that when I believe in things."

"Did George Challenge help you get elected? Mrs. Tuller said something this morning . . ."

"George Challenge? Don't mind his bowlegs: some say he's taller sitting down than he is standing up."

"Did he pull wires for you?"

"He's crookeder than a ram's horn. You remember what old Hosea Biglow said?—that rubber trees fust begun bearin' when political consciences come into wearin'? That's George Challenge for you."

"Did he help you?"

"Nobody can get elected, not even as dog warden, around here unless Mr. Challenge nods in his direction. Just the way you can't buy fresh meat at the market without the little blue pure-food stamp on it. Can't you see 'George Challenge' stamped across my forehead?" Mr. Avered's eyes were like those of a small boy, appealing for help.

This was degrading; Hester wanted no more. "Then your witnesses aren't worth much," she said cruelly. "The giant is for you anyhow—he made a speech for your drive last night. And now it turns out you're George Challenge's poodle. Your witnesses are no good to you at all."

"There were others who saw the crowd of woodchucks. Don't worry, girl. There are others up there right now looking at 'em. And you'll see 'em soon enough yourself, buck teeth, shoe-leather hides, and all." She had said she feared the teeth, the skins, the skulls; so, Hester thought, cruelty always answers cruelty. She wanted to make amends, but before she could, he had taken a startling jump.

"Now tell me about you," he said, with a kind of gentleness, as if she had not been attacking him; though there was, to be sure, a note of determination in his gentleness.

■

HESTER almost had to stop and think who she was. She knew she was standing beside a handsome older man in a woodsy place, among buoyant young trees that were menaced by sweet-smelling, murderous vines; she and this man were waiting; they were employed in an outlandish experience; they were alone, all alone, glimpsed in their green privacy only by the indifferent sun. "Now tell me about you," he had suddenly said. Hester cast about for an easy, evasive answer, for she had been trying for weeks—for the whole period of Eben's courtship, certainly—to discover exactly what she was, to make sure of her identity, to try to find out whether it matched, or complemented, or could be melted wholly away by, Eben's, and so far she had not found any insights she could depend on, she was still only guessing at herself; she would have to put off Eben's father's demand with some vague reply. She thought for a moment of her own father, of one of the last times she had seen him. She had been about twelve years old—it was half her life ago! The family—mother, father, Hester, and Pete—were living in the national capital then, in three dark rented rooms in a house of orange brick on an avenue named for a state. It was midsummer. Her unemployed father sat on the edge of his bed in the back room perspiring in an undershirt, some seersucker pants, and a pair of slippers; she was sitting in a straight wooden chair with a cane seat in the next room, which was connected with her parents' by a doorless archway, trying to read; he kept breaking in. "What're you reading?" he asked. A book by an English woman. "Good girl. Take care of your eyes, Hes," he said. "Have you enough light there?" She had. "Don't burn your eyes out, my Hes. You're going to need those hazel eyes. The world's going to need your eyes." The more his personal failure bore in upon him, the more convinced he became that his children had the potentials of success. The world would some day be grateful for famous Hes, for the great Pete. How bitterly she and her brother had learned that aspiration wouldn't buy groceries! That was probably why she was so afraid of Eben's undirected ambition. Yet how lovable, too, that overleaping naïve hopefulness had been in her broken father. "Eyes on the lodestar!" he had used often to exhort his children. Looking now at the blur that, coming into focus, became Eben's father, she wondered how Mr. Avered could be as complacent as he seemed, so satisfied with his small orbit.... She thought how, sitting at her metal desk on the seventeenth floor, she was always careful to have enough light for her hazel eyes to see by, just in case.... Mr. Avered lived here in his smallness perfectly satisfied with himself and openly contemptuous of Eben's efforts to "better" himself.

"I've always lived in cities," she said.

"Can't hold that against you," he said.

"It makes me feel awkward here."

"You don't seem so to me."

"I'd be lonely here."

"You can't lick loneliness by huddling up with half a trillion strangers, can you?"

"I don't know. Where can you? Do you have any friends here in Tunxis? I mean real friends."

"I have a lot of neighbors. I'll go that far."

"I mean friends."

"I had a friend once," the Selectman said.

"Who was that?"

"My wife, Mrs. Matthew Avered."

"Why the past tense?"

"I don't know, we've taken our ways. I talk all the time and she hardly says a word, unless it's to tell me I have a goneness about me. She's so tired most of the time she can barely stiver along from day to day."

"She seems wonderfully placid to me."

"She is. She's as calm as a pond that doesn't have any inlet or outflow: some call it stagnant. ... Whoa, girl, we were supposed to be talking about you."

"I've always lived in cities," Hester said, smiling. "My father wanted to be a lawyer. Some of the time he was a clerk in post offices. Toward the end I guess you'd say he was a bum—no good to anyone, anyway."

"You're just right for Eben," the Selectman said. "We Avereds always try to marry the daughters of tramps and hobos.... How did you get to know so much about people?"

"Out of books," she said. "Whenever I read, I'm careful to have plenty of light, so I'll be sure to see everything that's there."

"I used to read a lot," the Selectman said. "Did you ever read the poems of Patmore?"

This was a real surprise to Hester. "We had to read some of his sonnets in college," she said. "All I remember is, I liked his name better than his verses: Coventry Kersey Dighton Patmore—*that* I'll never forget."

"Well, girl, you're about to tie yourself down, you ought to read his long one about marriage. Then pick it up twenty-five years later, the way I did night before last, when I got thinking about you and Eben, and see whether it sounds the same to you. One grows and learns."

Hester felt an onrush of anxiety. What was the Selectman trying to tell her? Why did everyone always traffic so much in hints, why couldn't people speak out their straight thoughts? Why was everyone here trying to discourage her about Eben? Hester's defenses rallied to a quickened drumbeat of her heart. She began to be defiant. Let them try, she cried to herself, let them just try to discourage me! And she said to herself for the first time that she was sure about Eben. It did not matter to her that she felt, in her turn, not a real softening of the spirit that could be called love, but determination.

"Listen!" the Selectman said.

Up to the left the noisemaking had begun again, and soon Hester and the Selectman could hear an order to move forward being passed down the line, then Coit shouted it, and Hester volleyed it on to the dancing teacher; and they stepped into the woods. Gradually the honeysuckle thinned away, and she and the father of her suitor walked through bare-floored green gothic chapels. Off to their left Coit, instead of whistling, was singing now at the top of his voice:

> "Oh, I'm a hayseed,
> A hairy seaweed,
> And my ears are made of leather
> And they flop in stormy weather;
> Gosh all hemlock,
> I'm tougher'n a pine knot ..."

■

AND THAT ONE," the Selectman said, "is a beech—you could put your girl-hand around its trunk now, but it'll grow to be enormous. It'll beat out all these taller pig-nut trees around it, they'll gradually be overshadowed and weakened and then some fall equinox they'll plop over in a big wind, and when I'm dead, and Eben's dead, and Eben's son is dead, and the son's son is an old man, this tree'll stand up here over everything and cock its snook at the world—the paltry world. Whenever I feel pleased with myself, to the point where I can see I'm boring my neighbors, all I have to do is take a look at one of these beeches and I get humble pretty quick, humble and a little bit scared, because time is one thing to a beech tree and another thing to me. I put so many things off! Do you procrastinate?"

"Oh, I do!"

Hester felt a sudden, unexpected touch of the kind of poignancy which she had regarded, all through her adolescent years, as the earliest throe of romantic love, but which she recognized, now that she was more experienced, as being no more than the painful thrill of discovery, the pang of new acquaintance—with sometimes a fillip of desire thrown in. Any hazard there may have been in this incipient feeling was abated, and even made slightly ridiculous, by Coit's lewd whistling and singing to the left and the dancing master's musical halloos to the right, as well as by an occasional startling bellow from the Selectman right beside her and, afterwards, a dutiful, responsive shriek from her own throat. She understood that the emotion she directed toward this man was partly admiration and partly pity. Eben had told her more than once that versatility was his father's curse: that while he was not quite broad enough or brilliant enough to be the kind of universal man New England had once produced in its out-of-the-way villages, he was, still and all, an extraordinary jack-of-all-hobbies, versed in various country lores, professionally inconstant—now an insurance salesman, now middleman for truck farmers, briefly a smalltime speculative building contractor, once town librarian, often a summer-month real-estate agent, and now, because so available, a public servant; never successful in Eben's terms, yet never improvident, either. Hester savored the word "goneness," which the Selectman had said his wife used about him. She was grazed again by that sweet sensation of incipience—whereupon, dispelling it altogether and shocking her uninsulated sensibilities, the Selectman suddenly imitated the clamor of a crow with horrible fidelity.

"When am I going to see a woodchuck?" Hester asked, inwardly a-tremble.

"Let's see. Division Two ought to be going through Romeo Bacon's old meadows, where the burrows are, pretty directly now. Anytime after that. Pretty soon, I'd calculate."

"I told you," she said, "that I was afraid of the woodchucks' teeth. Now I'm scared of something else."

"What's that, girl?"

"Mrs. Tuller."

The Selectman gave out a single descending arpeggio of laughter, as if Hester's idea were utterly ridiculous; then abruptly he was serious and thoughtful. "As a matter of fact, I think I see what you mean," he said. "Mrs. Tuller must have half a bushel of brains in that head of hers, but I guess her heart's no bigger than a French pea. It's a funny thing: no one in Tunxis is more self-sacrificing than she is; she's famous for her labors of mercy. She's a teacher, to begin with—she lives her life for other people's children; couldn't have any of her own, or her ballet dancer couldn't give her any, one or the other. She's a devoted teacher—but ouch! Strict! She's strong as an orang-outang, as any pupil she's ever had'll tell you. During the war there was a time when every one of the town's doctors was off in the services, so what did she do? She appointed herself a medico, degrees and laws be damned. She has a motorcycle; you should've seen her in those years flying to sickbeds, with the saddlebags on the back busting with junk from the drugstore and her white smock flapping in the wind and her thighs shaking like laughing blimps. She didn't kill a single patient, but it was pretty well understood that so long as she was in charge, a sick person had to get worse, and I mean miserably worse, before he got better; she had a way of seeing to that; she favored mustard plasters and emetics; she was a firm believer that New England folks could only be cured with counter-irritants. She's always been a flower-sender and a train-meeter, and whenever someone passes on under a certified doctor's hands, she's the first to inflict condolences on the bereaved—and she knows how to make 'em felt, too. She was a Cherevoy; that family was of Acadian descent, her ancestors were shipped down here from Nova Scotia with the Acadians that were dumped in Connecticut twenty years before the Revolution. Maybe she's never forgiven the Anglo-Saxons for that outrage. Maybe she's furious at the world for giving her Friedrich Tuller. Maybe she hates herself because her head's so big. You're right, girl, watch out for her, don't let her take your skin off on the pretext you need your back scratched. Her kindliness has a murderous edge to it. Yet I can't help saying she's a wonderful woman; Tunxis would be dull and wishy-washy without her. I'll do anything for Mrs. Tuller—as long as I can keep my distance from her."

Ahead the trees were thinning out and the underbrush—bayberry and blueberry and humps of gleaming cat brier—was becoming more profuse, and Hester could see that they would come out soon onto a partly overgrown meadow. They were still walking forward at a very easy pace, and all across the hollow could be heard the sounds, unnatural for human beings, of the sluggish pursuit. Hester felt increasingly apprehensive, as with part of her mind she listened to the Selectman's words about Mrs. Tuller, and with another part she imagined a herd of wild boars bearing down upon the line between her and the helpless dancing master, and with yet another part she thought how almost fearfully beautiful this early morning had become.

"Mrs. Tuller said some awful things about the Avereds," she managed to remark.

"All the time she acted as if she were praising us, didn't she?"

"Oh yes, she called you a saint."

"That I am not, girl," he said, and all at once he had floated off in that deep daydream of his; staring, staring.

"Do you think we could go all day without seeing any woodchucks?" she asked, wanting to draw him back.

He did not answer for a long time, then he turned his face to hers and said, "I'm sorry, girl, I was off in the next county when you said that last. Would you care to say it again?"

"No," Hester said. "It wasn't important."

Just before they reached the edge of the abandoned meadow, a new order to halt the line came down from the left, and the Selectman, saying he wanted to walk up to see if anything was the matter, left Hester alone.

■

AN ORDER to move again came quite soon. Knowing now what she was supposed to do and how to do it, Hester was less fearful of ridicule than she had been, but she was still afraid of being tattered by enamel chisels; she felt like a primitive, like a woman from the troglodytic era—afraid of being eaten alive. She realized only now how comforting the presence of the Selectman had been. She missed him actively, wished he would return; but he did not come.

The field into which Hester now advanced was a new terrain to her. It was ragged, half way between cultivated, which once it had been, and wild, which again it would soon be—somehow forlorn-making: it reminded Hester that sometimes men try to do more than they are able, then they grow weary and give up and don't care. There were still large patches of strong, tall, enclumped timothy grass in the enclosure, but among them had sprung up new growth—numerous tall lone-standing cedars, saplings of wild cherry and pignut, and seedlings of maple and birch and oak; as well as aggressive pigmy forests, closing in on the good grass, of milkweed, cat brier, and poison ivy, which she skirted. There were, besides, four tall swamp maples in the field, one near each of its corners; these were so regularly spaced that she guessed they must have been transplanted there, when the field had been used for field crops, to give grazing animals shade.

Hester's slow course across the field took her toward one of these maples, and when she was about thirty feet away from it, she suddenly gasped, she froze, her skin tingled all over, her heart tried to run away from its cavity. She saw a woodchuck under the tree, just to the right of the trunk.

The animal was standing up on its hind legs, in profile to her, facing the sun, measuring the full length of its spine against the maple bark. Its head was tilted arear; its mouth seemed drawn back in a kind of grin, a grimace of complacency. Its eyes were three-quarters closed. Its forepaws were spread apart and limply hanging. The sunlight, slanting in under the branches of the tree at this early hour, lay full on the animal's round belly, and the direct light, together with the modulation in the color of the woodchuck's fur, from a dark rusty brown on the stomach to near-black against the tree, made it seem prosperously rounded, a comfortable pillow of a thing. The figure was one of utter well-being; it was a caricature of guiltless human indolence. Hester realized that the animal was taking a morning sunbath. It must have been driven with the others from its home, it was in mortal danger; yet here it leaned, a sleek hedonist, almost unbearably comfortable, to judge by those pulled-back lips, its danger far, far out of mind.

Hester lost her tenseness. The bear-mouse monk! What an amiable enemy!

For a moment Hester wished she could change places with this bliss-ridden beast. She, too, was a sunlover; she never got enough sun. When the summer sun warmed her body, prone on a sandy place, it seemed that her nerves were melted into common flesh, her brain was fused into a soothing, soft, idea-less juice; she enjoyed a warm liquefaction of all anxiety. She became something simple when the sun was on her. She understood that this sun-soaked simpleton on a beach was a contemptible creature, and all the centuries of man's patient climbing had not been suffered, Gethsemane, Chartres, King Lear, The Magic Flute had not been experienced, in order that human life might culminate in the repose of a girl's figure on the sand under the sun—a figure of languor, sexuality, irresponsibility, and brimming fullness of self. Yet what heavenly retrogression! She thought it was perfectly expressed in the pulled-back lips of the sunbathing woodchuck, showing the near-hurt of true pleasure.

She thought of the month of March in the city; how running across a sleet-sloppy street, with the filthy slush splashing up on her iron-cold stockings, she had to hug herself, as it were, in her own tense arms for only comfort; her hands and feet were in perpetual pain all through the chilly time; she frowned constantly—and dreamed of the summer sun. Now she felt wholly identified with the woodchuck before her. If only she could, as he, crawl into a burrow lined with leaves and straw and sleep the winter away! She dimly knew that her wishes did not mean precisely what they seemed: she supposed she wanted to be an infant on the warm breast of the beach, and she would even gladly be a foetus in the wintertime. How often she had heard the ideas of the modern psychologists spent in city chitchat like shiny, tinkling quarters, dimes, and nickels, by people who, like her, had never even read the essential books. Backward and downward from the arts! Man the beaches! To the womb!

She mocked her desires, and felt them still.

The woodchuck stirred. Its right paw went up and scratched its ear. It yawned, and then tilted its head a little to the left. The eyes were still drooped. Above the slouching belly the animal's chest swelled up and then seemed to burst in a deep, deep sigh of contentment.

Hester could help herself no longer. She laughed out loud.

Instantly the animal was erect and alert. Its small black eyes looked at Hester with a glittering defiance and hatred. The mouth was still drawn back, but now the agony was not of pleasure but of antagonism. Seeing the animal full-face, Hester was for the first time confronted by the enormous teeth. Her amusement was driven scurrying, her flesh crawled, glands prepared her for a battle to death. The woodchuck held its inimical pose for a few instants, then seemed to collapse into swift retreat. Its black back rippled across the field for perhaps twenty feet. Then the animal stopped, rose erect again on its haunches and looked around at Hester, as if it wanted to make sure that the monster it had seen had not been a fantasy. Hester imagined she saw a look of derision on the bear-mouse face, and she grew a little angry.

"Get on, you bastard!" she shouted, her back thrilling to another charge of adrenal fluid, and she stamped her foot on the ground.

The woodchuck ran skimper-scamper away. Hester moved forward with new confidence in herself.

■

AFTER THE CAUCUS Eben had been peevish, Hester remembered. He had led her to the car, where they had waited in the front seat for his father to join them, and though Eben had held her hand, as he always did in dark places, he had not seemed to be conscious of touching her; his voltage had seemed very low. His hand was limp and moist.

"It'll take him an hour to get here," Eben said, she recalled. "He'll have to argue the whole thing over two or three times before he can tear himself away. I know him."

"I could have choked that Sessions person," Hester said.

"He was the only one in the whole bunch who made any sense."

"You're trying some kind of joke on me."

"No, it's true. What this hick town needs is a few people with hard heads. Everybody's got mattress stuffing in the skull around here—including the famous Selectman."

"Eben! Your father was terrific."

"Just because he kept his temper? Do you think that makes somebody terrific? Think of the nonsense he was talking! Why, this whole woodchuck drive is child's play: it's a Boy Scout outing. Tunxis needs a woodchuck hunt about as much as Central Park needs a squirrel shoot."

"Why don't you try to get along better with your father?"

"Because he's elected to live in another century from ours. And I don't think that solves this century. I just can't get along with a man from the last century, and what's more, I won't. I think it's for him to make the effort to catch up, not for me to slide backwards."

"Are you saying that you're better than he is?"

"No, I'm saying that I talk a different language. He's a foreigner here. He's got to accommodate himself."

"A foreigner! You have a few prejudices of your own from the last century, Eben. Besides, you may be wrong about your father. He may be more up-to-date than you and I are. How do we know what's really modern?"

"I know that we're watching the world fall apart, and he moseys through life as though we were on the threshold of a golden age. Oh, for God's sake," Eben burst out. "I'm tired of listening to him and thinking about him."

The Selectman did not take an hour to get back to the car; he appeared in less than ten minutes, while there were still quite a few other cars to be driven away. "Hello, love birds," he said with a remarkable casualness as he opened the door to the driver's seat. He took off his walnut-colored coat, threw it in the back seat, loosened his necktie, and slid behind the wheel.

"Congratulations," Hester said. "You were wonderful."

"I don't want to talk about the meeting," the Selectman said with more anger than he had shown during the whole evening. All three were silent as they drove home. When they reached the house, Eben's father was abruptly rather cheerful, and he said, "Let's sit on the screen porch awhile and talk. I need a potion. Miss Hester, it'll do you good to sit in a rocker on a porch while Eben and I blow the soot out of your ears with some Tunxis gossip." But gossip, as it turned out, was not to be the fare. The Selectman went inside the house and switched on the parlor lights, and on the porch Hester and Eben settled themselves in a metal glider. The Selectman returned soon with three tumblers, each partly full of dark liquor.

"Isn't there any ice in the house?" Eben asked irritably.

"Ice in the icebox, where it always was," the Selectman said, "if it's your notion to spoil good West Indy rum."

"Rum!" Eben exclaimed contemptuously.

> "Rum-a-tum-tum,
> The farmer drinked some,
> Rum-a-tum-tum,
> The farmer's strick dumb,"

the Selectman said singsong, and took a sip from his glass. "I wouldn't give whisky hell-room, and I advise you to follow the example of your venerable father."

Eben stamped angrily into the house after some ice. As soon as the screen door slammed behind him, the Selectman moved onto the porch swing where Eben had been sitting with Hester and said, "Let's send Hamlet to bed and talk awhile. There's so much to discuss!"

"If you mean Eben," Hester said, "you'd better take it up with him. He may take it into his head to send the King of Denmark to sleep."

"The King of Denmark?" the Selectman asked, off

guard; then quickly he cried, "Oh!", and after another moment's thinking he said, sounding quite startled, "Listen, girl, don't talk that way."

When Eben had come back and had eased himself without audible complaint into the chair his father had occupied, the Selectman said, "We ought to have some apples; rum and apples go together like cement and sea sand. Old Ira Leaming—he was John Leaming, Senior's father, he was found frozen to death near the fire tower up on Beggar's Mountain standing up leaning against a tree with his gun tucked under his arm—anyway, when I was a boy Ira Leaming had an apple orchard clear down to where Sodom Street cuts through the town now, where he raised McIntosh apples that give farmers so much trouble nowadays with the blight, sweet as maple syrup. They were the best stealing apples anywhere around. Son, did you ever have gumption enough to steal an apple?"

Eben did not answer.

"Stolen apples are better tasting than store apples," the Selectman said. "Son," he then said, "it seems to me you're kind of stand-offish toward your venerable father. What's the matter, boy?"

Hester answered, "Eben says the matter is that you live way off in a different century from him."

There was a silence, during which the Selectman's face, being turned away from the parlor light, showed nothing; finally he said, "A different world, anyway, I guess. I live in the world of what I consider values; he lives in the world of what he considers realities. He thinks my values are obsolete, I think his realities aren't any more real or true to life than those Gorgon sisters that had snakes for hair."

For a moment Hester thought she saw what the cleavage was—the father living in the world of stern education, personal reticence, love of nature; of respect for property, idiosyncrasy, privacy, and poetry; of literal horsepower and the slow walk; of rigid family life; of frugality and thrift, of the Classics and the Bible, of charades and early-to-bed—the son living in a prosy, urgent, intrusive world, a world of "realities": of revolution everywhere, of war or military preparings and posturings, of fear for the future; of cities and science, of jets, reactors, and ultra-high-frequencies; of cool rationality and nervous breakdowns; of the shifty images of TV; of ads, giveaways, strained budgets, gadgets bought on the installment plan; of speeding tickets and drunken picnics and sexual frolicsomeness in the small hours. The opposition was clear in Hester's mind for only a flash, then she began to see that her idea was too simple: there were qualifications and shadings and loopholes, for in the father's world there had also been seething repressions and horrible social injustices, there had been rationalizations and pretenses and fake decencies smothered with heavy decor, while in the son's world there were miracles of progress ... and now she heard Eben, too, exploring the same doubts.

"Stolen apples taste good," he said, "so where do your values fit in with the Ten Commandments? 'Thou shalt not steal.'"

"Stealing apples wasn't stealing, that was just exercising boyhood rights and prerogatives under New England common law."

"Does New England common law make provision for all the other sins, too?" Eben asked.

Hester noticed that the Selectman paused again and then did not answer the question. "If you're asking me where I got my values, son, I don't know whether I can tell you right out. The Congregational Church drove a lot into me, then before he went mad and they put him in his wooden cage, Parson Churnstick drove a lot out again, by going too far with his nonsense. This man,

Hester, was a fanatical Sabbatarian. You weren't supposed to walk fast leaving the meetinghouse, even in the rain, and once he denounced Belle Booge, who's Belle Sessions now, from the pulpit for running a comb through her hair on the street on Sunday, as if she'd been a common slut about to have a come-by-chance child. That was enough to cool us young ones off on a certain brand of religion. ... Your grandmother gave me a lot of my values, son—she called 'em just plain horse sense. I got some in school from the best teacher a boy ever had, Jared Andrus. I've learned a lot from Anak Welch, stubborn as stone though he be. I've learned from doing wrong." He paused. "In fact, it seems that the only real specific for evil-poisoning is evil itself." The Selectman stopped and sat there in Puritan rigidity.

"I keep coming back to the Ten Commandments," Eben insisted a trifle shrilly, pressing his father during his strange moment of discomfiture. "It's all there in condensed form. If you don't live by a code like that ..."

"You people in the city live on capsules," the Selectman said, suddenly cool. "You have too simple a view of the Bible, son. The Ten Commandments are in Exodus, twenty. The very next chapter, Exodus twenty-one, tells us believers how to organize polygamy and slavery, and that's where it says, 'Eye for eye, tooth for tooth, hand for hand, foot for foot, burning for burning, wound for wound, stripe for stripe.' Oh, I know that book, boy. There are some harsh home truths about human nature in that book, son; it would pay you to read it, instead of talking so slick and glib like some gowk who's just taken a vitamin pill and read a condensed article and thinks he contains all the world's victuals and all her knowledge. Don't forget the serpent of brass and Lot's daughters and the mess of pottage and Mordecai and the thirty pieces of silver and how there wasn't a man jack in the crowd who dared cast a stone at the adulterous woman and how the multitude shouted to Pilate for blood—all those things are in there alongside your beloved capsule."

Hester felt the tension between the two men, and she understood that the elder had been somehow stung, but what underlay the strain she could not know. It struck her that the assigned rôles were reversed—that Eben was arguing for a specific set of values, while his father seemed to be urging deeper realities on him. It disturbed her to feel, as she did, that the contest was being waged at least partly for her benefit, and she wanted it ended. "Weren't you two going to tell me some local gossip?" she said.

The Selectman, too, had apparently had enough, for he said, "Aren't you weary, son? Why don't you march off to bed? I've some questions to ask your young lady."

"And leave Hes alone with Selectman Avered?" Eben said. "Fat chance."

"Then I guess it's me," Eben's father said, accepting defeat with an agility that Hester could not consider flattering. He arose, said his goodnights, and retired.

Eben, who moved to the swing, seemed moody and disinclined to talk. Hester, knowing that his feelings had many currents and eddies, decided to let him drift. Finally he said, "I guess I ought to warn you, Father's rather famous, or used to be, for girl-chasing."

" 'Warn' me? I can take care of myself, dear Eben."

"I'll never forgive him for what he did to Mother."

"What did he do to her?"

"He squeezed all the vitality out of her, somehow, with his goings-on. Even I can remember when she used to be a regular vixen."

Impatiently Hester changed the subject, and in due

course, after they had talked awhile, Eben embraced her and kissed her. She felt a sudden access of desire, stronger even than usual. Eben was tender; he denied her as always, but not before working his way through her defenses until, far beyond surrender, she clamored for utmost captivity. In his denial, murmuring that that was for marriage, he seemed strong, utterly male and unmanageable, and, Hester realized when she had gone frustrated to bed, surprisingly like his neo-Puritan father.

■

ACROSS A TUMBLED WALL of glacier-rounded stones, beyond the field with the four maples where Hester had seen the woodchuck, the landscape again grew more fretted and entangled, the second-growth became thicker and taller. The terrain still sloped forward, but more gradually now, toward the base of the hollow. Repeated calls had come down from the left to move more slowly, and yet more slowly, and yet more slowly. In the dark thicket, with her private woodchuck somewhere ahead, Hester became anxious again, and her heart leaped when she heard, then saw, the Selectman coming down the line. He was grinning; he was a welcome sight.

"I saw a woodchuck!" she called to him, as if she had seen an eclipse, or a whale, or a unicorn in a garden.

"We have the whole caboodle running along up there," the Selectman said, pointing backwards over his shoulder with his thumb. "So Beauty has seen the Beast? How was he?"

"Oh, he was so comical—sunning himself against a tree."

"All over being afraid, then?" the Selectman asked, falling into step beside Hester.

"Well—"

"That's good, girl. Don't stop being leery of them." The Selectman seemed intensely serious, not trifling now; she remembered how he had teased her about being afraid, before, with his story of the old woman, Dorcas Thrall, and her fear of birds. "They're horrible!" he said. "Once I was walking in a field up here with a stick in my hand, and I saw a mother woodchuck with four fat little ones. I went after 'em with my staff. Well, the mother herded her babies to the mouth of their burrow in the wink of an eye, and she jumped in, and then she turned and pushed the babies back out into the field, so I'd get them, not her. . . . Don't stop being leery of 'em."

"Thanks, I won't," Hester said, not without conviction. She thought for a moment of the Forward-Avered word, "wicked." Infanticides; wicked, wicked. "So you organized this drive out of hatred of the evil things," she said.

"Oh Lordy, no," the Selectman said. "You mustn't think that I'm some kind of Captain Ahab. No, no! I only look for good and bad in people. This drive's just a practical measure."

"But I have an idea that 'values' were involved in your mind when you set about planning it. Weren't they?"

"Values are involved in everything we do." Suddenly he took one of his leaps in thought—and later she wondered what his train of mind at this moment had been. "Are you a virgin?" he asked.

"No."

"My son Eben?"

"No."

"You mean he wasn't the first?"

"I mean he wasn't, period."

"Ahem," the Selectman said, as if to rebuke, or at least intercept, an impulse he had had to laugh. "How many?"

"You asked me a simple question and I gave you a simple answer. Do you have to hound me?"

"We live in a world of realities," the Selectman ironically said. "Does Eben know?"

"He's never asked."

"I'll have to have a short talk with that boy—not about you, Miss Hester. I just think his curiosity ought to have a whetstone applied to it."

"I think he has a very lively curiosity," Hester said, "about important things."

"I worry about that boy's curiosity," the Selectman said, moving cautiously out of the mood of impudent intimacy into which he had plunged—warned away, perhaps, by the cool lack of emphasis in her last phrase. "His curiosity's too mechanical. I remember once when he was just going from baby to boy, just between grass and hay, his mother was trying to teach him to say prayers on his way to bed, and he wouldn't stop bouncing around, so she said, 'Ebenezer, you have to keep still and speak clearly when you say your prayers, so God'll hear you up in the sky; He lives up in the sky, you know.' The boy, instead of asking who or what or whether God is, instead of a big, central question, just asked, 'Will an airplane hit him in the ear?' That's what I mean. He's always been that way. Side issues."

Hester said, "I think that was a pretty central question—the conflict of science with faith, after all. You don't give your son credit."

"I hope Eben marries you," the father said, walking close beside Hester as they moved out into a clearing, where a sudden, cheerful light fell on the strolling pair.

"Why do you say that?"

"Because you give a feeling of confidence; you seem to know where you are. And"—he gave her a comically voracious ogle—"because you're an eyeful."

Hester was puzzled, because for some minutes she had felt an ambiguity in all that her companion had said and done; perhaps because of Eben's "warning" the night before, she had now either detected or imagined a flirtatious note in his words and acts. She could not tell whether he had been turning over in his mind the possibility of some harmless woodland toying, or meant what he said and truly and selflessly wanted her for a son he loved and had set a canopy over his feelings in the Yankee way; and because the ambiguity tortured her, she felt maladroit, wordless, shy.

"Hey! You hogs! Hey! Hey!" the Selectman startled her by roaring to the woodchuck world. Then mildly he pointed up toward a stretch of Thighbone Ledge that had come into view in the clearing, at a great, deep scar in the dark brown traprock. "Look at the quarry," he said. "They worked it for about twenty years and got the best basalt out of the ledge to use for roadbed on the county highways and then abandoned it. That's New England for you—we've uprooted its meager wealth, and all that's left is a lot of water-filled pits and empty mine shafts and worked-out fields that weren't worth working in the first place—and folks, of course." He seemed wholly taken up with this thought, for his expression was sober and deep, and Hester was annoyed now, not only with him but also with herself, because she could not deny that she was disappointed; her vanity had been let down with a bump. (And later she was annoyed with herself, or at least troubled, because in these moments she had not given Eben a single important thought.) She hated not knowing whether she had been flirted with; if she had been, she resented this sudden little lecture on the conservation of the earth's resources.

"Folks!" she thought. "Fossils, you mean."

■

FOR SOME TIME Hester had been threading her way through scattered patches of cat brier, and now directly ahead of her in the next field she saw a widespread expanse of it, a sea of glaucous leaves, glistening vines humping in choppy waves over bushes and boulders, only here and there an islet of grass or underbrush not yet engulfed by the vicious tide. She remembered the brier vines that Andrew had showed her the day before, with golden-green spikes like copper carpet tacks all along the sinuous stems; and she remembered Mrs. Tuller's warning: "Do not plunge too valorously. . . ." On her left and right, Coit and the dancing master were working inexorably forward, making their eccentric woodchuck-repellent noises, and occasionally, as well, she could hear Anak Welch exercising his bovine throat with tragic-sounding baritone lowings. She was alone again; a message had come down the line asking the advance men to report to Division Two, where there was some tactical problem, and the Selectman had run off with a boyish whoop. She had walked forward in a kind of daze, puzzling over what had just happened to her, or rather what had not happened to her, and thinking about Eben and the future, and about the Selectman and the present; and about ambiguities and uncertainties in others and in herself; and all the time she felt somehow bad-tempered and displeased with the way life was treating her.

As she crossed over into the new field and came close to the cat brier, she saw that the growth, at least on its outer edges, did not appear to be closely interwoven, and that by threading back and forth, skirting between the many hummocks and knots of vine that made up the whole obstacle, it would be easy to move through it; from a distance it had seemed much more compact. She started in, and made her way for some minutes without so much as being brushed by a waxy leaf, remembering to warn the woodchucks of her coming with a shout from time to time. Then all at once the mounds of vine grew taller and closed in; she came up against a tight and extensive entanglement.

There was nothing to do but go around; she would go Coit's way, she thought, around the left—and at the thought of the bully she experienced a strange stab of curiosity and pleasure. With many a twist and turn, in a sort of waltzing detour, she progressed, somewhat forward of sideways, along the near edge of the impenetrability. She had only gone a few yards, however, when she saw a well-beaten path, clearly one of the woodchuck trails the Selectman had talked about at the caucus, and had urged the hunters to use, that led into a kind of funnel running deep into close-knit brier towering over her head. She assumed that this much-used animal trail must go all the way through the cat brier patch, so she turned and followed it. The funnel became a high-walled soft lane, winding, she imagined for a moment, like an eighteenth-century informal garden path to some out-of-the-way Fragonardish playroom of shade, where girls with their legs frilled in lace swooped high on swings pumped by desire-flushed swains. Cheerfully she tooted and yapped at the woodchucks, and heard, from the calls of her companions, that she was still fairly well in line.

After a bit the vines opened up somewhat again, into another area of clustered and mounded islets of brier. The path underfoot seemed less trafficked, then Hester saw there were several paths here wending and winding among the dangerous heaps, and she began to feel mazed. Still, oriented by the noises her friends kept venting, she moved, as she thought, forward. Gradually the vines thickened once more, the spaces between the clumps narrowed.

Hester thought for a moment that she ought to turn back again and escape and circle the whole troublesome field, but then she imagined she must be nearly through to the far side, and she was suddenly afraid of getting lost if she tried to retreat and of falling far behind the picket line.

She came up against a tight barricade; turned and met another; reversed herself and met another. She was encircled, bewildered. She found a place, toward the direction of the drive, it seemed, where the vines were at least shallow, and she decided to get a leg up and over and try to wade forward. The vines plucked at her jeans and pricked her legs. Still, she made some progress, and once she had a glimpse ahead to open meadow and saw that she had not too far to go. She felt encouraged and wallowed onward, ignoring many scratches, and for a moment came to a tiny open place where grass grew and through which, she fancied, a trace of a woodchuck path ran. Then she plunged, she realized, too valorously forward into the growth beyond, and soon was thoroughly caught. The vines embraced over her head. She pulled at them and tried to lift her knees and move her feet. Her heart raced. She felt stung and bitten and angry. She was able somehow to wriggle and stagger a few feet forward.

Then she fell and could go no further. She seemed tied down. She felt distended and enormous; she felt like a Gulliver lashed down by fabulous miniature powers.

Terror shook her. She tried to rise and back away. Her arms seemed bound, she could not move. She put her forehead down on a forearm and sobbed on her couch of thorns. Then, as she heard the dancing master, Coit, and Anak Welch calling, whistling, calling, she knew she had been left behind and she raised her head, thinking of trying to shout to them.

She lowered her eyes. Directly ahead of her on the ground among the vines, not two feet from her face, she saw the dry, whited skeleton of a woodchuck. She screamed, but knew at once that her cry would be thought merely part of the hunt, part of the day's play.

The blanched skull before her was turned to one side on the dry vertebrae, as if the animal had, at last, simply gone to sleep.

■

ON THE WALL of the beach terrace, carefully posed among some delicate shells and fronds of coral, on a doily of seagrape leaves, was the skull of a sea turtle, as big as a cow's skull. It was whiter than the sand of the beach, white as the spindrift on the wave tops. Picking up the skull, their hostess, who was tan as a mulatto, so that the dry bone left a pale calx on the glossy skin of her forearm, told the others how a sea turtle begets its young: When the huge creature comes up to lay its eggs, she said, it labors up the beach leaving a trail like a bulldozer's; the mother makes a mussy nest, a hill of sand, with twigs and seaweed on it—but that is only a decoy-place, for she moves away then and prepares another crater and lays her eggs (they hurt her so much, or parturition makes her so sad, that she cries immense tears) and leaves that place as tidy as she can and goes back down to the water. "The eggs are rubbery," Mrs. Mandeson said, reposing the skull; "they'll bounce on the terrace here." While the eggs hatch under the heat of the sun, the mother waits offshore, she said, and when they have emerged from their eggs the blind baby turtles turn around two or three times and then home, as if by a kind of radar, straight for the sea. The mother is waiting there offshore to keep the barracuda away.

"How do turtles make love, Professor?" George Mandeson asked his wife.

"The usual way," she said, "I guess."

"Is it usual to be wearing a tight-fitting house when you make love?"

Hester lay on a mat of woven rushes, half-hearing and aware that she glistened, for she was bearing some of the weight of the Florida sun, and the effort made her perspire; she was oiled, too.

"Listen to the rut of the waves," Eben said. He was in a good mood—living for sensations on this vacation trip that he and Hester had arranged to share by purposeful coincidence; for all sensations, that is, save one, for he was a Puritan boy and proving himself splendidly in his physical restraint toward Hester.

"Boy!" George Mandeson said. "There's power in them thar waves."

"How many tons do you guess a wave weighs?" Eben asked speculatively. "I mean from here to the end of the spit, one wave hitting the sand?"

"If only you could hitch a power take-off to a wave!" George said.

Hester noticed that George talked frequently about strength, and that he was big and firm himself. His body had a terrible rippling grace; when he moved, it was as if someone dropped a stone in the middle of him, making irresistible undulations spread outward all over him. His brain was his underdeveloped muscle. The Mandesons were older than Eben and herself, and away overhead economically. They were thirtying, ten years married and ten years childless, and they had a small house on this island on the West Coast, and they argued quite a lot, especially after drinks, of which they intook quite a lot. How lonely, Hester thought, they must be! She and Eben had gone unwarned one night into a nightplace called the Golden Olive, where the tariff was far too steep for them; and this lonely tarnished pair at a nearby table had invited them over and, hearing of their unmarried, hitchhiking, motel-housed adventure, had asked them urgently forthwith to spend some days at their cottage. George had a powered skiff and had inspected the power plant at Fort Myers and could tell you all about the power play series developed by the Philadelphia Eagles; he was obsessed with vital forces. He and Ruth were from outside Philadelphia, from what they called the wrong side of the Main Line, which Hester, having heard George's talk, thought of as a power line. Ruth was of the kind whom men fearfully love and women openly hate: beautiful and brilliant. There were tiny cracks around her eyes and on the upper curves of her cheeks, like those that appear in lacquer long kept in a too-hot room. She knew most things and would blandly talk about the other things that she didn't know, and Eben's eyes sparkled like stupid little firefly traps whenever he was around her.

"I've got to dunk myself," Hester said disgustedly, standing up. "Who's with me?"

"I'm ahead of you," George Mandeson cried, and he exploded from where he lay into a sudden full gallop down the beach, crashing his dolphin shoulders at last against the very stomach of an overfolding wave, in contempt of the water's might. He swam several yards under the surface, came up spewing air, and turned treading his legs to wait for Hester. She walked down the beach moving her hips warily and with her arms lifted and elbows back taking more time than she needed to put on her bathing cap; she had a queer feel-

ing of submissiveness approaching the brute in the
water—and she decided ("anyhow" was at the edge of
her mind) that she was peeved with Eben for being
such a lap-dog at the beck of their hostess; all through
this trip she had felt a growing resentment of his Puri-
tanism. Hester squealed and jumped as the waves hit
her thighs, and she swam breast-stroke to George, who
made sea-mammal noises at her, slappings and wet
snorts, and she splashed him, and he said, "What're
you two doing tonight?"—for the Mandesons had generously set freedom of action as a condition of the
young pair's stay.

"I don't know what Eben's got in mind. I expect
he'll decide to be tired tonight."

"Why don't we all go down to the Golden Olive and
have some drinks and a bite to eat?"

"Too expensive."

"This is on me."

"You're doing too much for us, George."

"I don't do anything at my expense that isn't fun for
me."

"An altruist," Hester sarcastically said.

"Hey, take it easy," George said with leaden suspi-
cion, for he did not like to be teased, and the unknown
(a vast realm to him, it appeared) seemed to terrify
him.

"You know, just below soprano in the choir," Hester
maliciously tried on him; she had by now a deep-seated
faith in his stupidity.

"Hey! What the hell!" George protested, his sense of
manhood abused; he splashed Hester. To admit the
truth, she thought, his voice was a little squeaky for
such a ram.

"I'd love to go," Hester said, "but you'll have to persuade Eben."

"Ruth can do that."

"That's a good idea," Hester said, laughing inwardly now at Eben and swimming away from George.

And that was the way it was done.

In a moment of clarity, while she was dressing alone in the tiny guestroom at the end of the house in the sedge by the sand, Hester saw George Mandeson for what he was. It would have been possible to think of him as the American ideal, a kind of manly Cinderella, up from nowhere in a hurry, up from being an ingenious mechanic, alias greaser, to being, at thirty or so, a man who wore leather sandals and linen pants and Hawaiian shirts in the palmiferous regions for two months every winter. Hester was sure that he had come up by a straight path—by hard work and by recognizing Opportunity when she stared him so close in the face that he could smell her foul breath; there was something about a patent on a gadget that would go into every cigaret lighter in every car in the land. He was what, according to the native myth, every clever girl who worked at a clerical job, every Hester and every Ruth Mandeson, dreamt of catching and dangling from her wrist: rich, healthy, dull, as patient and good-tempered as a little plated charm. But now Hester saw that he was nothing more than one of the pretty coquina shells on the beach, housing a small rotted tenant within—that get-fairly-rich-quick had as its complement more-more-more, and that George had seen the shape of the spiral above his head and it terrified and disgusted him because he was not equal to it; that he was stupid, stupid, stupid; that he had hidden from himself, without knowing it, in a busy pleasure hunt;—in short, that he was well on his way to becoming not the American dream but the American nightmare: a lush, a lecher, and a loafer. There was some putrescence in him. He was bad. He was startlingly attractive.

They sat at a table in the Golden Olive. A section of the roof had been rolled back so the customers could see a black velvet pincushion of night overhead. The orchestra was mercifully soft and persuasive. George had ordered gin and Schweppes Tonic Water, and when it came, Hester, a merest novitiate in the sisterhood of the gin-drinkers, sipped some of it.

"It tastes terrible," she said, making a citrus face.

"You'll have to educate yourself to this tonic water," George said with apparently unconscious grandeur. "It's an acquired taste."

"I can't help it," Hester said. "It tastes awful to me."

"It's British. For the tropics. It has something like quinine in it—keeps the fevers down."

"I can't help it," Hester said again. "Anyhow, this isn't the tropics; this is the intemperate zone."

Hester saw that George didn't even duck as that one sped close over his head. "The temperate zone," he said, gently correcting her.

"Yes, George," Hester said, feeling that awful submissiveness again, "the temperate zone."

Late that night, out on the sand, thanks partly to certain fevers that gin raised and sustained in easy opposition to the tonic from overseas, but thanks as well to a restlessness that was deep in her, deep in her, after a preliminary minuet of deception that had been eased by Eben's constant yawning at the nightclub and by an ache that pounced fortuitously on Ruth Mandeson's head, and also by the fact that Eben and Hester, being unmarried guests, were housed in separate quarters, she in the main house and he in the guest house, Hester, under the light of a sickle moon, terminated her virginity. Her disappointing collaborator in this ending was the stupid bull, George Mandeson. As she went to sleep in the pale blue guestroom later, with the bedlamp turned on to steady the room on its axis, Hester kept thinking how much, how very much, she loved her sweet Yankee character, Eben Avered. She would marry him and they wouldn't get rich and stupid, not very rich, anyhow.

■

THUS HESTER, entangled in the cat brier near the small bleached skeleton, lay in the presence of death and thought of lasciviousness under a hot sun and of the act of generation under a new moon, of golden olives and suntan oil and turtle eggs and squeezed limes and cheating kisses and more than kisses; in the presence of the bones in the brier. "I'm getting morbid," she said out loud, then started at hearing herself talk in a place where no one else could hear her. "Next thing," she continued, still audibly, "I'll be talking out loud to myself."

She decided (in order, perhaps, to keep fear down) that she was not very afraid. They'll come for me, she thought, they're bound to come back for me. When they stop for rest or for lunch, Eben'll look for me and they'll miss me and they'll come back for me. They know where I was in the line, it'll be a lead-pipe cinch to find me. No, she decided, I'm not particularly afraid, and she wondered what her abdomen was independently shaking about. Maybe it was laughing about the bone-headed stud, George Mandeson. Why was it laughing? She wasn't.

She tried again to work herself free. I was excited before, she thought, I'll go about it more carefully this time. She began to make cautious motions with her wrists and hands, but the labor was discouraging. Just to give her forearms mobility, she would have to exert a kind of patience she simply did not have, the steadiness of a knitter, the unhurriedness of a thrifty woman clearing a snarled wad of twine without snipping it. Damn it, she was just the wrong kind of girl to get herself out of a mess.

The little skeleton was right in front of her all the time. "Chuckie," Hester said, but not out loud this time, "were you like me? Didn't you stop to think? Did you thrash around till the toils had you?" Not out loud, not in a whisper, not even silently did Hester explicitly ask the woodchuck's relics what it had been like to die in the vines.

But we are different, Hester thought. We men and women think about each other. They'll be back for me.

Ha! she let herself complain. When do we think of each other? When we're afraid, when we need company, when we're afraid of losing something, when we're afraid of death—then we're selfless enough. All the rest of the time: bellies, genitals, if possible a heel on somebody else's neck.

And then Hester was thinking how pleasant it would be to be embraced by Eben's father. Here in the woods. He was experienced, compassionate, and troubled by daydreams; he would be a hundred times better than the Mandeson, the only one she'd had. It would be wonderful, she openly thought. Not here in the snarled vines, of course, but in the soft-floored forest.

She could hear the drivers calling and whistling in the distance. Their backs were to her and they were going farther and farther away. Eben's father was up there in that noise—and so, she thought with a little prick of annoyance, was Eben.

From here she heard the drivers' calls as a definite line of noise. If I were a woodchuck, she thought, I'd move away from such a racket—if only I could move. Then for a while she had a weird idea that maybe woodchucks think about each other, too; and she pictured a posse of them coming solicitously, with long

memories, to find their ossified sister chuckie caught in
the brier, but finding her, Hester, instead, and ... Hester felt the tremor in her abdomen again.

The calling of the hunters seemed to die out, and
Thighbone Hollow was silent but for the delicious fric-
ative whistling of a city of crickets. Had the line moved
so far as to be out of hearing? Or had it paused? Who
would think of her first?

Now Hester saw something curious. Under the cage
of the skeleton's ribs, lying nested in vine leaves, there
was a beautiful, queer globe of some kind, the size of a
small orange, a vari-textured ball whose surface was of
an iridescent light grayish color crisscrossed with delicate dark lines; it looked mysterious, semi-precious, a
monstrous jewel among the remains. She had a fanciful
notion that this woodchuck might have had a heart of
stone, but then she decided that this glistening thing
was too perfectly spherical to have been even an acci-
dental symbol of the seat of love. She determined that
she must have it, whatever it was, and she began carefully to plan how to reach out her left hand the two
feet it would have to extend in order to grasp the lovely
globe. If she could hunch her body around so that her
left shoulder would be thrust forward, like a pugilist's,
then if she could clear a way with her left hand to poke
her arm forward. . . . And soon she was working harder
to capture that eerie prize than she had worked twice
before to save herself from captivity.

Slowly, inch by inch by scratchy inch, she urged her
small hand forward. Now it was a foot away from the
pearly ball, now half a miserable mile-like foot, now
closer, now—ouch!—closer.

There! It was hard, smooth, heavy.

She began to draw her arm back, knowing that the
return would be even more tiresome than the reach had
been, for her loaded hand was bigger than it had been

empty, her fingers were tied down to their burden. Slowly, slowly.

"Hester! Hester! Oh, Hester!" Far away.

Pooh, it was somewhere Eben. He sounded like a scared chicken.

Knowing now for sure that she was safe, Hester decided to let Eben make the most of his great errand of mercy; let it last awhile; she just wouldn't answer for a few minutes. She concentrated on retrieving the woodchuck's treasure, while her brave but nervous Eben kept on bothering the welkin with her name off there.

At last her hand was back where it had started, and in it was this curious, pocked, resin-streaked, delicately lined gray globe, hers now; it had belonged to a woodchuck and now it was hers. It was a singular ball, very strange and fascinating.

Now Hester heard other voices calling her, with Eben's, and they were all much closer and would reach her soon enough. She listened for one particular hail, lay tense over her scratched left hand waiting to hear it.

Then she did. There it was, not far away at all. Eben's father's voice.

"Here I am!" she shouted delightedly. "Here I am! Here I am! Here I am!"

■

THEY FOUND HER a scant eight or ten feet from the outer edge of the brier patch. The search party—Eben, his father, Coit, Friedrich Tuller, and Mr. Challenge—told her through the spiny screen as they worked to free her that the whole line of the drive had stopped for lunch and that Coit had been the first to miss her. They had a couple of machetes, which some of the advance men had been carrying, and Coit and the Selectman hacked at the vines.

Hester was cheerful and talked to her rescuers about the path she had followed and about how she had become caught and about the skeleton lying there near her. She said nothing about what was in her hand.

Eben chafed and asked if she was hurt and whether she had been afraid; Eben's father was silent but worked hard to give her liberty. Coit teased her for a stupid city girl (evidently, being a talented bully, he had sensed the very point on which she felt most vulnerable); and the Selectman shushed Coit firmly. "Stop cruelizing the girl, Roswell," he said.

Soon Hester was free and could jump up and walk out onto open meadow. The searchers exclaimed over her scratches and her torn shirt, and Mr. Challenge said she looked like the tail end of a hurricane. She went straight to the Selectman and held out the odd thing in her hand and asked, "What's this?"

Taking it and scanning it, he said, "Where'd you find that?"

"It was inside the woodchuck, inside the skeleton of the woodchuck."

The Selectman tossed the ball up and caught it several times. "Never saw the like of it in my life," he said. "It's a spooky thing—fairly gives you a grue. We'll have to ask Pliny Forward what it is."

They did that. When they reached the shady grove where the line had halted—only about four hundred yards from where Hester had been caught—they searched among the long-strewn clumps of people sitting and waiting to picnic, for the young biologist, until they found him. The Selectman put the ball in his hand, and Forward asked where it had come from, and Hester told him how she had found it.

"You must be a lucky one," Forward said, revolving the orb in his hand. "Are you lucky by habit?"

"Well," Hester said, "as a matter of fact, no, I

wouldn't say so, I'd say that by and large I work for everything I get; after all, I'm a woman, no, I'm not very lucky."

"You will be from now on," Pliny Forward said; there was a light-heartedness in his voice, a mocking note. "This is a bezoar stone, and uncommon big for a woodchuck's. I saw a small one once, just a pint o' cider alongside this one. This is a dandy. It's nothing but a concretion of hairs and pebbles and indigestibles that the woodchuck ate by accident and coated with some kind of gum of his and built on up in layers—but it has magic properties. You must wear it as an amulet, because it'll ward off everything from bugaboos in your nose to the yellow creeping paralysis. At least that's what our ancestors, our old seedfolks as my mother called them, used to think. Don't know exactly what to think myself."

"Give it to me," Hester said a little sharply, and she took the bezoar from Pliny Forward. "Will it get you what you want?" she asked. "Is it like a wishbone or the first star of evening?"

"You can look on it that way if you want to," Forward said.

"Let's eat!" the Selectman said. "I'm as hungry as a graven image."

"I agree," said Mrs. Tuller. " 'For God's sake, let us sit upon the ground.' Is your acquaintance with Shakespeare sufficient to tell me what play that's from, Miss Hester?"

"Seems to me I recognize the line," Hester said abstractedly, while inwardly she addressed a vague wish, that had to do with herself and an older man who was troubled with daydreams, to the bezoar; she fervently pressed the round stone in her hand.

"Do you think you can eat, after what you've been through?" Eben asked her with a silly tenderness.

"Lead me to the trough!" Hester exclaimed.

"*Richard the Second*," Mrs. Tuller said, settling heavily to earth.

"Oh, of course," Hester said, as if annoyed with herself for forgetting, though in truth the only warrant for annoyance was that she had pretended to let slip from her mind something that had never been in it.

They sat in a circle and ate thick sandwiches that had been brought to the other side of the canal by Rulof Pitkin in his truck, had been ferried across in a skiff, and had been carried up the line and distributed, along with pitchers of milk and lemonade, and paper cups, by gentle busybody ladies of the village of Tunxis. While the hunters ate in clumps, a thin picket line of watchers stood out toward the woodchucks to give the alarm if any of the animals tried to go back toward their burrows. Anak Welch was the outguardsman nearest where Hester and the others sat.

"Did you see those damn fools showing themselves on the skyline up there on Thighbone Ledge?" Roswell Coit asked the chewing circle. "Don't our people know the first thing about cover?"

"I doubt if groundhogs can see that far, Ros," the Selectman said.

"Oh, they can see all right," Pliny Forward said. "A woodchuck can see a single clover leaf from a hundred yards away."

"Maybe I could train one to help me hunt for four-leaf clovers," the dancing master said. "He ought to be able to see a four-leaf clover from four hundred yards away, right?"

"Those kernel-heads wouldn't get up there on the skyline like that if the woodchucks had a few rifles," Coit sullenly said.

"We were talking before you came," Pliny Forward said abruptly to Eben, as if something about Eben had reminded him of the topic, "about the marmots' love life."

With Hester so close by, this affirmation seemed to make Eben fidget, as though he had just discovered he was sitting on an anthill. "Hadn't somebody better relieve Uncle Anak?" he said. "He'll want some lunch, his stomach's as big as a cheese vat. I better go take his place."

"Monogamous," Forward said, fixedly eyeing Eben, holding him pinned on his haunches with the intensity of the gaze he shot out through his green-rimmed glasses. "Oh, yes. They start going steady with a member of the opposite sex at the age of one year. And they're very faithful beings: the incidence of separation and divorce is very low among woodchucks, very low."

"Uncle Anak must be famished," Eben said.

"We ought to tell people to keep down off that skyline," Coit said, apparently brooding now more about the fact that no one was listening to him than about the hazard of careless cover. "That's the first thing any rook learns, keep off the lousy skyline." He was quite angry; he was Hester's idea of a sergeant.

Mrs. Tuller leaned over and murmured to Hester, as Coit began to argue his sudden obsession with two or three drivers on his side of the picnic circle, "Roswell's giant brain don't accommodate itself to projects that are the least bit casual, like this. Fact is, the boy ain't as bright as he might be. I believe he owes money on his I.Q."

But, Hester thought, he was the first to think of me when I was caught in the vines.

"And every spring, along about May," Pliny Forward said, still drilling Eben with his attention, "the faithful lovers produce a litter of four or five babies. As regular as clockwork. Would you like to hear how they do it?"

"I'm going to take Uncle Anak's place," Eben said, standing up with an awful effort, as if he had a bag of cement on his shoulders. He turned his flushed face for a moment toward Hester, and said to her, "See you later."

"Every single spring in May," Forward said to the reddened back of Eben's neck as Eben stumbled out of the picnic glade.

Hester said to the Selectman, "Eben called the giant 'Uncle Anak.' Is he a relation of yours?"

"No," the Selectman said, "he's nothing to us but friend. All the younger generation round here call him 'Uncle,' I guess it's out of awe of his great size—or maybe to acknowledge there's some kind of enormity in every family in Tunxis. But 'Uncle' Anak is part of what's behind your dre'ful Eben, as much as if he was a relation. Do you know how stubborn Eben is? Well, Uncle Anak's the stubbornest man I know; otherwise he's the salt of this quarter of the earth. Stubborn? One day when I passed his place I saw him out turning the hay in a meadow—kicking it up with a fork to get some dampness out of it; when a squall hermed up and it began to rain. Well, I stood there by a pair of bars in the fence and watched him go right on and turn the whole rest of the field in the downpour. Afterwards he walked over to me and said, 'Guess you'll put me down for addled, Matthew, turning hay in the rain, but I told myself I'd turn this whole field this very afternoon, and vummed if I didn't do it.' Our Anak has a temperament like cornmeal mush: he's always having to let himself cool off, but he's really soft through and through. He's so sentimental you could stick a cat's tail plumb through him and not ruffle it. He's not soft physically, though, not as far as courage goes. There's many a strong wild colt he's caught and shod in other days round here, many a wild steer he's yoked, and many a time he used to tie up his neighbor, Parson Churnstick, a devout man but powerful even in his late years and sometimes crazy. I believe Uncle Anak stands six feet seven in his cotton socks. He can do anything with his hands—build a coop, a cart, a plow, a keg: anything made of wood and iron. He seems to run into a heap of accidents, I must say—built a triphammer shop once, to do some of his metal work, and lost his thumb because he was so bound and determined to see his machine work that he tried to hold the bed-piece under the hammer before the bed-piece had been secured. The hammer worked satisfactory—a couple of knuckles' worth too well. His conscience, by the bye, is ten feet tall. One night several years ago when he kept cows, he forgot and left the barn doors open; it was midwinter. He punished himself the next night for his lack of consideration for the creatures by opening the doors again and sitting all night in a straight chair in the blast of a January nor'wester. Of course the doors were open on the cows again that night, and I guess some of the poor creatures got the sneezes and worse; but not Anak—his conscience was too clear for *him* to catch anything. I guess you'd have to say he's somewhat restive as a townsman. Seems to keep juggling a few lawsuits with his neighbors all the time, sort of testing their agility. Yet no one is more listened to in town meeting. As I guess you saw last night, he's reverend-looking with those big ears outspread like a benediction, and he's slow and careful of speech, and what he says is solid. His views are unpopular, but his influence is great. He's a Democrat in a rock-Republican town, and he wouldn't change his principles if you offered him a ten-room house made out of mother-of-pearl with ruby window lights. Stubborn! He was driving down to the capital once in June, way in the next valley, three hours to drive in those days, and I'd asked him to carry a letter by hand to a doctor friend of mine in the city. Of course Anak forgot, till he was home after dark and just turning in his driveway. Well, he wheeled around and went all the way back to town and banged the man out of bed at close to midnight and put the letter in his hand the way he'd said he would and got back here in awful small hours. That's how set he is. Just as set as a cement pavement. Shush! Here he comes."

The huge man came close, sat down with a groan, and, protesting that he'd lately lost his appetite, ate enough sandwiches to picnic a large and wholesome Sunday-school class.

Soon it was time to resume the search, and the drivers were asked to go forward to the picket line and take up their stations again. Hester managed things so that she walked up to the line with the Selectman, about whom she had been thinking during the morning, and with Roswell Coit, who had, it seemed, been thinking about her. She carefully carried the bezoar in her hand.

"Did you hear about Dorcas Thrall?" Coit asked the Selectman.

"What's she been up to?" the Selectman asked. "She's coming to our house tonight."

"D'you mean you didn't hear about Grandma Thrall and the chicken hawk yesterday?"

"I've been busy getting up this drive."

"I thought you'd be one of the first to hear," Coit said.

"Well, you know how sometimes you don't have a chance to swat the flies on your own back stoop for a week at a time," the Selectman said.

"That's funny," Coit said, "with you people bein' so close to her."

"I've been busy," the Selectman said.

"You must've been busy, not to hear."

"Oh yes, I've fair chased myself around a tree this last few days."

"I thought you'd have heard."

"Well, you know how 'tis."

"Yeah, I know, but still."

"Sometimes I don't hear what *I've* been doing till about a month after I do it."

"Well, you're a busy man, Mr. Avered, you sure flog yourself with work."

"Oh, I get by."

"No criticism meant. You get by, sure you get by. I just thought you'd have heard."

"You thought wrong, my boy."

"All I can say is, it's God digged strange."

"I can't help that. A fact's a fact."

"Didn't say it wasn't."

"I've been busy."

"So you said. I heard you."

"Don't think I enjoyed chasing myself around the tree."

"Who said you did?"

Then for some time the men walked along flanking Hester and saying nothing. It seemed to Hester that the two were preposterously angry with each other and that the subject of Dorcas Thrall was now closed, as well, perhaps, as many other subjects; she had a queer feeling that these two New Englanders might never be able to reach each other again—perhaps they never had. She felt sad about it. She liked them both!—the Selectman because he was the sort of man she enjoyed thinking about, the Coit because it was already clear that she was the sort of woman he enjoyed thinking about; they were her East and West who could meet perhaps only through such as she.

"This Dorcas Thrall," Coit said to her at last, evidently having decided to cut the Selectman out of further conversation, "she's ninety-one years old, they say she's ninety-one—old as rape and thievery, anyway; and always been scared of birds."

"This girl knows all about her," the Selectman curtly said.

"Yes, I know a little about her," Hester said in a friendly way to Coit.

"In that case—" Coit said, and clamped his mouth shut as if he had slammed down the engine hood of a car.

"But I haven't heard about yesterday," Hester said.

"I suppose you've been busy, too," Coit bitterly said.

Just then the three of them broke from the thin woods they had been negotiating into a clearing, and in the center of the clearing they saw Eben locked in mutual terror with a woodchuck.

The animal was crouching on the ground and Eben was standing over it, and both figures were ambiguously posed—either menacing or craven, it was hard to say which; or both were both at once, maybe. Each seemed to be trying to bluff the other and to bolster the self. The woodchuck was pressed flat to the ground, but its legs seemed under a spring-like tension, ready at once to pounce or bolt. Its head was raised, and its teeth were chattering in the hideous way of nature, both human and at large, that threatens when it fears and fears when it threatens. This was a direful rattling sound the scared beast made. As for Eben, he stood hunched forward, his elbows bowed and his fingers tensely outstretched, his knees visibly trembling, towering over the animal, Hester thought, like a figure in a nightmare she had often as a child, of a terrifying-terrified djinn that could do her great evil but might at any moment be driven into its home, a dark-glassed bottle, by a rub on a ring that was somewhere, somewhere. Eben was as pale as autumn smoke. He seemed unaware of the approach of the three—or dared not break his hypnotic relationship with this animal that made its vicious teeth so audible.

Hester glanced at her companions. She expected the bully Coit to be laughing, but on the contrary, he himself had blanched, as if awed and even a little frightened by this uneasy poise of flesh and flesh. The Selectman was evidently stricken with a father's shame; he stood for a few moments blushing and shaking his head.

No sooner had Hester looked back at Eben than, from beside her, the Selectman rushed forward and with a downswooping motion picked up the woodchuck by the scruff of the neck, lifted it in the air (it was much smaller, Hester saw, than the one she had watched sunning itself against the tree), and threw it forward into the edge of the further woods. At the moment of its landing, as if the wind was being biffed out of a thrown rubber toy, the woodchuck emitted a high-pitched brief whistle-like scream, and then could be heard scuttling away at a nice pace.

"You great gorming lummox!" the Selectman said harshly to Eben—more to vent his embarrassment, Hester thought, than to curse his own flesh and blood. "Let's get up into line."

Now Hester found herself walking out of the clearing and through thin woods alone with Roswell Coit.

"Your boyfriend was nervous," Coit said.

"Eben lives in the city. He's a city man," Hester said as proudly as she could.

"I remember a joker at the Volturno—that was about the dirtiest fightin' we had, at the Volturno, unless maybe Salerno—anyway one time the colonel told this joker, this Sanchez, he told him to go down by the river to a place there and do a little cleanup snipin', all by his lonesome. Sanchez stood around on one foot and other foot, and begun to sweat and he got the trembles. The colonel didn't tolerate no chicken-do, and he said to Sanchez, said, 'What the whoozis a matter with you? You Chrissakes scared, Sanchez?' So Sanchez, this wonderful spic from Jersey, he says, 'No sir, Colonel, I ain't scared—just shakin' with patriotism.' Sometimes it's hard to tell what makes folks look nervous."

"Eben used to hate you," Hester deliberately said.

"I don't hold him a grudge. We used to go fishin' quite a lot, down at Catspaw Pond, me and him and young Quinlan Leaming. They had pretty good striped dace and calico bass there, and a slew of sunnies. Quinlan and me used to think Eb was awful fussy, namby-pamby. He had to have his angleworm tidy on the hook. He wasn't sissy—he was regular, but small and hated trouble, and Quinlan and me, we loved it. Hallowe'en night—you should've seen the candle tallow on the big store windows and mailboxes down all over town! Eb didn't like to amplify around that way, and in school he was always farse to make the teacher take notice of him: he was too damn bright and full of sweet-gas for us common folks. And listen—his hand-writin' on the blackboard!—nothin' but curlicues and arpicues. So you can see we used to get after him whenever we could; usually he'd run or hide on us, but if he had to, he'd fight like a judgment. . . . But look how wrong we were, look at us now: Quinlan you don't hardly hear from, he's got a terrible streak of lack in his character, and me—well, I'm just a puke of misery besides Eben."

Hester looked hastily at Coit's face and saw an enigma. He had spoken his last words in a flat voice, and she could not tell whether he meant what he said, or was playing for sympathy, or was being sarcastic.

"What do you work at?" she asked.

"Outdoors work. I have to be outdoors. Since the service I can't abide to be cooped up."

"You ought to be a policeman," Hester maliciously said.

"I thought of that," Coit said, with a sadistic twinkle coming into his eyes. "That'd be good work. I thought of that, only I had some bad trouble, a bad run-in, with the M.P.s in the service, and the Legion fellows all know about it, so I wouldn't hardly get past the muster. I thought about that, though."

"What's your complaint against Eben—that he's too hoity-toity, or what?"

"I don't like these brainy coots, they make me feel squawmish. They don't shake hands hard."

"In other words you're afraid they may be better than you."

"I used to like Eben Avered," Coit said, and Hester saw that now he was serious, almost pathetically serious. "He could stand up to anybody. We had a game with our sleds—we used to coast down two ways, either there was scoochers, that was squattin' on the sled, or there was bellyguts, that was lyin' down frontways, and we'd get a line of us on either side the runway with sticks in our hand to hold acrost the runway on a slant, and the thing was to try to get under the scoocher's or the bellygutter's sled-runners like with a crowbar as he passed and offset him in the snow. There never was a time we could knock Eb off, never. He was nimble! I'm in mind of another game"—and slowly the muscular bully was melting away before Hester's eyes into a rather fat boy, too big for his age, everlastingly proving himself—"that we called haily-over. We picked up teams and got on opposite sides of a barn and threw a ball over top of it and hollered out a number on the other team and if the number didn't catch it, he had to come round to our side, till everybody'd been captured that way. I remember one day we were playing it, Eb wasn't with us. The ball was coming overhead, my number was called, I was just about to snag the thing, then what do I see but Eben Avered coming out of Booge's pasture in his overhauls with a bouquet of piss-abeds—I guess you'd call 'em daisies—in his arms? I never did catch the ball, it could've clapped me on the head. He said they were for his mother, so I sassed him for a mother-lover, and he dropped the piss-abeds and come after me, boy oh boy oh boy. He can take care of himself when he has to. I don't think those flowers were for his mother at all; he was just covering up in my opinion."

"What do you think of his father?"

"There's a man I don't trust. This woodchuck round-up!"

"Why don't you trust him?"

"Nobody's perfect."

"Why don't you trust him?"

"He just ain't trusted in this neighborhood."

"Why?"

"All right, then. There's an item of a little slip he made once; or rather, he got found out that he'd made it."

"What kind of a slip? What do you mean?"

"If Eben ain't told you about his own old man, it stands me in hand to talk about the weather, or double-yolked eggs, or something or other. You ask your boyfriend—when he stops shakin'. And when you ask him, he'll start again, like as not."

They had come to Hester's station in the line, and had been standing there talking awhile. Now the commotion of the drive began once more up to the left, and Coit hurried off to his neighboring post. The line began to move.

■

HESTER THOUGHT as she walked of games she had early played: city games, games of loneliness. You all lined up on opposite sides of a room, a big room, as spacious as sleep, and there was going to be some kind of rush, and piano music starting and stopping, and after the rush and the chords you found yourself clutching the hand of a boy—which one?—and they told you he was your true, your only love; but you hardly knew him. You hid alone in a coat-closet under some shelves, crouching among the galoshes trembling with hope that the door would crack and light would flood you and you would be found. You fled on a playground to the count of one hundred. The games always made you feel alone, and you didn't want to be alone; all you wanted was to be known and felt, to be close to the others.

That was not Eben's worry, it seemed. Eben, in his haily-over and sled-gantlet and all his open-air play, must have struggled to hide his talents, must have cherished mediocrity, must have groaned in his bed at night wishing he were dull as the others. How terrible to be what all wished to be! Hated for nimbleness, hated for intellect. Hester remembered what one of her friends had said about Eben shortly after Hester had met him: "He's unbearable! So busy trying to keep from being a genius." That girl had been talking about a pretentiousness she had seen in Eben, but on another layer there was this other horror that Eben suffered from: the horror of becoming what everyone wants to be and tries so hard to be.

Once in the city she and Eben were going to the movies, riding part way on a bus, and Eben said quite casually, "I got a raise today."

"Oh, Eben!" Hester said, and slipped her hand under Eben's arm.

"Five dollars a week," Eben said, sounding solid.

"Move over, John D. Rockefeller," Hester said.

But at that Eben took offense. "Let's not go too fast," he said.

"Have I said something again that I didn't understand?"

"Just because I'm a bit more prosperous than I was yesterday, you're going to start not liking me. I know how your mind works. You're just like everyone else, like all the ones at the office; they hate me now because of this puny raise. They all would crawl to Mecca on their knees for a five-dollar raise, but let somebody get one, and suddenly he's an outcast. Before he gets a chance to pay back the money he borrowed last month, he's already got airs, his britches are too big, they hate him. They hope he gets fired."

"I guess I am just like everyone else," Hester dismally said.

"I think you might have the decency to sympathize with me."

Hester began rather methodically to cry. "You don't know what you want, so you get mad with me when I agree with you," she said, sniffling.

"There's an old lady up in Tunxis," Eben helplessly said, "who prays every night that none of her sons or grandsons will ever be rich. Mrs. Dearthick. She prays every night for her boys to stay poor, and I think she's going to have her way just by main force of praying; though I must say they're co-operating with her, they have no talent for making money stick to their fingers."

"All I meant was," Hester said with a saline, moisty affectionateness, "you'll be a millionaire before you know it; you're my favorite plutocrat." She blew her nose.

"Take my father," Eben said. "He's a failure. I don't know what it is, the minute it looks like he's organized for life, he makes a mistake that sets him back to where he started when he was my age." But suddenly Eben tumbled from these heights of condescension and was miserable. He shook his head. "It baffles me," he said. "Father's so happy."

Then Eben did something Hester had seen him often do: He went all the way home in his mind. Frequently when he felt a city tension, when he wanted to vacate an argument, when he was mixed up or angry, he did this runaway to Tunxis that seemed to clear his mood. He had already started back when he had thought of Mrs. Dearthick and of his father, and now he said, "Speaking of britches being too big, did I ever tell you about Father's prank with Uzal Belding's pants?"

"No, Eben," Hester said, blowing her nose again. "No, you never did."

"You see, Uzal's mother was fat to begin with. One thing that Beldings did was make cheese and sell it, and they economized on a cheese press—never did have to get one—by Mrs. Belding sitting on the driver of the hoop and doing her knitting. I was much younger than Uzal, but I remember I used to go into their house sometimes to get cheese or eggs for Mother, and there Mrs. Belding would be up on a new cheese like an ottoman balanced on a teacup. Uzal was fat enough in school. He dropped out at ninth grade: they said he was always cheery, like all roly-polies, still down deep I guess he couldn't stand the teasing he laughed out loud at with his face. Anyhow, he dropped out of school and took up walking from village to village with a box of magic tricks and a steropticon and I think he sold cards of gingerbread, too. When he went from house to house, he was something to look at! With his box on his back, he looked like one of the castellated elephants that my father had in his chess set as rooks. He got bigger and bigger, outstripped his mother by a ton—they could have used him as a hydraulic press to bale rags for the paper mill in Treehampstead. By the time he was about twenty-five and I was ten, Ros Coit and I and some other kids used to follow him around and hoot at him. He was a peddler of the old wooden-nutmeg school—drawling, snuffling, haggling away over pennies. Well, this one time someone found out he'd left a pair of pants at Boyd's to be dry cleaned, and Father, either Father or Anak Welch, got somebody to sneak them out of Boyds' shop and on Sunday morning, just when church was letting out, Uncle Anak and Father and Judge Pitkin all three got into the pants, their left legs in its left leg and their rights in its right, and they got Frank Cherevoy to play the Legion drum and just as the people were pouring out of the church, they marched up and down the green, the drummer in front, rub-a-dub-tup-tup-Joe-Joe-Bunker, and the three gents lock-stepping along in the pants behind. It was a sight. Mother'd had me in church with her, we were on the front steps when they came, and she froze up and nearly broke off my shoulder pinching it because I laughed with everybody else. That wasn't too good for Father in the town; that particular laughter on the Sabbath backfired some. Uzal became sanctimonious later, gave up his box and began distributing religious pamphlets and begging for candy around the township. Finally they advertised him for an impostor, or something of the sort, and he died a couple of years ago in the corrective institution over near Whigtown. Poor coot!"

"Your father sounds like fun," Hester said.

"He's a very serious man," Eben said, "essentially."

■

THE SUN coasting down the slope past the meridian threw enough heat onto the woodchuck drivers in steamy Thighbone Hollow so that Hester, in her torn shirt and blue jeans stiff with newness, with the bezoar in her hand, perspired, flagged, and wished the afternoon done with. She suffered especially, for perhaps half an hour, as she went through some thick underbrush, where her only entertainment, besides recollection of things past, was provided by some blackberry bushes, nastily brambled and sweetly fruited, from which she picked the enormous, purple-black, ripest berries, and ate them as she struggled. She had never seen or tasted such swollen, ready drupelets. No one came along the line to visit her all afternoon. She felt languid, and though she kept up her share of the noise of the drive, she began to lose her interest in, or at least her apprehension of, the woodchucks. From time to time a halt was called. She sat down whenever she could, for her legs were becoming heavy and dull.

Once, at last, while she sat during a pause, at about four o'clock as she guessed from the sun, she heard someone approaching from her right, from the direction of the canal. It was Mrs. Tuller, with tiny pearls of sweat on her huge forehead as gray as oystershell. "Where's that Coit boy?" she asked. "How far along is that rascal boy?"

"He's right up here," Hester said. "If the line was moving, you'd know. He makes a noise like a monkeyhouse."

"He *is* a cage full of monkeys," Mrs. Tuller said. She cupped her hands around her mouth and called to Coit. He answered promptly and ran through the woods down to her.

Mrs. Tuller told him that the line was approaching Job's Creek, which was now perhaps a quarter of a mile farther along. She said that there was one plank bridge across the creek to each division, and that Four's bridge was situated near where this upper end of the division would reach the stream. When an appropriate command would come down the line, she said, and it would probably come at the end of this halt, then, as the picket line would start to move again, the center of each division would lag back, both in pace and in noise, while its two ends would loop forward dinfully toward the creek. Thus four sacs would be formed, and after another halt, giving time to check the soundness of the pockets, they would gradually be tightened toward the bridges, until the woodchucks within were driven across to the other shore.

"As soon as you two on this end of our division get to the creek," she said, "swing to your right downstream along the bank. You'll come to an old stone wall after a bit, that runs spang down to the stream. Hide behind it, on the upstream side of it, and wait there. The bridge is just below that wall, so the rest of us'll work whatever woodchucks we have in our sac up against the wall and along it to the bridge. Your job is to make sure none of 'em try to cross over top the wall. Keep hidden, so the animals'll come along unabashed. If they have a mind to get over the wall, jump up and make a racket. Don't chase 'em, just wave and dance around on your side of the fence. You know:

> 'Ha! ha! ha!
> And sadly sing. . . .' "

Hester grew excited at the prospect of facing the pursued at last.

"How's your arithmetic, dear?" Mrs. Tuller asked her. "D'you think you could count the creatures as they cross the bridge?"

"I can try," Hester said.

"They might be in clumps and bunches, you might have to do some fast addition."

"I can try," Hester said again, nettled at being made to feel like an elementary-grade scholar.

The agile, bigheaded schoolmarm hurried away up the line, her buttocks bobbling and curtseying to each other, as if to swift musical counterpoint, and soon, evidently having conferred to her satisfaction up yonder with the anchor of Division Three, she came bouncing past downwards again, announcing that all was set. "All set," she said mock-heroically, in tones of Pallas Athene, "to smash the groundhogs' bridgehead!"

Before long, indeed, the confirming message, to form pockets, came down the line. Coit, going off to his station, said cheerily, "See you by the crick."

■

THOSE AT THE ENDS of the divisions who were pulling forward the drawstrings of the pockets hastened now, with renewed eagerness, and the quarter mile remaining to the brook, if the distance was that great, seemed to Hester to be quickly left behind. She found herself with a fast beating heart on the near bank of Job's Creek, which was only a rill in the woods, perhaps six or eight feet across, but with a vigorous current that had cut a deep, definite, and fairly straight path in the loam of the forest floor; from its banks, here and there, dead root-masses protruded, and the rivulet protested in whispers at the many rounded stones in its mattress.

Coit came along. "You been eatin' berries," he said.

"Did you ever find such big ones?" Hester asked.

"I can see the juice on your lips, where it dried."

Hester drew the back of her hand across her mouth.

"Don't bother," Coit said. "It looks O.K."

They walked downstream together and before long reached the wall Mrs. Tuller had described. Many of its stones were dappled with fine moss and lichens, and here and there honeysuckle hunched across the long pile in hedge-like masses. The ground beyond the wall, once cultivated, had grown up into woods considerably junior to, but no thinner than, those on the upstream side of the barrier. A few feet beyond the wall, the bridge lay across the stream—just three heavy planks tacked side by side to crosspieces.

"Why don't we set down while we wait?" Coit asked, pointing to a place where honeysuckle offered a dry couch. Hester settled down with her back to the wall, holding the bezoar in her left hand. Coit sat on her right. There was an awkward silence.

"What about the old lady and the chicken hawk?" Hester finally asked.

A flicker of sullenness crossed Coit's face, but then, at once, cheerfully he said, "That old aunty is tougher'n a boiled owl, I never saw the beat of her. Last Friday night she showed up at the Grange dance, and there she was at next to midnight out on the floor cuttin' up didos alongside of us young ones—and she's supposed to be ninety-one."

"What makes people live so long?" Hester asked.

"It has to be in the family," Coit said.

"They say it's in the mind," Hester said.

"You know all about Aunty Dorcas and birds," Coit said with still a trace of resentment.

"Mr. Avered told me she'd been scared to death of birds all her life."

"That's what made this thing yesterday so rich. She has a slew of cats—I guess she figures they hate anything with feathers onto it just as much as she does—and one of them is a kitten, been weaned about two weeks. Well, old Dorcas was exercisin' her back bendin' into her laundry tub in the kitchen yesterday washin' a sheet when she heard this kitten squallin' like it was bein' murdered, out in the yard, so the old Thrall looked out the open door, and it was bein' murdered, a thunderin' big chicken hawk was on the back of the thing, bareback ridin' it to death, and peckin' and snatchin' at it. I dad! The way she tells it, it didn't take her long to skip out there in the yard on light feet, and scared of birds or no scared, she squatted on that big thing—did you ever see a chicken hawk close to?— 'cause it looks as savage as a meataxe; I'm scared of the things myself. Anyway, this bird-leery old body landed on the hawk like a thousand of brick and she took aholt of its neck and wrung it like a hen's till it flapped round and in no time it was ready for the pot, so to speak, though I don't guess even Aunty Dorcas would have the stomach to eat such a bob-wire creature. But she killed it dead, and she's tickled as a gimlet. Says she was still scared most of the way off her hooks, though, later in the day, when she saw a sparrow on her sill."

"I'm sort of afraid of woodchucks myself," Hester said.

"You're just like your boyfriend," Coit sarcastically said. "You're city people, that's your trouble. That was your excuse for him, don't forget."

"I'm a lot more apprehensive than Eben," Hester said.

"I wisht I lived in the city," Coit said, looking longingly at Hester. "Do you like it in the city?"

"I love it—but what's the matter with Tunxis? I'm beginning to like Tunxis."

"I'll tell you exactly what's wrong with Tunxis. Couple weeks ago, I was standin' with some of the fellows down by Eells', that's the drugstore there on Station Street, and this car drove up, it was an old battered thing, and this joker with a long pursed-up neck like a turkey-gobbler's stuck his head out the window and asked us where he was and where he was goin'. Young John Leaming was standin' there, he's got a mouth like a pickerel, and he looks like the Day of Doom, he's so sour, but he funs people the whole endurin' time, so he said to the stranger, as sour as a frost grape he said, 'You're in Tunxis and you're goin' straight to Hell.' Well, this old gump smiled as clever and cheerful as you please, then he squizzled up his face and he said to young John, said, 'Thank ye, bub,' he said, 'I thought from the looks of the countryside and the natives round here I couldn't be any great distance from that place.' And off he went like he was satisfied. There was more truth than comfort in that comeback, that's the whole trouble with Tunxis in a nutshell."

"Hell is wherever a person lives," Hester said. "Anybody knows that."

"I like blackberries," Coit said, looking at Hester's mouth.

"I never ate such big ones," Hester said, wondering what sort of stain was on her lips.

"Can I have a taste?" Coit asked, and before Hester understood just what he meant, he had crawled toward her, and put both arms powerfully around her, and had begun to kiss her savoringly on the lips.

Hester set the bezoar down on the ground beside her in case she might find it necessary to put her arms around this active young man. His bold tongue began to inquire for the taste of berries in her mouth. He had a faint smell of leather about him. The thought came into Hester's mind that with any luck at all, this might have been the Selectman, and at that she squirmed and pulled her face away from Coit's and said, "Watch out! Mrs. Tuller's liable to come any minute."

"I still like blackberries," Coit said, settling back with a glower.

"The John Leaming you speak of," Hester said, trying with quick dry talk to make a eunuch of Coit, "isn't he the owner of the land we're on?"

"He has title of this land, bramble bushes and all," Coit said, "and I still like his berries."

"His father certainly was angry at the caucus last night," Hester said quickly, drily.

"All the Leamings are famous for their tempers," Coit said, with a fine aggressive complacency on his face again.

■

Mrs. Tuller must have had enough of trotting up and down the line, for this time she sent George Challenge as her deputy to test the readiness of the arc of Division Four. When Hester and Coit heard someone coming on the far side of the wall, they got to their feet and saw the weary-looking politician coming tick-tock on his bandy legs, swaying like the arm of a metronome.

"Spread out! Spread out, you two," he barked. "You've got a hundred and fifty feet of stone fence to cover there, till the line tightens up, then Tuller and Anak Welch'll come over your side the wall. Spread out! We're trustin' you two. Young lady, ma'am," he said to Hester, "you're to count the creatures as they go by, is that right?"

"I'm going to try," Hester said.

"Keep down and just peek over top the parapet," Challenge said. And uttering other official admonitions, he labored off down the line, tick, tock, tick, tock.

Hester and Coit crouched behind the wall nearly a hundred feet apart. Once as they waited Coit turned his face toward Hester and gave her a ridiculous, cheek twisting wink, as if to seal an understanding between them that he would be back for more fruit of her lips.

"Seems like they're dawdlin' a longful time down there," he said in a loud voice after a while.

"Sh-h-h."

At length the noises of the drive began again, far down the line at first. Later the stalkers of Division Three, not far away at Hester's back, began to shout and whistle, and once she thought she heard a brave faraway roar from Eben, and that led her to wondering where the Selectman was. The sounds of Division Three were closer and louder-seeming than what came from Mrs. Tuller's people lower down, and for a time Hester was fearful lest the woodchucks from below might be turned back by the racket upstream.

Apparently Coit had the same idea, for he called mockingly to Hester, "Your Eben's making quite a hullamaloo up there."

Hester shushed Coit again.

Eventually, however, the uproar above receded and the one below advanced and swelled, and Hester became excited. In a few moments she would see a dreadful crowd of marmots. She felt afraid, and to her surprise she yawned.

She began to make out Tuller's blithesome tootling and the cattle moans of Anak Welch, and before long both those men were on her side of the wall, a-crouching silent, and the rest of the line could be heard tightening, closing.

There one was! And others, too!

Hester saw then a whole curve of advance scouts of the woodchuck force. These scouts would run forward liquidly a few feet at a time, then rise on their haunches with their forepaws in prayerful poses and glare awhile, heads steady, each in a single direction, then they would fall and run again, and next time up each look another way.

Hester heard a hiss to her right. It was Herr Tuller, motioning to her and Coit to squeeze down toward the stream. All four above the wall crept along toward the brook, as stealthy as the furry quadrupeds on the other side of the barrier, until they were posted only twenty feet apart. Hester, peeking, saw that others of the line had begun to approach beyond the wall and to the right. Then behind the point of the marmots' scouts she saw furry, rippling masses. She yawned enormously.

Out in front was a great bull of the species, ranging this way and that in his leadership. Hester saw him look at the stream and look at the wall and listen to the line of drivers, which had halted and was quieter now, to give the animals time to decide to use the bridge. The big one and his band were encircled, and he swayed, like a being behind bars, while back of him his scouts marked time and the ranks all paused. The leader darted straight at the wall, and Hester missed what happened next, because, as Coit and Tuller and huge Anak rose up and bellowed at the poor thing, she ducked and hid from it.

When she was on her knees again blushing, she saw the leader run along the stream away from the wall until he reached the bridge, whose planks he sniffed in a leisurely way. He walked slowly three or four feet out onto them, then turned and in a rush ran downstream on the bank, but Mrs. Tuller shrilled at him from beyond as if he were a naughty boy, and, alarmed, he ran up again toward the wall. This time Hester managed to stay up and chatter at him as her three flankers roared. The leader ran back a few feet. Then he and the scouts and many of the other animals all at once broke in a pack directly away from the stream, but the line of human beings on the right pressed together shouting in awful unison and holding firm; Hester saw George Challenge standing square and solid on his short bowed legs like a Queen Anne lowboy.

The woodchuck wave pulled back, and with a deliberateness and hauteur that seemed insulting to all human life, the leader walked to the bridge and crossed it in stately ease. One, Hester said to herself.

Three scouts followed scuttering over the planks. Two, three, four, Hester counted.

The line of drivers resumed now a murmuring all around, and other woodchucks dared to run across the open wooden bridge. Then a general rushing eagerness to cross set in, and Hester had her head full of figures, and she felt dreadfully sleepy. One woodchuck fell off the planks and drowned. Hester yawned and counted. Several times small groups, unfavorable to the bridge, tried to rush off this way or that, but each time the drivers discouraged their escapades; and the circle tightened continually, and at last all the animals save the one that had drowned were on the other side. The people then walked across the planks congratulating each other, and four men pulled the bridge over after them.

Hester was quite a center of interest. About sixty-five, she reported, give four or five either way. Yes, about sixty-five.

It puzzled her that after all her curiosity, fear, and fellow-feeling toward the woodchucks, after all her complex and disturbing sensations during the drive, her response to the thrill of the noose at the bridge had been drowsiness.

Not until the division had secured the last of its work, and Hester was walking down toward the canal with Coit in the crowd of well-pleased drivers, and it was too late to go back, did she exclaim, "Oh, damnation! I left my bezoar stone up there by the stone wall."

She was inappropriately sad and angry for some reason, and she began to try to beat out the reason from the underbrush of her mind, as if it were a dark wild beast that would go to ground, and all she could find was a sense of the failure of her idea of love, a vague feeling that in some way her idea, and even her love itself, had proved during this day not adequate to her needs. "Oh, well," she said at last, having had no encouragement from Coit, "maybe I can find it in the morning."

The members of Division Four, enjoying a pleasant deceleration of heartbeat after the tense last few minutes of the drive, convened at the juncture of Job's Creek and the canal, where, while some chatted easily in the shade of the enormous sycamore tree, others were ferried across the canal in two large skiffs to the shoulders of the highway beyond. Nearly half the division was across the water before the first drivers of Division Three reached the sycamore, Eben among them.

"Didn't they give you folks sandwiches?" Mrs. Tuller in bluff tones asked Manly Sessions, the captain of the group. "Never saw a crowd of rapscallions look so down in the mouth."

The teacher's friendly barb was not well received. She was informed, with tight lips all round her, that Division Three had not driven a single woodchuck across Job's Creek; it hadn't seen ary creature in the last hour of the drive.

This calamity of Division Three increased the good humor of Division Four, which began to pour onto its inept fellow unit a spicy dressing of sarcasm and fun—did so, that is, until drivers of Division Two appeared with glum brows and on their behalf their bitter-eyed captain, John Leaming the younger, reported that his unit had sent only seven woodchucks across its bridge; whereupon the jokes ceased, as cicadas fall quiet under the first of a drizzle.

And then, when the drivers of Division One came down, the Selectman out in front of them, with a face as gray as summer mildew, in a very great hurry to hear the tallies, and when it was learned Division One had rounded up only sixteen woodchucks, and when, taking into consideration the approximateness of Hester's count (which, sorry as she was for it, she could not mend), the total of the entire day's drive was set at about eighty-eight—after these dismaying turns, all signs of gaiety vanished. The number was very small.

Where now, Hester thought with a sinking sensation, were the Selectman's four hundred black-backed fleeing animals? Where, for that matter, were the huge Anak's quietly affirmed half that many?

Eben, who after the bad summaries of the day's work had an intimidated look on his face, as if he had been caught very much in the wrong about something, guided Hester by the elbow to one of the trucks parked at the highway's edge and pressed her to board it, which she did. The truck was soon full of people who were not leaders, unaggressive people who all seemed rather ashamed of themselves and anxious to depart the scene of ignominy as quickly as possible, and its driver, responding to their almost sneaky ways, pulled it away in haste from the knot of captains and self-appointed counselors and congenial pushers who stood shouting at each other between the canal and the highway, arguing about the fiasco, searching explanation but only finding fault.

Three

HESTER STEPPED DOWN the narrow and worn wooden stairs, noticed in passing that Uncle Jonathan in the close hall had lost his face and that some of the clock's curious wooden cogs were scattered in disorder on the floor beside it, and then, as she turned into the sitting room, saw the Selectman, his face lustrous after a scrub, dressed once more in his flannels and walnut-colored coat, sitting in a rocker with a magazine spread in his lap to catch the dust of his labor, rubbing one of the cogs with a scrap of sandpaper, and humming a tune she'd never heard.

"Come in, my dear," he said, looking up.

Hester had lolled long in a lukewarm, rust-tinted tubful of water, and she felt refreshed. She had put on a silken dress with little formal flowers strewn across it, her favorite of this summer, and she traveled in a capsule of honest cheap soap smell. Eben, who had had to wait for the tub, was not down yet. She walked self-assured.

"You look kind of tuckered out," the Selectman said in the teeth of her freshness.

"I feel it in my legs and my back," Hester said,

knowing better, by now, than to be disappointed by anything the Selectman might say, but being so, none-theless. What a chary man!

The room was a frugal place, this family room, with nothing overstuffed, all backs straight and wood consid-ered good enough to sit upon; and there was nothing sentimental, no appeal to the past, no spinning wheel or cobbler's bench or other reminder of times when life was simple and crude work was everyone's. The things in the room were made of wood, metal, and cloth to be used. The rug was hooked in a dull pattern. There were some books in a cabinet with a wiremesh front. Over the mantel was a reproduction—incongruous here, Eben's protesting touch of younger years, surely—of an impressionist painting, by Manet or Monet, perhaps, Hester thought; she never could keep those two straight.

There were sounds from the kitchen, and Hester said, "Do you suppose I can help Mrs. Avered?"

"She keeps a lonesome kitchen," the Selectman said. "I think you'd better stay here and help me."

"I'd like to show that I can be of some use in the household department," Hester said. "I can boil water, honest I can."

"Aunty Dorcas'll be looking in soon," Mr. Avered said. "I'm sorry we aren't having some young people in for you to meet, Tunxis young ones, but Eben's got himself citified and he's floated away from the ones that used to be his friends, he hardly knows them now. Aunty Dorcas can tell you anything you want to know about Tunxis and the Avereds, for better or for worse—for worse, no doubt. . . . Say! I can't get over that chicken-hawk epic. You don't think Ros Coit was pulling your leg, do you?"

"I don't think he could," Hester said smiling.

"She's got some spunk," the Selectman said; then he, too, smiled at what Hester had said.

"You've found out the matter with the clock," she said.

"These consarned black oak cogwheels in Uncle Jonathan get all warped up like potato chips when we begin to catch thunderstorm weather. Don't know why they didn't use common-sense cherrywood."

"Do you have to work every minute day and night?" Hester asked, suddenly irritated, at what she did not know.

"Would you have a rum toddy?" the Selectman calmly asked, putting the cogwheel and sandpaper on the magazine and the magazine on the floor beside his chair. "It'll limber up your back muscles."

"That's absolutely necessary."

Eben came down while his father was out mixing the drinks. "How pretty you look!" he quickly exclaimed, and he went to her chair and kissed her on the cheek; and she thought of rough Coit.

"How's he seem?" Eben asked, bobbing his head in the general direction of the back of the house to indicate his father.

"He seems about usual," Hester said.

"I doubt if he'll ever be the same," Eben said. "He doesn't relish being wrong."

"Who does?"

The Selectman came back with three warm rum drinks. "Ice in the icebox," he said cheerfully to Eben, "if you want to cool off your gizzard." But Eben took his drink warm and murmured that it was good.

"What did you people decide about the drive?" Eben meekly asked.

"They settled on leaving the final decision up to me whether we'd go ahead tomorrow or not," the Selectman said. "They told me to digest my ideas on it along side of supper, and then let 'em know by phone."

"I take it, then," Eben said, "that they're not very enthusiastic about going on the rest of the way."

"Most of 'em are very enthusiastic about not going on the rest of the way."

"Why don't you give it up?" Hester asked in a voice whose heavy note of compassion startled her.

"Because," the Selectman bristling said, "as I told those lazy so-and-sos, a thing that's worth beginning is worth finishing. I mean to say that a thing that's worth trying to do at all is worth trying to do well from beginning to end. Else why exist?"

"In other words," Eben said, sounding more tender toward his father than Hester had ever heard him be, "you've already made up your mind."

"Well, no," the Selectman said much more mildly, looking here and there around the room, as if for a speck of guidance, "I haven't decided, really. I'll just have to think it over. . . . What puzzles me to beat the band," he added with great weariness, "is how so many trickled away. . . ." He began then to stare in his way of dreaming. "I wonder, I wonder," he muttered at one point.

Hester thought of Uncle Anak turning the hay in the rain—he'd said he'd turn the whole field that very day, and "vummed if he didn't do it"; and now the Selectman had to decide whether to finish what he'd said he would. Yet this choice of the Selectman's was, in some way, different. There might be purpose in destroying eight-odd woodchucks, even if they were but a fraction of the colony, but Hester saw that for the Selectman the issue transcended such practicalities; the issue for Eben's father had by now drawn into it many terrible considerations: of personal confidence, of trust, of sacrifice, of the gift of power, of common responsibility, of interdependent life, of friendship, love, and self-esteem in Tunxis. The choice was far more complex, Hester saw, than it had seemed on the surface just now when she had made her silly, pity-ridden suggestion that he simply quit this drive he had been thinking about for a decade, and she felt, suddenly, a glow of embarrassment for herself and of admiration for him, who was so very troubled but so very deliberate.

At two sharp raps from the front door knocker, Eben and his father both hurried to the hall. Hester, hanging back, heard greetings, heard a small but firm treble against the two deep hellos, and then:

"How're you feeling?" Hester heard the Selectman ask.

"Poorly," the voice of Dorcas Thrall said. "My food don't set well, Matthew, I kind of gullop up a lot of air about two hours after I eat. Otherways, I'm fit as Mrs. Tuller's bull fiddle."

"Your appetite's too good," the Selectman said. "You shouldn't gorm into your food the way you do, that's the why and the wherefore of that air you get, Aunty Dorcas."

"Flatterer!" Dorcas Thrall said after a little protesting cackle. "You're the worst one for handing out the taffy I ever saw."

"Come in, Aunty Dorcas, come in," Hester heard the Selectman say. "Come in and meet Eben's girl. Eben's and my girl." Hester heard that, and she saw Eben coming in from the hall turn and give his father a quick patricidal look, which the Selectman, with a hand on his son's shoulder half shoving Eben into the sitting room, did not trouble himself to see.

Dorcas Thrall was slender and short, and Hester, stepping forward with hand outstretched, was struck at once by the thought that the old lady's face was

like a bird's—though perhaps, she realized, the idea
might have been induced by what she knew of Dorcas
Thrall's terror; at any rate, the nose was narrow,
sharp, and pointed, the eyes large-pupiled and dark,
and the chin nothing to speak of, so that she looked
like a nice little birdy. She did not wear all of her
age; for although her face seemed somewhat dry and
around her eyes there were a few of the small skin-
folds of an ancient human being, her lips were
scarcely creased and pulled at all, and her cheeks
looked soft, and she had no hanging dewlaps.

Mrs. Avered came softly from the kitchen wiping
her hands on her apron, and she kissed the old
woman on a cheek, and Mrs. Thrall patted her shoulder and then said to Hester, "You never in your born
days saw a girl as pretty as this one"—patting Mrs.
Avered—"as pretty as this one when she was ten
years old. She looked as tasty as a sherbet. A big
sateen ribbon right here," and Aunty Dorcas reached
up and touched the right side of Mrs. Avered's hair;
"always that ribbon!"

"Pshaw, Aunty Dorcas," Mrs. Avered said.

Hester swallowed despair as she contemplated the
decay, the rotting of the heartwood, the falling away
into dullness, that Eben's mother had all too obviously suffered since the hair-ribbon time of her life,
for in her born days Hester had seen a million women
prettier than this one who now stood before her with
a splash of spilled gravy on her apron—a million
women simply more alive; and Hester was afraid of
that decay, wondering uneasily whether the Avered
men had had anything to do with it.

When all were seated, Dorcas Thrall said, "Did
you hear about my triumph—my triumph—over the
forces of Darkness?"

"We heard you mashed a Cooper's hawk, if that's what you mean," the Selectman said.

"I brought something to show you," the old woman smugly said, reaching into her handbag and drawing out the pair of shanks and fierce talons of the chicken hawk she had assassinated. "He acted as if he felt ashamed of what he'd been doing to that poor kitten, while I was wringing his neck," Aunty Dorcas said.

She offered the cruel claws for view, holding them up in her delicate-looking hands that were streaked with the tiny blue veins of old age.

■

EBEN'S FATHER, having served the roast all round, got up from the table, went into the kitchen, could be heard descending the cellar stairs, mounted them again, and came back with a galvanized iron pail in his hand, and in the pail, nested in cracked ice, Hester saw the neck of a bottle.

"Bubbles for beautiful ladies!" the Selectman cried, looking at his wife and, Hester egotistically thought, not meaning her. Still standing, he took the bottle from the pail and began to worry the cork with his thumbs.

"Shame on you, Matthew," Mrs. Avered said, in a rebuke that had no real scolding in it. "The extravagance of you!"

"You should have heard Seth Parmely down at the store," the Selectman said, "when I asked him to sell me this. 'Champagny!' he shouts at me. 'What the hell fur?' I told him Eben was coming home. 'So,' says Seth, 'the boy's been to the city to see the elephant, now he's comin' home and you're scared of him,' that's what he said. He said he hated to take my money for such nonsense."

"I'm honored," Eben said, with an edge of effort to his voice. The cork shot out, hit the ceiling, dropped to the floor, and rolled to a stop under Hester's chair. When the Selectman had poured helpings to all in jelly glasses and had taken his place again, Eben raised his portion and apparently trying to be gallant said, "To the beautiful ones!" He bowed toward Aunty Dorcas, and the old woman giggled and shook her head, and everybody sipped laughing, and Mrs. Avered, choking on the wry, strange, expanding liquid, coughed above her glass and shed a tear.

Suddenly during the main course the Selectman began to talk like a man hard pressed by pocketwatch and calendar. He fell into a queer, luxuriant, reminiscent mood, and Hester thought he must be fighting through his decision on the woodchuck drive in some oblique way. "I'm contented," he said. "I want to live forever like you, Aunty Dorcas." He said that he wanted no end to his senses, for everything he saw or touched seemed magical to him, and he told of having gone to several doctors when he had felt fine, a few months before, to make sure that he was healthy; he had gone all the way to the city to see one of them. He began to talk of his happy boyhood. "Did you ever whip apples?" he asked Hester at one point. "My heavens, that was fun. What we'd do, we'd take some of the sucker shoots from an apple tree, we'd get some tough, supple green saplings by cutting off suckers, and we'd cut them to about this long"—he held his hands about three feet apart—"and whittle a sharp point, like a pencil's, on one end. This was in August or early September, when the apples were fairly big but still green and hard. We'd stick the sharp point into the apple, so the apple was skewered onto the stick, then we'd rear it back and (this worked like the catapults the old Romans used) we'd whip it forward. It would fly off and follow the most marvelous trajectory. Up! Up! Up! Like a baseball when it's been properly connected with, Aunty Dorcas, you've seen that happen on your television. It used to be an extension to the strength of our arms." Later he said, again to Hester, "Do you remember that powder you could throw on a fireplace fire, some kind of salts that would give you flames of different colors—blue, green, red, yellow flames? Did you ever have any of that? We used to do it winter nights in the kitchen stove. Brilliant green flames!" His outwardly mellow frame of mind seemed thin and unreal to Hester. "Do you know my favorite form of art of all times?" he asked his tablemates. "The frescoes we used to put on the walls down at the Manross School when we were boys. We used to draw funny-faces of old Jared Andrus and the other teachers with a tallow dip and then we'd bring them into relief and shade them by rubbing hard with different-colored wool skullcaps. The fuzz of the knitting came off on the wax. Do you know who was our best artist, Aunty Dorcas? It was Corydon Jones."

"Gracious me," Dorcas Thrall said. "He was a pokerish-lookin' thing."

"He was a cripple," the Selectman told Hester. "Gnarled up like an old crabapple tree."

Aunty Dorcas said, "I forgave Frank Churnstick a lot of things he'd done in his clear days, after he lost his mind, but one thing I never forgave him was readin' that hobbled-up Jones boy out of the church."

"Ha! I'd forgotten that," the Selectman cried, seeming almost to pounce on Eben. "You and your code! Parson Churnstick. ... Wait a minute, wait till I get The Book." The Selectman pushed back his chair with a clatter and left the room.

"Matthew! Matthew!" Mrs. Avered sadly said.

"What a one for looking things up! Forgets to eat his meals half the enduring time."

The Selectman came back with a Bible in his hand, riffling the pages as he walked. "Let's see, let's see," he said when he had sat down. "Oh, that was shameful: it was long before his trolley hopped the wire, too."

"Pshaw!" Dorcas Thrall said. "Even in those middle days he was too pious to eat black pepper."

"Here it is. Listen to this, son, you with your capsules. Parson Churnstick got up in the pulpit one Sunday and out of the blue he pointed a finger as long and thin as a string bean at Corydon Jones—church-meetings were that poor boy's only entertainment—and he said the cripple couldn't come to meeting any more, and then he read out of the Bible, he read this: 'Whosoever he be of thy seed in their generations that hath any blemish, let him not approach to offer the bread of his God. For whatsoever man he be that hath a blemish, he shall not approach: a blind man, or a lame, or he that hath a flat nose, or any thing superfluous, or a man that is brokenfooted, or brokenhanded, or crookbacked, or a dwarf, or that hath a blemish in his eye, or be scurvy, or scabbed, or hath his stones broken.' Well, Corydon Jones had most of those things wrong with him, except he wasn't blind and I couldn't say as to his stones, poor rascal. Parson Churnstick snatched that passage right out of context and threw him out then and there; I guess the parson just couldn't stand looking at a monster in his pews week after week—maybe he felt as if he was looking at himself in a mirror. Things aren't as simple as you think, my Eben."

Eben flushed.

Dorcas Thrall said, "Frank Churnstick was wholesouled as you and me when he was a young man, you'd have thought his head was made of hard-beam or ironwood. The borers sure got into it toward the end, though."

"Your end of Division Four'll be going by the abandoned church tomorrow," the Selectman said to Hester; then he pulled himself up short: "—if we go ahead, that is. I'd like to show you the old church."

"Some woodchuck drive!" Eben exclaimed with more or less repressed vehemence.

"All I can say," the Selectman replied coolly, "is, I hope we keep the ones we have, if we go ahead."

"Here's to your creatures, Matthew," Dorcas Thrall said, raising her glass. "Never had any use for 'em."

■

WHAT'S YOUR PRESCRIPTION for a good old age, Aunty Dorcas?" the Selectman asked as they sat over dessert. He looked ashen and had begun to perspire. "You're going to live an eternity. What's the secret?"

"The first hundred years are the hardest," Dorcas Thrall said merrily; evidently that was her standard response to good wishes for her permanence. As she answered, she dropped a gobbet of apple-slump off her spoon into her lap. "Dear me," she said, shaking her head and scooping it up, "what an old slopdozzle I'm gettin' to be." Then she said respectfully to the sweating Selectman, "I calculate the main reason an old pelter like me has run on so long is that I'm not scared of dyin', not a bit. Bein' afraid of dyin' is the most killin' pastime there is. I remember when my brother Walter died—land of Goshen! that was forty years ago ... forty years ago ... a good lifetime right there, but I remember it as if it had happened yester-day—I sat beside him nine days, and in the end he just got soggy and wasn't there any more. I can't be bothered to shake and shiver about going to sleep like Walter; I've done it every night now for plenty of years, and glad to do it. I was just addin' it up the other day. Countin' naps and snoozes, I've gone to sleep close onto thirty-five thousand separate and distinct times. Why should I be afraid of one last doze?"

Death is nothing to her, Hester thought, but a hummingbird at the lip of a trumpet of honeysuckle would throw her into a panic. She thought of the city-panics Miss Morris was always having. "Some people," she said, "think they can keep young just by taking care of themselves. I have in mind La Morris," she said to Eben. "She's my boss," she said to the others.

"She's a bad egg," Eben gloomily said.

"People don't set out in life trying to be bad eggs, Eben," Mrs. Avered said in kindly reproach.

"She's on the Yoga and yoghurt circuit," Hester said.

"Carry me out with the tongs!" Aunty Dorcas said. "What's that?"

"Miss Morris goes to a class and takes these exercises that were invented by Yogi philosophers to help settle their minds. You should hear her tell about the class! Flabby women with little purses and lapels of skin and fat behind their arms and between their thighs—as if she weren't one of them. They stand on their heads and sit cross-legged and roll their stomachs and dream of being firm young virgins. Oof! Then on the yoghurt end of it: Miss Morris eats like a growing dog most of the time, till all at once she'll have a fit of dieting and eat nothing but yoghurt, not a blessed thing but yoghurt."

Suddenly Hester had a perverse impulse to shock the circle of Puritans at the table; it seemed suddenly important to her to shock them, for perhaps she would one day belong to them, and she must try them now, try them, shake them, see if she could stir their settled underpinnings. Especially, for some reason, she was aware that she wanted to shock the Selectman.

"Miss Morris thinks if she keeps hunting long enough, she'll find the Fountain of Youth," Hester said. And she told of a day she had gone with Miss Morris to see a hormone doctor. She described the doctor's splendid office, hung with modern paintings, and the doctor himself, behind a huge carved desk bountiful with dictating contraptions and secretarial buzzery. Hester had gone with Miss Morris because that morning Miss Morris had pleaded nervousness and had asked for company on a round of errands, as she often did. Hester told how the doctor had explained to Miss Morris the effect on a body and mind of hormone deficiencies. "Then he started talking about his injections," Hester said. " 'We have to watch things pretty closely,' he told her. 'One danger,' he said, 'is that even many years after the menopause, there may be a marked reassertion of the libido.' Miss Morris didn't know what that was, so he explained it to her and then he said, 'This can be a sweet thing,' he said, 'or it can lead to tragedy. Now, I don't want you to think I can make you over into a young woman. Human tissues,' he said, 'are resilient and capable of being kept healthy, but rejuvenation of most parts of the body is not to be dreamed about.' Then—listen to this!—he said, 'There is, though, one interesting exception. Certain of the hormones bring about a miraculous restoration of the vagina. I had a patient of sixty-five who, after a few months of treatment, had the vagina of a twenty-year-old girl.' "

"One of the hens looks to have some mites," Mrs.

Avered promptly said to her husband. "Do you think we ought to dust the chickens?"

"Women are the limit," the Selectman said pleasantly enough to blushing Hester, who was not sure for a moment whether he was referring to Miss Morris or to what his wife had said. Then he went on: "I try to be a good husband, but I swan, I can't tell how the wind is liable to blow from one minute to the next—whether it's chickens or what. Remember that time, dear, last winter?" he said to Mrs. Avered. "It had snowed about twenty inches," he told the others, "and it was cold enough to freeze two dry rags together, so Mrs. Avered said to me, 'Matthew,' she says, 'don't you think you ought to shovel the snow off the front path?' So, I always try to be obliging, I say, 'Yes, dear, I do.' 'Well,' she says, 'in that case I suggest you bring up some cordwood from the cellar.' "

"Ayeh," Dorcas Thrall said sarcastically, "and our Selectman—our Selectman, he's as consistent as Puritan virtue, be'n't he?"

"I'm getting old, Aunty Dorcas," the Selectman said with sudden sickly despair. "Last week I was supposed to make voters on a Saturday and I got my days mixed up, I showed up at the courtroom at eight o'clock Friday morning, according to scoodle as I surmised, but of course there just never was ary voter there to register, no matter how I'd wait, it was the wrong day. I'm too young to be old."

"No harm done, Matthew," Mrs. Avered said. "Everyone gets a lapse here and there."

"I wasted the better part of a morning," the Selectman protested. "You can't call Friday back when Saturday comes. You know what the poet said about the Moving Finger. . . ."

Hester felt a deep and delicious pity for Eben's father; then she caught Eben looking mysterious swords at her.

"Shall we go in the sitting room?" Mrs. Avered said, picking up her dessert plate and reaching for Eben's.

■

WHEN MRS. AVERED joined the others after having washed the dishes (she dispatched them with remarkable speed, having refused and ridiculed Dorcas Thrall's suggestion that Eben and Hester wash them), the Selectman fetched a bottle of cider brandy and the jelly glasses he had used for the champagne.

"How about a little winkum, Aunty Dorcas?" he said.

"Just a smile of it at the bottom of the glass, please," the old lady said. As the Selectman poured helpings around, Aunty Dorcas said to Eben, "Must've been a tidy elephant you saw in the city, boy. Your father's outdoin' himself for you."

"It's not all for me," Eben heavily said, and Hester thought that was true.

"Shall we play a game?" the Selectman said. "Would your scruples permit you to gamble for some straight pins, Aunty Dorcas?"

"You know me, Matthew, my conscience lets me gamble—I'll gamble—with anything but my worldly cash," Dorcas Thrall said. "Why sure, let's jostle some pins awhile."

The game was a simple-minded one. At her husband's request, Mrs. Avered got the Selectman's felt hat and a card of pins. Eben's father dealt out the pins, ten to a player. Two at a time, pair after pair, the players would place a couple of pins parallel to each other on the brim of the hat. One adversary would tap the side of the crown with his hand, making the pins jump, and the opponent would follow, until one pin fell across the other; the one who crossed the pins won them both. The Selectman had placed himself beside Hester. At first the players all concentrated on the contents, and the tappings were followed by words of advice, groans of despair, cheers, and laughter. But eventually eyes wandered from the circulating hat, and the company began to talk.

"Aunty Dorcas," the Selectman said, "do you think I'm George Challenge's poodle? That's what this young saucer of a girl called me this morning."

Dorcas Thrall, with the hat in her hand playing against Eben, looked rather sharply at Hester. "Poodle?" she then said, twitting the Selectman. "No! Challenge's mule, maybe."

"Is that crook Challenge still running this town?" Eben asked, tapping the hat carefully.

"The Selectman runs the town, son," Mrs. Avered said, firmly for her.

"Bah!" Eben said.

"He's not exactly a crook, son," the Selectman quietly said.

"Well," Aunty Dorcas said, "he's not the most sensitive man I ever saw. His nerves—his nerves are very deep, I must say."

Hester remembered that in the woods that morning the Selectman had said that George Challenge was as crooked as a ram's horn. But: "He's not a crook," the Selectman now said. "He's just a combination of lazy and shrewd; he can sojer and he can peddle. Hester, this fellow's so lazy he once broke one of those nail-keg staves he has for legs just walking across his office. That was when he was a Tax Collector. He got up and started across the room with nothing in his way and stumbled and broke his leg, and everyone said it was just from the effort of moving his carcass. And what a weeper he is! That's part of his trade, too. You tell him some sorry yarn about your troubles, and lo, his head is waters and his eyes a fountain of tears. His main source of wherewithal has been setting up petty estates, and I declare, it's wonderful the way he grows fat as a consequence of bungling the legal process and juggling the Republican town committee."

"He's a crook," Eben said. "In my kind of language, he's a crook, and he runs this town."

"It's hard to catch a weasel asleep, I'll grant you that, son," the Selectman said in an even voice. "I was going through the town records some months ago, trying to make head or tail of our Tunxis finances, and I came across an item where George Challenge, when he was Collector, had a two-dollar per diem allowance for the trouble of dunning folks for their dues, and at the end of the year—that must have been six or eight years ago—at the end of the year he filed for three hundred and sixty-nine days of expense money. I said to Mr. Challenge when I ran across the item, I told him, 'There are only three hundred and sixty-five days in a year; how come?' 'Oh, you mean working days,' he said, smooth as margarine; he said he'd worked a few extra days—some holidays and Sundays! I swan, I really believed he'd never studied a calendar."

"There!" Aunty Dorcas shrilled. "I crossed 'em!"

"This town'll never amount to a hill of beans," Eben said, passing the hat to his mother, "so long as you let yourselves be run by a second-rate hack like him."

"The people here," the Selectman said, showing annoyance for the first time, "have more sense of responsibility about their town than the residents of some much bigger places that I can think of. Much bigger. And always have."

"Phooey," Eben tormentedly said.

"The trouble with you," the Selectman said, quite

angry now, "is that you don't know enough to knock two pins together on a hat. These people in Tunxis are willing to work for each other. Why, look here." The Selectman stood up and crossed to a bookshelf and pulled open the mesh door and took out one of a number of ledgers with cracked and curling spines. "We were talking about Corydon Jones at supper. Well, here's a case, let me find it. . . . Here's just one example of how this town learned way back to take care of its own. . . . Here: 'Voted,' here's what it says in the minutes of a town meeting, I was going over this the other night, 'Voted, that the Selectman's office be directed to take charge of Parliament Taylor, and conduct with him as they shall think most for his comfort, and will be least expensive to the town, whilst he remains in his present delirium, either to set him up at vendue to the person who will keep him the cheapest, or dispose of him in any other way which may appear to the Selectman more convenient, and for such time as he may think reasonable, and on the cost of Tunxis town.' You hear that?"

"What does that prove?" Eben said. "What in hell does that prove? After all, that was a long time ago, that was in another world, and anyhow, what did they propose to do with the town idiot there? They put him up for sale! Oh, God! Everyone's so mixed up! Nobody knows what we're coming to—and you sit there reading me eighteenth-century town records."

"Grow up," the Selectman said, in a father's commanding tones.

"Nobody knows what the score is," Eben said, "least of all this hick town."

"Grow up," the father said. "Do you hear me, or do you want me to come over there and put some hearing into you?"

This made Hester feel rebellious; she was on the

point of protesting that Eben was no longer a child and should not be treated as one, when:

"If I could offer a suggestion," Aunty Dorcas said, "why don't these young ones go across to my house and turn on the television set? The latch is up, and"—she added with nonagenarian innocence—"the settee's comfy."

"That suits me," Eben said in an unenthusiastic voice, standing up. "Come on, Hes, let's watch a ball game."

"Aunty Dorcas is the only person I know," Mrs. Avered said composedly, "who has a television set and still lights her way to bed with candlewood."

"Don't stay too long," the Selectman said, meloncool. "We may have another hard day tomorrow."

■

THE PITCHER UNCOILED, the white ball rode spinning down the bulb-lit alley toward home plate, and the batter leaned on the night air as he pulled the bat around. Then parts of the picture became molten, viscid, elastic; the batter in the act of swinging put forth a horribly distended arm which reached, bat in hand, brutally out over the grass of bunting-land toward the pitcher, who had suddenly shrunk and stood quaking rhythmically on the mound. The weird distortion on the screen seemed to Hester a gesture of retribution, a hitting back at torment on behalf of all those who stand forever having difficulties pitched at them. She laughed.

"What lousy reception!" Eben said disgustedly. "It's hopeless." And he got up from the stiff little couch and went to the machine and snapped it off.

"What's the matter with you tonight?" Hester asked in the dim place.

"What do you mean?"

"You're so grumpy."

"You would be too, if you were me."

"What's wrong with being you?"

Eben still stood by the television set in the darkened room. His feet were at the edge of a trapezoid of light that fell onto the parlor floor from the hall lamp. The room where the old lady dwelt smelled faintly of balsam and mold.

"I knew it was going to happen," Eben dejectedly said.

" 'It'?"

"I knew you'd fall for his line."

" 'His'?"

"You know who I'm talking about. You're in love with him."

Hester stood up. "Really, Eben," she said, "you're beginning to sound like that crazy parson—what was his name?"

"You don't deny it."

Hester found herself thinking for a moment about Roswell Coit, about the powerful, vindictive, envious, childlike man who had embraced her under the lee of the stone wall by the brook. "I'll grant you, your father's a fascinating man," she said with a deliberate light-heartedness.

"You're in love with him!"

"I'm sorry for your father because there were so few woodchucks at the end of the drive today—that's about where the truth lies." Then Hester asked with sudden energy, "What is love? What's it to be in love? I was trying to figure that out in the woods all day today. I'll bet you can't tell me the answer. I'll bet you don't even ask yourself the question."

"It seems to me," Eben said, driven by Hester's attack into conciliation and pomposity, "that if we're going to approach marriage with this kind of background—"

"Don't bother your head about it," Hester said. "Who's not going to marry you is me. Don't even talk to me about it. I wouldn't think of marrying you. Let's go back to the house."

"You don't give me a chance to say what I mean."

"After you say what you mean, you try to cover it up with what you wish you'd meant."

■

THE SELECTMAN seemed glad to have them back. "Well!" he exclaimed. "That was a short nine innings. What was the matter—dull game?"

"No," Hester said, "no, it was fine. Three to one for the Red Sox in the fifth."

"Was it wobbling?" Dorcas Thrall asked. "Some nights that screen's unsteady as thunderation."

"No, Aunty Dorcas," Eben lied, cheerful as a bluebird, "it was O.K. Good signal."

"My gracious," Aunty Dorcas said, "don't you children have anything to talk about? When I was your age sparking—sparking—used to take us a longful while. Lands alive! We could sit and droop our heads and just get ready to talk longer than you two've been gone all told. I guess there's no such thing as shyness any more."

"Of course there is," Mrs. Avered said. "Eben always was a shy one."

Now Eben looked as cheerless as a low-lying cloud.

"See here, Matthew," Dorcas Thrall said, rising by stages to her feet, "can I take this girl in the kitchen and talk to her a piece? Could I talk to her? You asked me to come look her over tonight, and here I've done nothing but listen to you gab and gossip. Come along, dear, let's chitter awhile, I want to look you over."

Hester, blushing, said, "I'm game," and followed the old woman.

When they were settled on kitchen chairs, Aunty Dorcas asked, "Now! How do you like Tunxis?"

"People seem so—so—so almost cruel here," Hester said.

"Ayeh, maybe; maybe," Aunty Dorcas said reflectively. "We've had a long learnin' in mean rascally behavior round here. The Pequots were the first to give us lessons; they used to cut gashes in a person's muscles and put live coals inside, and they'd make people eat parts of themselves."

"Oooh," Hester said.

"So you're going to marry little Eben," Aunty Dorcas said in an unchanged tone of voice, as if she were still talking of Indian tortures.

"I—I guess so," Hester said.

"Well, child, if you've found the pearl you want and are inclined to sell all your worldly goods to buy it, advice is useless, advice is worse than useless. That doesn't stop people from givin' it, though, and my advice to you, young lady, is, go ahead and marry this boy and then leave him be; these Avereds have to be let alone, you can't hobble 'em, they have to be themselves. You'll be miserable as any housewife, but you might as well marry. Listen! I know these Avereds like the inside of my coat-sleeve that's frayed. Why, I carried your Eben's father pooseback all over Tunxis when he was an infant. I had a little sneakin' hanker for *his* father, only I wasn't pretty enough to suit him. He was a man for you! His stature was ridiculous, a small man, he was always the titman in his class in school, a regular runt. But a person! He didn't care a continental what people thought of him, and bad luck never bothered him, and he had a plenty: Whenever it rained porridge, it seemed his dish was always upside down. He was a great one for learning; he called the outhouse—no plumbin' in those days, dear—he called it Avered University. 'Well,' he'd say, 'I guess I'll go out to the college and study awhile.' He could do more work on a stretch than any man I ever saw. He had a watermill when he was young, and once when a landslide the other side of Beggar's Mountain cut off the railroad—they had a landslide over there that cut off the railroad—he ran his mill day and night for the neighborhood a whole week long, and he trained himself so's he could turn a grist into the hopper, lay down on a bench with an old turnip watch he had hammerin' alongside of his head, and he'd sleep till the split second when the last kernel dropped out and no more, then up and at it again. He carved his own gravestone, said you couldn't depend on your survivors to say anything good about you on your headstone, so he'd have one handy of his own composition. I forget right now what he wrote on it. There was a mighty big donnick in a meadow on the Pinney farm that one of the Pinney children was killed sleigh-ridin' into, and the Pinneys told Reuben Avered he could have the boulder if he'd kindly remove it from their eyesight, so he split it up and made a good profit out of posts, lintels, underpinnin's, and whatnot—and 'twas out of that donnick that he took out a choice piece for his headstone and memorial, and now he lies under it, dear small creature! I'd give my bond and swear he got to Heaven, though he'd broken with the church when they decided to support the meetin'house by sellin' the pews instead of rentin' 'em. He said he didn't want God on the basis of short-term financin'. He never once went back."

"Tell me about Eben's father," Hester said.

"Oho!" Aunty Dorcas said, "he's a puzzler. I remember once when he was a boy he come over boastin' about his father's house, said it was big, boastin' how his father was plannin' to put a mortgage onto it—like addin' a piazza or a cupolo, I guess he thought."

"What kind of trouble did he get into? Someone told me he was caught out in some trouble once."

"Mercy, child," Aunty Dorcas said, looking at Hester as if assessing her. "Mercy. . . . Oh, well," she then said, "I guess you're old enough to tell milk from cream; to judge by your stories, you can bandy the human anatomy around, right down to the last particular—I didn't understand half the words I wanted to, when you were talkin', and didn't want to understand the ones I did. Anyway, Matthew's little accident doesn't take any tellin' at all. It was just one of those things that happens to soft-hearted people. It was the night of a storm here one fall, oh, 'bout fifteen years back, there was a wind that'd blow all Hell out by the roots, and Matthew said he'd better run up to see how old Aunty Dorcas was makin' out all alone in her house. Well, he visited me by a hell-fired roundabout route, 'cause the next thing anyone knew Roger Booge, who thought he was just makin' the rounds of his animals with a flashlight, found his daughter Belle in her shimmy and one Matthew Avered pullin' on his pants in under a sheep shed out of the wind and rain. No sheep in that shed, it was a cleaned-out one. Matthew, poor soft-hearted individual, he's got a soft heart, he was just detourin' to my house to look to my safety—but Roger made a fuss all over the county! That girl of his, Belle, she never was no good. My father was a lawyer, I remember he used to say when a girl would get caught that way, 'In the court of law,' he'd say"—Aunty Dorcas put into her voice a juristical pomp—" 'they call it flagrante *delicto*' (I think that was it) 'but between us,' he'd say, 'between us, I call it "in heat." ' "

Hester felt a surge of outrage at Aunty Dorcas for telling this valuable story in such an offhand way. Then for a tangential moment she thought of Coit by the wall in the woods. I should have slapped him, she decided to herself; yes, I certainly should have slapped him. "I suppose that hurt him in Tunxis," she said out loud, of the Selectman.

"Hurt him? Well, he's the Selectman. But people just can't seem to take him whole the way they used to. Most times we take into account everything a person has done and said when we weigh him for market, but it only takes one little caper like that to make people stop thinkin' about the rest of a man, even though they may have gone in for some of the same themselves and not got found out at it."

"Do people trust him?"

"Nobody trusts anybody any more. Nobody trusts anybody."

The two talked a few minutes longer, and Hester thought the old woman liked her, because it was easy for her to listen to Dorcas Thrall.

When they went back into the parlor, Mrs. Avered was splitting an apple. "Have a taste of apple, Aunty Dorcas?" she said, giving the halves in her hand to her husband and son.

"Don't mind if I do," Aunty Dorcas said.

Mrs. Avered cut a second apple in thirds. She gave pieces to Dorcas Thrall and Hester, and kept one herself.

"You're a thrifty being," Aunty Dorcas, chewing apple, said to Mrs. Avered, "to cut up your helpin's accordin' to the size of the customers." Delicately she unlocked a slender belch. "See what I mean?" she said to the Selectman. "It was a good supper," she said to Mrs. Avered.

"Can I walk you home, Aunty Dorcas?" the Selectman said. "I know you're just raring to stay up, but it's time for us tired old folks to hit the hay, isn't it, Miss Hester? We're stiff in the hams, Aunty Dorcas, and we've got a hard day ahead of us."

"We have?" Eben said. "My God! You don't give up easily, do you?"

"Of course not, son," Mrs. Avered proudly said. "You ought to know your father better than that by now."

" 'Tis a wise child who knows his own father in this day and age," the Selectman said, with a trace of a not-very-happy smile on his face. He stood up. "Could you hold on just a minute while I make a telephone call, Aunty Dorcas? I won't be a minute."

Hester, glancing at Eben, who had dark circles under his eyes, was oppressed with a sense of lost opportunities. She had suddenly, at the end of this day, a feeling something like one she always had on leaving a holiday place: that she hadn't done half the things she had meant to do, that she loved the view, that she would have to come back and relive what she had enjoyed and make amends for what she had been too lazy or unknowing or complacent this time to do; yet already understanding that she would never come back again, because there were other places and moods to visit if ever a new chance came. Toward Eben, who looked so tired munching apple in a chair, she had a heavy feeling of unkept promises and unrealized intentions; of choices that could never be revisited.

Before he left the room to go to the telephone, the Selectman stooped to pick up off the floor the magazine with the cogwheel and sandpaper on it, and Hester saw him wince, as if with an imaginary pain that came from heaviness of the heart, as he bent over.

Four

WE SHALL RALLY," Mrs. Tuller had said, "at the chestnut," as if everyone in the wide world knew that tree.

The drivers had met again on the common in the dark before day, and Hester had stood again beside the whipping post, stiff, half awake, fearless, and dull. She hated doing things a second time; once in a parlor game in which the players had been asked to list on a sheet of paper their likes and dislikes, she had headed her roll of the latter with "Repetition." Mrs. Tuller's briefing, Coit's cavils, the onloading into Pitkin's truck—all were familiar and boring and a waste of the minutes of a young life. They had been ferried at last to the new days workplace on the far side of Job's Creek.

The sun was upping now. Hester and Mrs. Tuller and Anak Welch walked in the van of the group along the bank of the creek through a saffron thicket, and Mrs. Tuller complained of the humidity of summertime Tunxis. "I finally decided," she said, "that the only way to keep my 'cello from splittin' open at the glue was to treat it like a brood of chicks and keep a light bulb goin' alongside of it."

"The summers are gettin' wetter and wetter in the air and drier and drier in the ground," Anak Welch said sadly, shaking his head, as if the plan of the universe had lately been changed and was now too much for him.

"I can't understand our Selectman bringin' us out here today," Mrs. Tuller said, as if the ways of the Selectman were, like those of the weather, forever unpredictable, fickle, and fit for commonplace talk.

"What did he say when he called you?" Anak Welch asked.

"He said folks who start a thing ought to finish it."

"That's plain bullheadedness."

What about the day, Hester wanted to ask the huge man, but didn't dare, the day when you turned the hay in the rain?

"I tell you one thing, Anak," Mrs. Tuller said. "I think a person ought to be civil to another person on the phone. Land's sakes! The way he ordered me to get the chain of phone calls started, why, he made me feel like the dirt under a bed in a lazy woman's house."

"He was tired," Hester tiredly said.

"Yes, child," Mrs. Tuller said with a kindliness that made her implicit censure seem all the sharper, "we were all tired right to our marrow."

They came soon enough to a clearing. "Well, here's the old chestnut," Mrs. Tuller said, "God bless it." She sat down on an enormous stump.

"Do you mean that's all there is to the chestnut?" Hester asked Anak Welch. "Just a crumbled-up stump on the ground?"

"Law love us, girl," the big man softly said. "There's not a chestnut tree alive anywhere around—the blight left our woods in an awful hue, you know. This old tree used to mark one end of the parish in the hollow, that's why it's *the* chestnut, as you call it; you don't have to scorn the thing."

"I didn't mean to sound—to sound that way," Hester uncomfortably said.

"I don't know," Anak Welch said, a reddish, effortful look of worry spreading over his face slowly like a symptom of inner infection, "it seems as if we used to be a little easier about property than we are nowadays. Take this tree as a marker, now. Old Rufus Choate, you know, he talked about the happenstance way our boundaries used to go, how they'd go 'from a hill to a log'—I remember this 'cause I boned up on it for the open meetin' when we had our big fight with Treehampstead—'from a hill to a log, thence to a rock, thence to a hemlock tree, thence to a stump, thence to a savin bush, thence to a hive of bees in swarmin' time, thence to three hundred foxes with firebrands tied to their tails'—those were the property lines we used to have! Nowadays it's all accordin' to survey down to the last endurin' inch. Squabble, squabble, squabble."

Hester remembered that the Selectman had told her that this honorable big Anak had a way of starting lawsuits with his neighbors, and she asked, with mischievous curiosity, "Why do people quarrel so much?"

"They can't stomach the idea of bein' equal," Anak Welch said.

Mrs. Tuller had told the drivers in her division to resign themselves to a long wait this morning, because no one knew what difficulties the advance men might have in getting the woodchucks moving. It was assumed that some of the animals would have dug underground overnight, but whether all of them would have burrowed, and whether temporary burrows would have two mouths and therefore easy egress, and what mood the animals would be in, stiff-jointed and grumpy like the drivers, or restless still, no one could know.

Several people were standing around the chestnut stump talking with Mrs. Tuller, and Hester, who wanted to ask the enthroned captain something, edged into the circle.

"That's saving at the spigot and wasting at the bunghole," George Challenge was saying in a pleading whine. "He just has no faculty for conserving the town's money. If you put a barrelful of dollars behind the door of his office, he'd forget where it was. He's a poor tool for economy, and that's all there is to it."

Mrs. Tuller said, in a ponderous good-natured tease, with heavy sarcasm, as if tickling the politician with a crowbar, "You picked him, you pulled him right out of your fedora hat, didn't you, Mr. Challenge? After all, Mr. Challenge!" Looking around for approval, Mrs. Tuller saw Hester and abruptly she added, "But as I was saying, you can't expect a school to be built overnight."

This sudden change in the direction of the wind confirmed Hester in her guess that talk was again of the Selectman, and again carping—almost conspiratorial.

"I was wondering," Hester said, bending forward to put her face near the teacher's splendid head and murmuring confidentially, "whether I could get someone to help me cross back over the stream for a minute. I lost something over there by the wall yesterday afternoon."

"What did you lose, child?" Mrs. Tuller asked in a loud, earnest voice, which blew Hester erect and invited the whole circle into her business.

Hester felt the blood climb her face. "I left—I left that bezoar stone over there," she said.

"That what?"

"Oh, I guess you didn't see it," Hester said. "It's a thing, a ball, out of the inside of a dead woodchuck."

"Land of Goshen! A gallstone, dear?"

"Not exactly." By this time Hester was in a twist of embarrassment, and Mrs. Tuller, though firmly shelved on the chestnut stump, seemed to be advancing steadily against her. "I just wanted it for a souvenir," Hester stumblingly added.

"Do you think this—this dingus out of a ground-hog is worth the risk of settin' up the bridge again? You know, my dear, we can't afford to let a single one of our precious wild boars"—Mrs. Tuller jerked her head in supposed direction of the marmot pack—"out of the bag. We've got few enough as it is."

"It doesn't matter," Hester said, shocked by the laughter that ran around after Mrs. Tuller's sarcastic speech. "I don't need it."

"I'll help her find it," came a sudden offer in the voice of Roswell Coit. "Come on, Avered's girl," he said. "I'll jump the crick and you can tell me from this side where to look."

Hester willingly turned away from the council at the stump. Coit took a run and a sturdy jump, but one of his feet fell short and plouted into the muck at the far edge of the stream, whereupon climbing out he swore at women in a generalized way.

"It's just above the wall," Hester called to him, and then she couldn't resist saying in a voice of brass, "I think you ought to know where it is, my dear Mr. Coit."

Coit turned his head, looking first, to Hester's perverse gratification, at the group around the stump, evidently to see whether any had noticed her loud remark; satisfied that none had, he glanced at her and said, "Noisier and funnier, please."

Coit searched and searched but could not or would not find the bezoar.

While Coit hunted, Hester thought gropingly about the Selectman, whose sad eyes, lost in perpetual dream, and whose lips, moving around enigmatic words, had visited some secret closet of her mind during sleep the night before; but she could not find its door now, she had lost all of the dream save an afterglow of pleasure. She had scarcely seen the man this morning, for at four o'clock breakfast in the kitchen at the homestead, she had been far from wakeful and had tried to keep her surly nose in her coffee cup, and he, brisk yet generously untalkative, had hurried her so he could go along to the Grange Hall and stand firmly there as the volunteers gathered. She had in the kitchen, however, a clear impression of his calmness; apprehensive herself on his behalf, she was surprised at his tranquillity. She was stabbed, thinking of it, by a strange, ruthful thrust, by a pity so keen that it drove into her chest a sweet, hurtful physical sensation which by now was her reflex to thoughts of him.

"Nope!" Coit called. "Nowheres."

"That's strange," Hester said.

Coit, coming back toward the stream, said, "I guess old Pliny Twinkletoes Forward must've sneaked out here in dead-o'-night to steal it for his museum."

"But he didn't know I'd lost it," Hester slowheadedly said.

"Well, then I guess the whole thing just didn't happen at all," Coit said, shrugging, "I guess you never had the thing at all," and with a grunt and an "Up she goes!" he leapt across the rivulet.

■

FOR HESTER the beginning of this day, after its fine sunrise, was paler than that of the previous one, in every way less vivid, perhaps because less strange, less fearsome. Once, looking at the pallid sky through the sallow treetops, she thought she must have been more sensitive the day before, and she thought: Fear is a great friend to beauty; anxiety propped up my eyelids yesterday. . . . *This* morning her thighs hurt, she had seen wild woodchucks aplenty, these rustics of Tunxis were not quite such formidable strangers as on the previous day—ergo, the woods seemed not nearly so awesome and magical as they had the day before. Anyway, it was a hot morning, and humid, and a rank smell of ferns and skunk cabbage and cresses along the stream touched the day with a kind of vegetable rottenness; it was scarcely the climate of ecstasy.

This morning Hester was put in the line between Coit and Anak Welch; Coit was the leftmost anchor of the division again. There was much muttering about vigilance. Everyone seemed to be tired and stiff, and many complained openly about having been brought out again, and as the line commenced to move, the drivers' shouts were rather like groans.

News came that the woodchucks, perhaps dispirited and exhausted by their forced march the previous day, had dug themselves in overnight only superficially, and had now surfaced pliantly enough and seemed willing to pioneer further along the hollow, so long as pressed from behind.

When the line first started, Hester felt a new stirring of queasiness as she reminded herself that the main pack of woodchucks had crossed the bridge before her own summing eyes, the previous afternoon, and must still be directly ahead of Division Four; then, suddenly on the edge of nausea for a moment, she remembered that the Selectman had told her, after supper the night before, that she must be very careful, if she came close to a woodchuck, to examine herself afterward for ticks and fleas. She had a deep horror of crawling insects, and the Selectman's thorough description of a dead woodchuck, shimmering with vermin, made her feel ill now as she stepped through the undergrowth.

The air of the new day was insipid, still, and irritating.

During one of the early halts, Anak Welch sauntered casually up the line to Hester's post and, after a long tongue-tied period, during which he often shifted stance and sometimes grunted or carried on transactions of phlegm in his upper caverns, he abruptly, slowly, and mildly asserted, "You're the one who's goin' to marry the Avered boy."

"Well...," Hester said doubtfully.

"He's a fortunate young man."

"Thank you," Hester said, supposing herself congratulated.

"Don't thank me, young lady, I wasn't tippin' my hat to you, I don't even know you. What I meant to convey was, young Eben's always been fortunate in his choice of parents, they're a comfort, those two—though I must say his father's a stubborn man."

Hester recalled the Selectman's emphasis on Anak Welch's own stubbornness ("as set as a concrete pavement," she remembered his saying), and, since it was not like her to support embarrassment with silence, she flippantly replied, "He thinks you're stubborn as a stone."

"Oh, he does, does he?" This young lady seemed to

require consideration, and again the enormous man withheld speech during a long period of ballast shifting, which was almost, Hester thought, a beautiful dance—a pantomime of caution.

"I never saw the beat of that man for takin' down his friends," he finally said. "The next time you see him, young lady, kindly tell him for me that he can go to ballyhack, and a good trip to him." On the surface, at least, the big man seemed genial.

"I'll do that," Hester said.

"Watch out for Matthew Avered on your wedding day—you'd better not get married in Tunxis. He's a great one for funnin' people—or thinks he is. Let me tell you what he done to me." Hester was perfectly willing to allow the tale, but the big man had some rocking to do first. "I was hitched young," he then said, "and all of us were full of blood in our veins in those days. It was wintertime, and durin' the night after the ceremony, when the doin's were all done, weddin' breakfast and all such, I drove off with Martha and a two-gallon bottle of rum in a sleigh; we had sheepskin rugs for the cold and it was pitch-black dark—very cold-an'-cosy, you understand; our destination was a certain house I'd taken a loan of near Treehampstead. Well, if you please, three successive places on the way, we found the road fenced right across, and each time we stopped, out came some he-neighbors, and at each place, each and every jackanapes was prepared to kiss either my wife or my bottle two or three times before any road-clearing could be got on with. We didn't reach Treehampstead till broad day, and my bride was all kissed out, so to speak, and Matthew Avered was behind all that, who calls me stubborn, the scamp. They said he thought up the whole game, it was his idea."

Word came down the line to move, and the noises

of the drive could be heard again. Anak Welch went away through the woods like a moose. As Hester walked forward, over ground that was beginning gently to rise, across the grownover fields of sometime farms, she caught a glimpse, now and again, of the canted steeple of the abandoned Church-in-the-Hollow ahead. She had not yet seen a single woodchuck this morning and, mindful of the disappointing catch of the day before, she was fearful that the animals might now be slipping unseen by ones and twos through the picket lines. With spaniel eyes, and with a frown of concentration, she watched for a few minutes every inch of ground she could scan as she moved; then, with a minor panic flooding her veins, she wondered what she would do if she saw an escaping woodchuck, and she was struck by a clear visual memory of the glistening long teeth of the animal she had seen sunbathing the previous morning, and she decided that noise was her only protector, and she redoubled her shrill alarms.

When the distractions of the landscape had dissipated this little flurry of fear, she began, because of what Anak Welch had said, to think about getting married.

She conducted a kind of parade review of young men she knew. Availability of suitors was no problem to her; she was presentable—"ripe enough to rattle," Mr. Bandylegs Challenge had said in the foggy, foggy dew the day before—and she was sure that she could set her cap and hitch her blouse for any of ten she knew and win him, and of the ten, at least seven or eight were easier and surer, more prosperous, more respectable, more conforming, more something—less troubling—than Eben. "Everyone's so mixed up," Eben had cried in anguish to his father the night before, meaning, she supposed, "I'm so mixed up." Yet those of her ten who were most certain they were not mixed up—ha! they were, if you looked deep enough, the truest of nastiness-machines. There was one who was not in the slightest measure mixed up politically—and oh, my, what a certainty festered within *him!* There was one in whom a rigid, inflexible religious orthodoxy ruled out any mix-up on any subject—all he lacked was heavenly grace. One was a know-it-all, one didn't want to know anything. One was positive that if you ate a portion of wheat-germ meal and drank a cup of hot cow's milk each night before retiring, nothing could go wrong with your world (but he was a terrible one for moving gastric bubbles out into the peopled world; he was really rotten inside). Eben at least had a certain nervous, mettlesome humility. Hester knew herself well enough to have caught herself in company, over and over, wishing she were with someone else, or at least having flitting daydreams of someone else, and she had to face the fact that more than any other, Eben—irritable, mixed-up Eben—visited her in such restless moments in the city, whenever she was with any but him, especially with one who considered himself at home and at ease in his times.

But that was in the city, and with others, and now, perhaps because she was thinking of Eben and was therefore with him in a way, she began to think of other men—of his father, and even of his grandfather, for all the good that would do her. She decided she was glad she had come for the weekend, because now, at least, she knew a persuasive, if not overwhelming, reason for marrying Eben: Eben had, besides his own humble flexibility, something back of him in his heritage, and therefore probably within him, that she considered the most important quality a man could have—lonely courage. It stuck out all over the strange Selectman; and Aunty Dorcas had said the Selectman's father, Eben's grandfather, "didn't care a continental what people thought of him." Hester remembered how, for a yestermorning moment, she had had a delicious managerial sentiment toward Eben; she loved him and would run him to her own satisfaction. Now, though, she knew that if he contained, as she thought perhaps he did, this quality his father and grandfather had had before him, this Yankee quality of an independence that could not be intimidated by any means, even by people who considered themselves not at all mixed up, then he would conduct his own business quite well enough, and hers, too, and she could depend on him—and this was an even more satisfying feeling than the other; though the satisfaction was somehow puzzling, especially in view of the fact that the feeling also contained a paradoxical element of pity, and because all at once she had a queer sense that the one who was closest to her heart was not Eben at all. In a moment of silly jealousy, Eben had told her that she had fallen in love with his father, and now she was beginning to believe that something like that might actually be happening, and she faced this possibility, which Eben had put into her head, with equanimity at first and then with a sudden surprising fervency. She could have Coit anytime. She would probably marry Eben.

Well, she thought with some satisfaction, *I'm* a little mixed up, anyway.

■

THE SOCIETY abandoned the place," the Selectman said, "directly Parson Churnstick kicked the bucket. We hadn't been coming to meeting here for about twelve years during the time he was off-and-on crazy;

we were kind of waiting for the Lord to take mercy on him. In the meantime, those as wished attended services in the church on the green, where there was some very sane and very stupefying preaching done every Sabbath morning. But not me, I just backslid."

They stood in the hot sun in front of the unused church. The Selectman had told Anak Welch that he was going to show Hester the church and had asked him to close the gap in the line until her return to it in a few minutes. It was conceivable to Hester that the building might once have been beautiful, out of sheer rightness, but now the tilt of the steeple above the paintless, weather-plated façade made all the lines seem to have been wrenched out of their former rectitude; they seemed out of plumb and plane in their various turns; the impression was of a great stagger.

"All the clapboards and all the twenty thousand roof shingles for the place came out of one pine tree that stood just about where we stand now," the Selectman said. "Imagine a tree like that! It must've been three or four hundred years old. They don't grow them that old now."

Hester listened with but half an ear to the substance of what the Selectman said; she listened, with the rest, to his tone, hoping she might hear, and even persuading herself that she did remotely hear, the sympathy and warmth of old-fashioned dishonorable intention. She pinned her hopes on the "soft heart" Aunty Dorcas had casually ascribed to him. She felt ineffably sorry for the man, and did not know why; she wanted to be comforted by him, and did not know why. Trying in the outrageous humid morning to imagine, as he commanded, a tree that had unfolded and clothed a mansion, she could only imagine how cool and grand it would have been to stand under the living tree with this daydream-ridden man on its soft bed of fragrant spills in deep, deep shade. "Do you suppose it's cool inside?" she asked, a vague design forming in her mind.

"Let's go in and see," he said.

"I'd like to see the inside," Hester said, masking with casualness the excitement behind her feigned curiosity.

On the front steps and on the low porch before the now doorless entrance, the Selectman took Hester's hand in precaution, for the beams beneath were obviously infirm; the porch danced under them in a dangerously cheerful way. Hester was willing to consider the Selectman's grip significant, something more on his part than an instinct for insurance against liability, and she pressed his fingers meaningfully in return, but he said in a flat, nasal, indifferent way:

"Last summer I came in here one time and there was a chuckie going up the center aisle. He wasn't singing hymns, understand, just nosing around, yet I tell you it was spooky; I wasn't born in the woods to be scared by a groundhog, but that gave me a nasty turn—it was one of the things that made me want to go ahead with this drive as soon as folks would cooperate. Church is no place for a woodchuck. I could just picture one of them up in the old tub of a pulpit giving forth on morality and damnation. Whoof!"

Still holding hands, the Selectman and Hester stepped through the doorway. Hester drew in her breath, for she had never seen such a harsh, austere place of worship. The room was surprisingly small. Four high, rectangular, paneless windows gaped in each side wall. The pews were not long benches but square boxes with little gates, each enclosure having room for about eight people; some worshippers must have sat with their backs to the preacher. The pulpit, dominating the congregation, was, indeed, a kind of iron-banded tub, chest high, perhaps six feet in diameter, set upon a single pillar with heavy spiral handhacked fluting on it; the whole structure, like a grotesque goblet, stood nearly twice as tall as Hester. Narrow stairs with carved railings rose from each end of the altar to landings level with the tops of the pews, then turned toward each other and met up behind the tub. Several feet above the pulpit a large square wooden slab, the size of half a door, hung on a lean-to slant from a slender iron rod that ran all the way up to a roof beam. A narrow, precarious-looking gallery, evidently with room for only one bench on it, clung to three walls above the window holes and was reached by a straight stair near where Hester stood against the Selectman. The interior had apparently never been painted, except for the pulpit, the face of the gallery, and the rails at the tops of the walls of the pews, all of which were a drab, grayish blue.

Outside, not far away, the sounds of the line starting up again could be heard, strange human shrills and bayings. Indoors, the floor creaked underfoot.

"It is cool in here," Hester said. "It couldn't have been any cooler under the big pine tree they made it of." He'll never give an inch to that sort of thing, Hester said to herself; I must be cool.

"Well, there're no panes in the windows," the Selectman said. "It used to be hot enough in here, there used to be twenty-four squares of glass in each one of those windows. Oh, it could suffocate a Hottentot in here. . . . The drive has started up again. Hear 'em?"

"Look at all the birds' nests on the rafter," Hester exclaimed, face upturned, with a put-on pleasure that would show herself to the Selectman as observant, simple, impressionable, a lover of natural things. Would he give an inch to that?

" 'Yea, the sparrow hath found an house,' " the Selectman said, withdrawing his hand purposefully from Hester's tender grasp, " 'and the swallow a nest for herself, where she may lay her young, even thine altars, O Lord of Hosts.' "

"You're a curious man," Hester said, ever so slightly angry.

"His mother and I never gave Eben much religious training," the Selectman said gravely to Hester. "We used to send him to Sunday school some, because everybody did it, but the pageants they gave at Christmas and Easter, with poems written by Sue Pitkin— she's a desperate old maid, cousin of Judge Pitkin's, that lives over on the knee of Beggar's Mountain— her poems put me off the thing, they were Satan's work, those poems, they'd turn the stomach of a billy-goat, so we stopped making Eben go, he hated it anyway." The Selectman paused. "I don't know," he finally said, "there's been a failure somewhere."

Hester, who was feeling wanton in the hot morning-tide and did not relish being moralized at, thought how different things would be with Coit as her present guide; but, being a resourceful girl, and generally unhurried, she decided to accept things as they were for the moment. "I've never seen square pews like these before," she observed with a charming enthusiasm.

"They had a committee to assign them," the Selectman said. "I remember when I was a boy, the first idea I ever had of the vicious way people insist on lining themselves up in ranks—So-and-so's better than Such-and-such, and Such-and-such is better than Whatshername—was one time when the pew seatings for the next year were announced; you see, the seatings were by wealth and social position because the Society kept up the building by a tax on the pews.

They had this committee that assigned the pews—
they called it 'dignifying the pews,' though it was the
most undignified, heathen rite you ever saw, well, it
was about as humane as child labor—and old Ira
Leaming was the head of it and he hated Father, so
the Avered family was demoted, we were put below
the Cherevoys that Mother considered just a lot of
savages, though they'd been rising socially as fast as
bread-emptyings ever since they'd taken over a spoke
works we used to have here in Tunxis. Mother kept
on going to church all the same, but you'd've thought
she was a-mourning. Us kids, we called these square
pews sheep pens, and that's what they were!"

"People up here are so hard on each other," Hester
said with a little feminine pout at which the Selectman failed to look.

"They are, they are. I remember one time hearing
how Parson Churnstick, not long after he accepted
our call, visited to preach over in Treehampstead and
he gave them one of his poignant goose-pimple talks,
and after the service one of the deacons over there
went up to the parson and asked him if he dared
preach like that at home. 'Yes, sir,' the Parson said.
'Why,' he said, 'this sermon you just heard was nothing but a hazel switch; when I'm home I use a sled-
stake on 'em.' "

"Mother used to say, 'God is love,' " Hester said,
her arm rubbing as if accidentally against the Selectman's.

"Old Churnstick's God was anger. Anger gradually
ate him up. The first sign he was going in the head
was a trap door he cut in the floor outside his bed-
room for nighttimes, so any intruder would drop into
the cellar, and the way we found out about it was one
morning when Mrs. Churnstick forgot and dropped
into the cellar and earned a game hip out of it. Fi-

nally Anak Welch—Anak lived next door—built him a big wooden pen off his parlor, and when the Parson felt some craziness coming he used to go voluntarily into the cage and be locked in. Anak and the Parson's wife used to read him his own sermons and talk to him about how much his mother'd loved him, and that usually calmed him. Sometimes Anak had to wrestle him to put him away, and they say during those wrestling matches old Churnstick used to think he was Jacob at Penuel, only there was a slight difference, being that this angel—Anak, in other words—had no trouble pinning and trussing this particular Jacob in short order, and the only blessings Anak gave him were Scotch blessings."

"Truly," Hester said, in earnest and out in the open, "when I told you that Mother used to say, 'God is love,' I meant to say that I hardly know where to turn. I guess I'm too young to understand what love really is, but I guess I'm learning; I've had a feeling lately that all the ideas I used to have about love weren't worth anything, weren't nearly big enough, and that's given me a feeling that the whole thing with Eben was falling apart—though maybe it's just really beginning. I don't know, I'm mixed up, right now I feel as if you mean more to me than Eben. What can I believe? I want to know what love is, I have an appetite for it, sometimes I have hopes that Eben does, too, if we could just understand more about it, but it's so hard these days. . . ."

"Dear girl," the Selectman said with what seemed to Hester an acute and painful tenderness, "I wish I could help you, but I'm no particular authority on the subject. What happened to Parson Churnstick and to this building—they bother me all the time, because I think they're a part of the breakdown of ordinary, everyday love that we see all around us. This church—

this House of Love—is simply abandoned. I couldn't teach Eben *this*. I guess you and Eben'll just have to struggle along on whatever leftover ethics you can scrape up for a while till you figure things out for yourselves. Lately I've been thinking quite a bit about—about love, I guess, in Nature and in people. You remember yesterday I was telling about the mother woodchuck that shoved her babies out of her burrow that day to protect herself—that was horrible! Yet on the other hand the woodchucks are apparently very strict and moral when it comes to 'being in love'; they're rigidly faithful, you won't find ary philanderer among 'em, at least that's what Pliny Forward tells us—you remember he was rubbing it in with Eben yesterday to tease him. I can't believe, though, that love is just what's convenient for survival; it's got to be something to live for, because we don't live very long, do we, Hester? I just haven't exactly found it in my born days—love, that is; oh, I've been 'in love,' but I mean the bigger thing you mentioned; otherwise, dear girl, I'd be glad to try to advise you."

He was smiling down at her with a sensitive, tortured expression, and Hester was just about to give in to an unruly impulse, when he said, "We'd better get out there and catch up to the line."

"I guess we'd better," Hester said, turning quickly toward the door.

Outside, as they hurried forward, the Selectman casually said, "A person could say that I'd had a narrow escape."

"What do you mean?"

"You don't have to be told what I mean. You know as well as the next one."

Hester laughed in a shamefaced way.

■

THE HEAT became appalling. As she climbed the uphill terrain, Hester felt herself become sticky and irritable. Then, in an unexpected moment of compassion, she felt suddenly terribly sorry for the woodchucks scampering ahead—all dressed in fur, they were, in this cooking temperature, and in nearly black fur, at that, which under the down-pressing sunlight must absorb a frightful temperature. Hester imagined herself in a fur coat—didn't they sell something called "sheared marmot" in the stores?—and the very thought made her feel faint. Why didn't the woodchucks die or go mad in their senseless, sun-struck flight? Hester paused in shade wherever she could. The hot, humid air was hard to breathe; it was oxygenated soup.

Three woodchucks were seen breaking through the line below Anak Welch, and for a few minutes, fearful always of encountering one, Hester was called upon to run here and there in a vain effort to recapture them, and afterwards sweat poured off her face and her shirt adhered to her back.

At last, in a suffocating glade, the branches of whose trees seemed to hold the noon air in a kind of death grip, the drivers of Division Four paused for lunch. Tempers crackled. Mumbling their sandwiches the leaders of the division exchanged recriminations over the three animals that had got away, and volunteers blamed the higher-ups. Hester saw the Selectman visit part of the argument; he left soon looking gray and offended.

Reluctantly the drivers began to go forward again.

At this end of the hollow, the mounded, rock-ridged land was largely wooded in descendant stands of the original native forest—feathery hemlocks, for the most part, and under them masses of wild mountain laurel clutching on branch ends dried relics of what must have been, a few weeks before, a glorious pink and white salute to the solstice. The generations of hemlock were all crowded together there: half-fallen giants still partly rooted and sustaining bedraggled crowns, heroic adults with straight trunks two feet thick, young leggy trees jostling each other and reaching for sky and for life, and delicate fans of seedlings outspread uncared-for underfoot—a fecund, optimistic society. The glossy leaves of laurel nodded limply in the heat. This was the finest part of Thighbone Hollow—everyone had said that at lunch; but it was not cool at all.

By slow stages the line reached the approaches to the funnel at the Lantern Flue.

During a halt Coit came down to Hester. "Seems like it's hermin' up for a storm," he said. "Did you hear that rumble yonder?"

"I did, I thought I heard thunder," Hester said.

"Look at the devil's darnin' needles!" Coit said, pointing at two flirting dragonflies. "When those things behave that way, you can be sure there's thunder comin'. It seems to tickle their diddlybumps."

"What'll we do if there's a downpour?"

"Get wet, I calculate," Coit said callously, and callously he added, "I imagine the groundhogs'll be nervy and kind of undone, 'cause they can usually go to ground when the cracklin' and boomin' begins, but this time, with no hidin' place at all, I imagine they'll twit and fling and kick and stram and carry on like glory-be. 'Oh, there'll be dancin' in the dingle, Suzy-pie!' "

"I don't like it," Hester said. "I hate thunder."

"Now that's just like a woman," Coit said. "Hates thunder when lightnin's the only thing to be scar't of.

Lightnin's very partial to hemlock trees, I've heard that many's a time."

"You're a nasty person," Hester said with a heat matching the day's.

Already to the west, up beyond the lace of the evergreens, could be seen awesome ranges of glory-capped cumulus. A gusty wind had sprung up, and the fragrant hemlocks gossiped.

"That's the funny wind," Coit said, "the wind before a storm. See how it's blowin' toward the thunderheads. Twenty minutes from now it'll be squallin' the other way. Just like a woman," he added with a smirk.

Still wearing a twisted faint smile, Coit stepped to Hester and without apology put his arms around her and confidently laid his cheek against hers. Hester, swiftly overcome by a silly, agonizing desire somehow to punish the Selectman for his resistance to her, and relying on the impression that she and this man who had the fragrance of leather were chambered by close-grown trees, slid her hands up Coit's shirt-back. Coit promptly kissed her; she closed her eyes and floated on her sensations in a void, where for some time she experienced this and that and the other thing, until at last she was convinced that a man's palm was on her skin between her shoulder blades, that her shirt was unbuttoned from collar to apron, and that steady fingers, which had found and had tobogganed down the zipper at the right side of the waist of her slacks, were now bargaining with the button of the waistband; and she decided she had chastised the Selectman more than enough and it was high time to open her eyes, and she did. A puff of the contra-wind just then lifted a whirl of humus dust off the forest floor and, with a whisk and a lift, threw a speck of it into one of Hester's newly unveiled eyes. The particle smarted sharply there.

As if struck by the heel of a hand, Hester's head flew back. She got her fists onto Coit's chest and began to push and rap. "Stop it!" she said in fierce undertones. "What're you thinking of, anyway?"

"Same thing you've been," Coit thickly said, releasing her, though not without having held her long and close enough to have made her realize he had sufficient strength to do anything he wanted.

Both Hester's eyes had turned on their faucets to flush out the hurt from one; she could feel the courses on her cheeks.

"Cry-baby!" Coit said.

"I have something in my eye," Hester said, "if you want to know."

"Oh, so that's why you wanted to stop," Coit said triumphantly.

"You ought to have your face slapped," Hester said, winking and fluttering her eyelids. "Ow, ow, ow," she said in pain and shame.

"Grab aholt of the lid and pull it down and count to fifty," Coit said.

A distant thunderbolt rolled down the rough alley of the western sky.

"Boi-oi-oi-oi-oing. Sounds like we're goin' to have a socdolager of a shower before we know it," Coit said happily while Hester tugged at her eyelid and wept.

Without having succeeded in clearing her eye, she buttoned up and tucked herself away. "You're a mean, nasty person," she said blinking as he stood watching with a grin on his face.

"No, not me. You've got the wrong pig by the tail. ... Did you get the grit out of your eye?" he asked with exaggerated gentleness, as if to dispose of her unsavory charge.

Even as he was asking the question, a man's voice began calling Coit's name from up the line. Both he and Hester then heard the shouts, and he turned and ran.

Hester found in a few moments that by looking sidewise, with her pupils rolled to the right, she could keep her eye from hurting, except when she blinked. While she stood tensely glaring in this sidelong way, Coit came back into her glen, and swiveling her oblique stare toward him she groaned, "Oh, God, here he comes again."

"They say to stay right here till the storm passes," Coit said, wholly impersonal now, bossy and pragmatical. "The main thing is not to let the woodchucks panic back through us. If you see a single one of 'em, holler out, 'Groundhog! Groundhog!', so the people on either side of you can close in and help hold the line, and if you hear your neighbor shout, move over toward him and begin to make a racket. Get the picture?"

"I get it, sugarlump," Hester said in what she hoped was a scornful tone, looking at Coit queerly out of the corners of her eyes.

Coit turned his face then and reciprocated clownishly with a stare that was just as twisted as hers. "I've got to go tell the others," he said, and slowly closed one of his eyelids over half his cater-cornered look; then he left her.

■

Something like a terrible weariness settled over the hemlock woods. The air had gone lax, and every needle on every branch was poised, hushed, drowsy as it were. Hester sat down on the ground, stirred and shifted until she had found a nest of needles that was clear of upjutting kneelets of roots and of prickly, crackling, fallen twigs, and then, like all life nearby her, reposed limp in the heavy, waiting, resinate air. Sitting that way, she could see under the branches of the nearest trees quite far forward into the woodchuck realm. Nothing moved save the great sound in the distance.

She wept slightly still at the irritation in her eye, and still looked askance at the slumberous world and tried to keep from blinking.

Coit went back up the line and passing, declaimed,

> "Molly had a walleye
> Saw things on a slant.
> She sighed fur Seth, and golly,
> You sure could hear her pant!"

Hester felt too sorry for herself even to try an answer.

Once in the city, Hester for some reason remembered in a moment (was it anger—fury—that she was inwardly turning over?), Eben had told her that he had never, not once, heard his father argue with his mother. "Aside from her, he's got a temper," Eben had said. "Oh, he can slam on the brakes and holler at the customers like an Irish bus driver, but I don't know, it seems that inside he's a peacemaker. People who're fighting send for him from considerable distances to settle their disputes," Eben had said; "and he manages it, too, I don't know how. The lawyers up home hate him, the way he does them out of the lucre of gain, why, he diminishes their business something awful. I remember one time Eli Pinney had an awful set-to with his wife, they were on the point of splitting up and getting a bill, and they decided to have Father in—this was long before he was Selectman—and I remember, I was home when Father came back from their house, and Mother asked him, 'Did you set things to rights, Matthew?', and he sat down to supper and took a mammoth helping of yellow squash that I can still see and smell to this day—sweet stuff! Lord how I love it!—and I distinctly remember he said, I was too young to understand what he meant, but anyway he said to her, 'Nothing wrong there, dear, that can't be fixed by Mr. Pinney giving his helpmeet a cordial servicing once a week or so. He agreed to try. They're quieted down for the time being. This is a fine Hubbard squash, my dear.' Mother said in that terrible calm way of hers, 'Charity begins at home, Matthew dear.' I sure puzzled over what they meant." Eben had studiously mimicked his parents, without satire.

Hester remembered how the Selectman had told her the day before that he and Mrs. Avered could no longer be called friends, and she wondered bleakly how much of real life Eben clearly perceived.

Then she thought she had one clue to the resentment the townspeople felt, even his close friends seemed to feel, toward the Selectman. Perhaps, through sympathy, he had come to know too much about them.

There was thunder again, louder but still deep and blunt, muffled, it seemed, by the yellowy, unbleached heaps of cloud that were fast drifting closer. Hester scanned the oncoming line of the storm with her sidelong vision, and began to be afraid.

At the edge of her small clearing, the skirts of laurel started to dance, though as yet Hester could not really feel the new breeze. Then she did receive a puff of it on her damp skin—a cooler air, and hasty. All at once into a gap in the green to the westward rolled the blackish lower edge of the cold front, with horrible rounded swift-whirling sarcomatous growths pushing down from its underside. One moment the hot sunlight slanted through the hemlocks, the next, was gone; riding the shade came a sharp little wind, under the force of which whole branches bent, and behind this cool puff followed sluggish whirlpools and eddies of the day's hot, stale atmosphere. Now there was an almost constant rumble from the pile of clouds.

Hester got up on her knees, as if that would make her more ready for danger, and she crouched, looking at everything, as Coit's walleyed Molly did, on a slant. She wished for Coit, for the Selectman, energetically for Eben; she wanted any company she could get.

A new hard flaw of wind hit the hemlock tops, making such a rough sound that for a few moments Hester could hear no thunder. Now she saw with what dreadful speed the squall line was coming on. She thought of the huge mosques of cloud, miles high, that she had seen from a distance, which were founded on nothing but this roiled, skidding base, and she trembled to think of those edifices crashing down on her and on these fragile woods, as they must.

The wind died for a moment. Suddenly Hester, as if taking a hard blow on the head, subjectively suffered a huge external flash and crack—the annunciatory bolt of the storm's arrival. At once the full force of a new wind squall pounced on the hemlocks. Hester put her hands over her face, then, hearing a new awfulness, she took them away again to watch warily and crookedly: Down through the woods from Thighbone Ledge walked the rain. It came as a solid advancing heavy hushing sound, a horrible moving wall of wetness.

The wind went from harsh to brutal, and the hemlocks moaned. Then rain fell. The drops seemed as big as jellyfish. In an instant Hester was soaked.

There came a series of blinding licks of lightning and flat quick cracks of thunder, and the gale and cloudburst increased, and Hester looking from side to side wanted to run away—but to what refuge? She stayed rooted, swaying like one of the trees nearby, and gasped for breath as the cold white rain hit her.

Close the windows! Close the windows! Hester thought of her mother rushing from room to room with a panic-twisted face, crying that thunderbolts travel on drafts; and Hester hugged herself in terror in this gale in the woods. The frightful flashes and claps were so near! Hester felt as if the terrible eye of the storm was looking for her, for her alone; then for a tiny moment she had a weird sensation of crouching beside her sopping self and laughing at herself; even if she lived and was not reduced to a charred basket of ribs and odds and ends by one of the tongues of flame, she was shortening her life to nearly nothing by being so afraid of dying—Dorcas Thrall had given the warning the night before. The terror almost made her laugh at herself, beside herself.

In the midst of all this, she could feel the whole time the tiny prick of foreign matter on her eyeball.

Suddenly, in a pause between bolts, she heard a chorus of excited whistling, penetrating the plash of the rain; thunder shut it out; she heard it again.

She was astounded. Was the line starting up at the very climax of the storm?

Then Hester realized that what she heard was straight ahead—the terrified shrieking of woodchucks in the lightning, thunder, and rain. It was worse for them than for her! On her hands and knees she became dutiful and vigilant. Her fear for herself diminished, and she became instead afraid for the Selectman; this new fright was not unpleasant. She watched for runaway groundhogs. For the Selectman's sake, they must not be allowed to escape in their frenzy. As the storm's noisy procession moved on, none of the screaming animals showed themselves. Gradually their crying died down. So violence was slowly drained out of the sky, and horror out of Hester.

■

THE spent clouds were fleeing to the east. Up from the floor of the forest came a pungent smell of newness, of washed earth and fresh life. Hester was amazed to see with her biased eyes that after all the murderous impact of the storm the frail new needles of hemlock still lay in order on the leaders and seedlings, as if freshly combed, and the leaves of laurel were unruffled.

All would have been summer peace, except that down to the right Hester could hear a confusion, an urgency of shouting that made her, at last, rise up alert from her kneeling position. She stood, dripped, and listened. People were running about down there and calling to each other and to the animals. Then she heard someone oncoming with clumsy haste, and George Challenge burst with rolling eyes into her little opening in the thicket. "We need help!" he forced out panting. And the drenched politician blurted out a report that some of the groundhogs had "gone plumb crazy"; four of them had attacked drivers down the line; one of them had bit young Ira Pinney, giving him "a nasty dig acrosst the shinbone"; and then the possessed animals had escaped, but might be caught again. Challenge's wild eyes, appreciatively excursive for a moment, took in Hester's shirt clinging wet to her flesh. "We need men to help us," he then gasped, resuming his excitement. "You stay right here where you are and don't let any of the boogers get back through here." And the short-legged puffing man crashed out of the hemlock circlet and struggled up the line.

Not long afterwards Hester saw a handful of men run crackling down through the woods with desperately earnest faces; she imagined that untried soldiers going into battle to be blooded wore expressions like those, and she thought that for people who had not wanted to come on this second day's drive at all, these runners were much interested in it—grimmer about it, indeed, than the Selectman himself. The shouting continued. Hester crouched again in order to be able to look forward under the boughs of the surrounding trees.

Across her line of still hurtful, still sidelong vision, some distance from her post, Hester presently saw the Selectman walking without haste down toward the trouble. "Hi!" she called out. "What's happening?"

The Selectman turned and peered into Hester's bosk. "That you, Miss Hester? Where're you hiding?"

"I'm back here," Hester said. "Is there anything I can do?"

"Much ado about four groundhogs," the Selectman said calmly, walking toward the enclosure. Hester hastily pushed her seaweed-hair back along the crown of her head, and stood up and waited. "It's not the end of the world, don't jump out of your skin, just four groundhogs got loose," the Selectman approaching said. "Did you get all wet and sozzled?" he asked, still hidden from her.

"I'm sopping, I'm a mess," Hester protestingly said.

The Selectman came through dripping branches into the opening and stood before Hester with glistening eyelashes and a drop of water on the end of his nose. "You're too young to have read the novels of Rafael Sabatini," he said. "I used to read 'em, when I had more time for reading, and my goodness, you could count on that same thrilling style in book after book. People have a way of getting over-excited in those books—and my neighbors here in Tunxis are the same way."

What a queerly various man, Hester thought—Sabatini and Patmore and the Holy Writ and FitzGerald of the Moving Finger! Then suddenly she became concerned over the contrast between the Selectman's calmness and the strange fanatical look on the faces of the hurrying drivers she had just seen.

"But I thought every single woodchuck was life and death to you," she said, hoping to rouse him somewhat. "At least I should think it would be, at this point."

"You look like a mermaid," he said, ignoring her thrust in a way that could not but give her pleasure; "but why do you glare at me that way?"

"I got some dust in my eye just before the storm. That was the worst storm I've ever been in. I thought I was going to be dead and buried any minute."

"We could've buried you in our family plot in the hollow."

"It's no joke," Hester said.

"I meant to show you the graveyard when we stopped at the church," the Selectman said, as if he had time of day to burn. "That's where you can see the real Tunxis. You know, in the old days up here, all the women were dead before their fortieth year—you'd've been a middle-aged woman right now, one foot in the grave with creeping age even if you hadn't perished in an electric storm."

"I am middle-aged. After that storm, I am."

"That was just a quiet little everyday thunderation. You must have too much shelter in the city."

"I wanted to see your father's grave," Hester said. "Aunty Dorcas told me he carved his own headstone."

"And footstone. He said his feet hurt in bed if he didn't have a footboard."

"What did he write on the stones? Aunty Dorcas couldn't recall."

"He put his name on both stones, and then he cut on one, 'His head was in the clouds,' and on the other, 'His feet were on the ground.'"

"Aunty Dorcas said he was a tiny man—it was nice he could make himself so tall in the end."

"I think you're fond of us Avereds," the Selectman baldly said.

"It's just like you to say that, instead of starting out by saying you Avereds like me."

"I try to be honest. A lot of folks say, 'I'm fond of you,' so's to hear what the retort'll be; the way most people write letters so's not to have empty mailboxes."

"Do you think people are selfish?" Hester asked.

"Not selfish, just anxious. Seems to me, this is the heyday of the worry-wart. People don't have to be so nervous about everything, but they are, and I always wonder why. Once I had to fly in an airplane—when Eben was at that camp in Louisiana and they thought he had the infantile, he's probably told you about the time he was so sick. . . ."

"Yes, he's told me."

"When I was in the airport over at the capital, somebody led me up to this little gillhickie like a slot machine, you could put a quarter in and get your life insured just before you took off. My heavens, they've even got nervousness mechanized nowadays."

"Don't you ever worry?"

"All the time. Sure, I put my quarter in. . . . Whenever Eben's around me, I guess I'm supposed to worry about not amounting to anything, but as soon as he goes back to the city it seems as if there're more important things to fuss about. What's eating him? Do you know? . . ." The sounds of shouting still came up from below, and the Selectman, breaking off, turned his head toward them; then, as if those noises, at least, were not worth worrying about, he looked back at Hester. "You look miserable, squinching that way," he said.

"My eye hurts."

"Let's see if we can fix it. Let's see if we can get the thing out once and for all."

As the Selectman moved toward her, Hester felt her opportunity. The sun was out to stay; there was a holiday twinkle in the wet hemlocks all around. Hester was exuberant, and grateful for the joyous speck in her eye.

The Selectman stood close to her and said, "Now, let's see, let's see." He lowered his face toward hers, and peered intently in her eye. "My, you've got a nice eyeball," he said softly. "It's been a dog's age since I saw such a clear white eyeball. You must be at peace with your Maker, Miss Hester." Then, putting one hand on her cheek and the other on her forehead, the Selectman pulled the lids of the smarting eye apart, and he craned and searched. His hands were hard, his fingers were mailed with callus; in spite of their tender restraint, Hester realized their enormous unexpressed strength—but she also sensed in them a delicate tremor which she chose to regard as the tiny flutter of some kind of fought-against eagerness. "I'm sorry," the Selectman said, deeply and quietly, "but I can't see a doggoned thing." Hester felt somehow too weak to assure him that the mite of grit was there; really, it was there. "Maybe it's bedded in the back of the lid," he said. "Hold on just a sec." He stepped back a pace, fumbled in a pocket of his soaked trousers, pulled out a limp box of wooden matches, and took one out. "I'd hate to have my life depend on lighting a fire right now," he said. "I'll roll the lid up on this. Do you have a hanky?" Hester pulled a dripping handkerchief out of a pocket in her shirt and handed it to him. "When't comes to snotrags, d'ruther use yourn than mine—on you," he said in burlesqued Yankee twang, wringing out the delicate cloth with his stubby forefingers and thumbs. "Now!" he said, "let's have a try," and he moved to her again. This time he stood dead against her; Hester, lifting up her face to him, drew in her breath and made herself as tall as her spine would allow. With his big clumsy fingers the Selectman tried to grasp the lashes of the upper lid. "Hold still!" the Selectman smiling said. "Did you ever try to catch a moth on the wing?" Near a flame, Hester wanted to say, near a flame, but she felt too weak—and knew it would be too stupid; she tried to stop blinking. At last he caught the fugitive hairs between the thumb and forefinger of his left hand. He drew the lid down, placed the match on its lower edge, folded the lashes and a little skin back over the match, and held them tight as he began to turn the match. The lid made an inappropriate sucking sound as it was pulled away from the eyeball, and Hester emitted a tiny, protesting, winsome "Ouch!" The Selectman's face was very close to hers and as it was turned a bit to one side, his lips were opposite hers, and Hester knew that now she was trembling more than he. She insisted to herself that his compassion, felt in the paradoxical delicateness of his rough touch, leaned far toward something else, something else she scarcely dared define. She thought, jarringly, of Eben, who had the same consideration in his fingers, though they were not shelled with the thick skin of handwork; the same touch, given yet held back—unlike the unstinting, smearing paw-touch of a Coit. Hester breathed against the Selectman's breathing. "Yup," he said (with suppressed feeling, she assured herself), "there the dang little thing is. Wouldn't come out because the lid got swelled up all round it." He spoke very low; she could taste his sweet hickory-nut breath in her own slightly open mouth. "Now," he said, "you'll have to help. Take ahold of the match in your right hand and mash down on the side of the lid with your left hand so it won't slip off." For a long, long moment, his hands were against hers; then he took his away. He rolled a corner of the handkerchief and lifted it to her eye. Hester felt his left hand cupping the back of her head, and she was brimful of hope and desire. He flicked the lid with the tiny linen tongue and kept up a murmur as he worked: "Out in a jiffy . . . that's a good girl . . . hold on now . . ."

There was a sudden crackling noise in the hemlocks at the lower edge of the open place. A breath was audibly drawn into a throat. Hester's free eye saw something that looked like Mrs. Tuller's black-and-white checked skirt flash between branches, and perhaps something else, too, and then there was a hurrying off.

"We almost had a caller," Hester said. "Or maybe two."

"Hold still!" the Selectman impatiently commanded.

"Sorry," she said.

"There!" he triumphantly said, and drew back. He held up the twist of handkerchief, with a dark trifle on it, for her inspection. "There's your little friend.

Nothing but a little black atom—but I suppose it felt like Plymouth Rock in your eye there."

Hester was bleak. The intruders had spoilt things—though she could not be sure that things would have been different had there been no intrusion; perhaps that was really why she felt let down.

"Who were they?" the Selectman stiffly asked.

"I didn't see for sure," Hester said, "but I think it was Mrs. Tuller, and I don't know who else."

"That's just fine and dandy," the Selectman sarcastically said. Then he said, "I guess we didn't hear anything sooner because of the way I was gabbing along about that smidgen in your eye."

"It feels a lot better," Hester sadly said. "Thanks a million."

■

THE DRIVERS moved through the fragrant, glistening, dripping woods toward the beginning of the funnel at the Lantern Flue. The woods, sloping rather steeply from an outcropping of Thighbone Ledge down to the canal, were light and open here, for the land had been cultivated in recent years; a sparse growth of sapling locusts and wild cherries, with a few older cedars, partly shaded the ground, which was bedded with water-bright grass and low thickets of sparkling milkweed. Compressed, as it moved, by the narrowing of the hollow, the line was gradually shortened so that, at last, the drivers were but twenty feet or so apart. A few woodchucks were sighted moving into the mouth of the funnel. A halt was called.

Hester stood dissecting a still-green milkweed pod with her fingernails, and was quite empty of thought, when a delegation came to wait on her: Mrs. Tuller, Anak Welch, George Challenge, Friedrich Tuller, and a woman and a man whom Hester did not know. Mrs. Tuller, whose face was sullen, peremptorily called Roswell Coit from his nearby post. All dripping, mussed, and beslimed from the rain, these hot-eyed Tunxis people looked to Hester as if they had just crawled up out of some primordial ooze; she didn't like their looks.

"Now," the schoolteacher commanded Hester, when Coit had arrived, "tell us exactly what he tried to do to you."

Hester looked at Coit, whom she supposed to be her fellow-accused, and she blushed, remembering how unbuttoned, how inwardly undone she had let herself become with him, and fleetingly she wondered what prurient, sneaky voyeur had been watching their embrace in the little clearing. She saw Coit grinning at her with his customary swaggerer's face; apparently, she thought, he expects me to brazen it out. Her eyes traversed the other faces in the circle; they seemed suddenly like so many boulders in an old New England stone wall. She thought of the row of faces on the stage at the caucus two nights before—hard yet yearning. For what did these hard faces yearn? For what? What were they so intent upon now? Why were they so exercised?

"Oh," she said offhandedly, her eyes turned away from Coit's, "I guess he was just trying to prove he's a man."

"There!" Mrs. Tuller exploded to the others. "Is that enough for you?"

The great Anak shook his head. "I can't understand it," he said.

"We saw them plain as day—they thought they were tucked away in the hemlocks!—didn't we see them plain as day, Roswell?" Mrs. Tuller said.

Half way between realization and incredulity, Hester looked quickly again at Roswell Coit's face; the complacent grin still resided there—had, if it had changed at all, nourished itself on the recent speeches and grown some.

"What galls me," George Challenge said in his pleading whine, "is the way he ordered us to round up those four creatures that had got away—I was the one who ran up there to him and you'd've thought he was talkin' to a common garbage collector the way he sent me down—and what did he do while we were breakin' our legs tryin' to catch 'em? That's what galls me!"

But—out of disbelief Hester still kept silent—the Selectman hadn't done anything; that had been precisely her disappointment.

"It's really too much," Mrs. Tuller said with a kind of conclusiveness that sent a chill to Hester's bowels. "We might've re-caught those animals if he could've been bothered to come down and help us. Law! With his own son's girl! . . ." Mrs. Tuller broke off and stared contemptuously at Hester.

Other drivers, evidently having seen the knot of people, and complacent about the woodchucks in this constricted place, had begun to drift up or down to the circle; Eben was among them, Hester saw. Hester blushed with rage and frustration and bafflement, all of which expelled from her, at last, a violent, stammering utterance. "Wait a minute!" she burst out. "Do you mean—do you mean the Selectman—and me?"

"Too late for innocence," the schoolteacher said in a kind of jeer. "You've already confessed."

"Confessed to what? I haven't confessed a thing!"

"What's this all about?" asked Manly Sessions, the captain of Division Three, who had lately sauntered down.

Mrs. Tuller's face seemed to turn a deeper shade of mad purple as she said, "We caught the Selectman tryin' to rape this girl."

"Oh-oh," Manly Sessions said. "Not him again."

"What?" Hester shouted, straining to control her tongue. She was afraid she would burst into tears. For a moment she saw Eben's face, pale as the flesh of an apple; drained of blood but full of belief. "What? What do you mean, rape?"

"Well," Mrs. Tuller said, as if yielding a mile of hard-won ground, "I guess it ain't accurate to speak of rape when both parties are willin'."

"You people are crazy," Hester said with conviction and vehemence—though the number of stones now in the wall roundabout made her heart sink. "He was trying to get something out of my eye."

The stones all split open and laughter came out; the circle laughed loud.

"Back this mornin'," Coit now offered, "they ducked into the old church. I guess they were in there half an hour, seemed like that much."

"That's true," Anak Welch said, "the Selectman even told me he was goin' to show the girl the church, asked me to cover her section of the line for her till they caught up again."

"He did?" the strange woman who had come up with the original posse broke out. She had heavy bangs that, hanging like a valance across her forehead, made her eyes seem tiny, inadequate windows. "Why, we could've lost some more of the woodchucks right then and there, thinnin' out the line that way."

"Guess he was tryin' her then," Coit said with that smirk of his.

Hester turned slowly to Coit. "You know I had something in my eye."

"How would I know that? Now just how would I know that?" The smirk held firm.

Hester had begun to tremble, because she did not know how to deal with the situation in which she found herself. Something seemed to have been wrenched loose in her world. She was used to living in a quiet world in which truth was abused slightly now and again for the sake of tact and social ease; this was all on too grand a scale. "Do you like blackberries?" she asked Coit.

"Not too much," Coit said. "They're liable to turn sour."

"Wait a minute," Anak Welch slowly said. "What tune are we playin' now?"

Coit shrugged. "She asked me did I like blackberries," he said.

"That's right!" Hester said, stepping over to Anak Welch and grasping the sleeve of his shirt. "Ask him what that's about till you get an answer."

"Well, what is it about?" the huge man gently asked.

He was looking down at Hester; he was asking her. She thought suddenly of what she had wished on the bezoar; she thought of her acquiescence to Coit; she thought of Eben; she realized that it was not her fault that this crazy allegation was not a fact. "Ask him," she feebly said, knowing that this little hope of hers was spent.

Mrs. Tuller, impatient with all these speeches that she evidently considered irrevelant, broke in, demanding, "Well, what're we goin' to do about this?"

"The whole town knows about it now," George Challenge said with less whine than usual, and he surveyed all the faces in the circle with evident satisfaction.

"I think people should know about it," Mrs. Tuller, who was obviously one to make such a thing possible, declared. "I think it's time to make a public example ..."

"Holy catfish!" Roswell Coit suddenly shouted, pointing off into the underbrush. "Look down there!"

■

DOWN THERE a whole crescent of woodchuck scouts was, for the moment, erect, a-begging, and all seemed to be staring toward the cluster of Tunxis people, with a comical pious look, as if appealing to them in a dignified way for tax-deductible gifts. Then the animals serially ducked down and could not be seen in the tall grass and undergrowth, but what could be realized and what could be seen were these: that the curve of upright scouts had been oriented toward a gap in the drivers' line which stretched from the clump of people to a point more than a hundred feet down toward the canal, and that, behind the scouts' screen, there was a widespread progressive disturbance in the grass tops, quickly moving toward the gap.

The circle around Hester became at once a cavorting, many-throated body, desperate for want of discipline. Everyone started running somewhere and crying something. Many people appointed themselves commanders, and called out orders at cross-purposes—this one, to cut the creatures off; that one, not to rush them; another, to shout but not chase; another, to skirt but be silent—so that all did various errands and were angry and practically useless.

The woodchucks meanwhile were of one mind. They moved in full rout toward the opening.

Hester and two or three others followed the instinctive Coit, who had darted off in the one direction that seemed to make sense—directly back along the hollow; for evidently he thought a wide loop could be thrown around the animal band, which was, one could see, certain to break through the old line. Much as he would shout for other followers, though, his leadership was spurned by drivers with notions of their own. It was for Mrs. Tuller to pursue circumstances from bad to worse and finally make them a splendidly worst. In an unthinking fury, as if releasing a pent-up anger at generations of irrepressibly contrary schoolchildren, she rushed, uttering warbling screams, right at the core of the woodchuck pack, and this hysterical headlong charge of hers had the effect, at first, of making the whole herd swerve toward the canal and away from the main concentration of drivers who might have encircled the animals; and then, despite moaning cries of warning from Anak Welch, she bore on with a hurtling, unstoppable rage and soon was right in the midst of the rippling island of fur. That was the disaster. The manageable pack disintegrated. Individual woodchucks ran off in all directions save toward the funnel.

Now the hunted and the hunters were pitted, as it were, one for one. There was no more herd. There was also no more line. Single persons ran looping and winding awhile after single animals, then switched to other individual quarries, for the creatures outnumbered their pursuers. Breathless, Hester ran heavily here and there to no purpose at all. The woodchucks slipped away as easily as sand through twitching fingers; their escape was a perfect demonstration of the occasional value to a group of disunity.

Very soon the creatures were all gone, and the uselessness of an un-co-ordinated chase was clear to every driver.

Gradually the still-wet villagers came together in the young dripping woods; their frustrated anger was immeasurable, and it was directed, with a sweet unanimity such as Tunxis had obviously seldom enjoyed in all its history, at the species *Arctomys monax*. These people were one in hating woodchucks. Their cheeks were red, their eyes like the ends of sharp sticks just withdrawn from fire. "Bastards! Bastards! Bastards!" cried Coit, and even Mrs. Tuller nodded slightly at the sound of his cursing.

Then Hester, who in this feeling was truly conjoined to Tunxis for the first time, saw and heard a strange thing happen, which all too soon separated her again from Tunxis. The wrath of the drivers turned away from the animals, which were now, as receptacles of temper, far out of range, toward the Selectman, who was more available.

Hester heard George Challenge utter the first suggestion of the switch. "This whole thing's as rotten as a dozy post," he said. "Just a lot of damned boondogglin' nonsense."

"It's that God-damned greenhorn lecherous Avered," Coit said. "What the hell, anybody knows you have to *shoot* woodchucks."

"If you'd ask me," Mrs. Tuller said, her eyes extruded, as if there were not room even in her capacious head for so much anger and eyeballs too, "if you'd ask me, an old-fashioned whippin'd be too good for Matthew Avered."

The faces in the circle turned with slow speculative interest toward Mrs. Tuller's scowling countenance, and Hester saw an awful concord flowing into almost all of them. The silence was prolonged; this seemed to be an idea with a slow grip, and even when it had taken hold, there was something about it that needed prolonged ventilation.

"A light public whippin'," George Challenge finally said in an apologetic whine, on a note almost of charity, "would seem to me to be a very practical solution."

"I agree a hundred per cent," Roswell Coit said with ill-hidden jubilance.

"Isn't this a kind of disgusting kangaroo court?" Friedrich Tuller objected in a high, strained voice. "What right do you people have to pass judgement?"

"I don't think newcomers and foreigners ought to meddle in Tunxis affairs," the woman with the bangs said.

"I came here sixteen years ago looking for freedom," Herr Tuller said. "How long is a newcomer new?"

"Let's not get shunted onto a siding," said Mrs. Tuller, who had had ample experience in committee work and knew how to keep things moving.

"We mustn't be carried away with haste," Anak Welch said with a fairness that seemed to give him physical pain. "Let's put on our thinkin' caps and try and do the right thing. I have to say that I lean toward the opinion that a public example would be good for all of us. I'd suffer for our Selectman if we did this thing that's been suggested, and I think that sufferin' would probably be good for me. It'd probably be good for all of us. But we oughtn't to be hasty."

"Whippin'd be too good for Matthew Avered," Mrs. Tuller repeated, quite satisfied with having invented this sentence.

"It's not as if this wasn't a sound traditional practice hereabouts, Anak—in the old days anyway," pronounced Judge Pitkin, the Town Counsel, the Selectman's close friend.

"Oh, it's an institution with a great deal of heft behind it," Anak Welch said in a troubled way. "I'll grant you that. A very respectable institution. Long honored here in Tunxis—though not anytime lately, that's the part I'd want to analyze. I just have a feelin' we ought to think this through pretty careful."

"Too much thinkin' gives folks the rheumatism," the woman with the bangs said. "You'd better make up your mind afore you get a crick in your neck, Mr. Welch."

The Selectman himself came running now from up above. "How many got away?" he asked with an uninformed coolness that seemed grotesque to Hester.

Hester was surprised, and then afraid, when she heard the slow, sober, cautious, kindly giant, Anak Welch, say sharply, "God damn you, Matthew."

"Am *I* to blame?" the Selectman angrily retorted, "From what I hear, some of you people got careless down here."

"We'll see about that," the big man said. "We'll tend to that in its own time."

"How many got away?" the Selectman asked.

"We'll settle up accounts when it comes time to send out the bills," Uncle Anak said.

"What are you all standing around this way for?" the Selectman shouted. "Do you want to lose them all? Get back to your positions and let's at least keep the ones we have!"

The drivers, with a sudden amazing sheepish obedience, resumed their line.

■

As HESTER MOVED UP the funnel, with the line constantly shrinking, so that Coit on the one side and Uncle Anak on the other closed more and more with her, she felt, above everything else, a heavy apprehension, a presentiment of something from which she would surely have to run away. She tried for a time to attract Coit's attention without getting Anak Welch's as well, for she wanted at least to make a reproachful face at Coit, and thereby somehow seem to justify herself; but the thickset, good-looking young man kept his eyes forward in an excess of conscientiousness, as if, by God, no woodchuck would ever get away from an alert young fellow like him.

The drive up the funnel was no work at all, and soon the line grew so tight that people began to drop out of it, and Hester, feeling very weak, was one of the first to resign. Toward the end a dozen men were all who stood pickets, and in due course they reached the gate—only ten feet across—and shut it, and then lifted planks off a ditch that traversed the opening, rolled the gate-wire down onto it, and filled it with dirt to complete the deep-fence around the enclosure.

The count was soon reported. There were but thirty-seven woodchucks in the corral.

They were such cheerful-looking, rotund animals!—only thirty-seven in number.

Hester, who had her eyes and ears open, neither observed nor overheard any further consultation among the drivers, but, as if some kind of agreement had been sealed between them in meditation, silence, and shared lunacy, a group of them went straight to the Selectman when the drive was over, and following closely, Hester heard Anak Welch say, "Matthew, I've got to tell you that we're very pent up at you."

"I don't blame you," the Selectman said. "I don't blame you."

Then Hester saw the Selectman's face—dark, weary, defeated, abject he was. Only thirty-seven woodchucks!

An annoyed crowd had gathered around in a moment, and its swaying, its almost breathing together, its palpable unified mob-life showed that a rumor had already run its course.

"We've decided we've got to take it out on you," the huge man said, obviously given courage by the many-eyed febrile entity around him.

"I can't say I blame you," the Selectman said, head down.

"You were very wrong," Mrs. Tuller said with a tight mouth and ice-pick eyes.

"Let's not discuss it right now," the Selectman said, raising defiant eyes and aiming them at the schoolteacher, whose gaze grew blunt and dropped. "What do you intend to do?" he asked Anak Welch.

Now it was the giant's turn to be abashed. He cleared his throat with a tiger's rumble. "We had thought," he said with extraordinary mildness, "of a scourging."

There was an excited indrawing of breath by some of the drivers who had not previously heard this thrilling news. The Selectman was silent awhile; he looked at the ground. Then dully he said, "Does Judge Pitkin know about this?"

"You're thinking about legality?" Anak Welch asked.

"I just hold the opinion that the Town Counsel should know about it."

"I'm here," said Judge Pitkin's voice at the edge of the crowd, in an unmistakable tone of adherence to the popular opinion.

"Oh, you here, Judge?" the Selectman asked with a calmness that gave Hester a chill.

"We want to be fair, Matthew," Uncle Anak said with a disgusting, shameful affection in his voice. "We realize there ain't been a floggin' in Tunxis for I-don't-know-how-many seasons. But—but—"

"We've taken as much as we're going to take," Mrs. Tuller said for the hesitant giant, and for all.

"Let's get it over and done with," the Selectman said.

Hester wanted to scream out against the mildness and politeness of this talk. She wanted to cry out that the citizens intended to flagellate this man for one thing while he thought they were to punish him for something entirely else. She wanted to protest against his taking on his shoulders the blame for the outcome of this drive, which he had been thinking about and planning for a decade; and against his silly, vapid invocation of the name of the Town Counsel—what a response for a courageous man! She wanted to proclaim his innocence of the gossips' crime, his absolute innocence, and Coit's lack of it; she wanted to announce her own. . . . She was silent.

■

HESTER WONDERED whether Tunxis had ever had such an entertainment as this. The Selectman stood on the lawn not far from the notice board—almost exactly at the spot where she herself had waited in the fog that morning so many experiences ago—and he gravely stared into an infinity that seemed nested in a sugar-maple tree across the way; he seemed to be gazing at mysteries, at the deepest paradoxes of life, whilst the townspeople busied themselves with happy, constructive errands of preparation. Rulof Pitkin was sent whirling off in his truck to Leamings' Service Station to get a big pair of lug wrenches to take the notice board down with. Manly Sessions had gone away in his Chevrolet for a length of rope. Four clustered male elders of the town, exuding the sweet gravity of mortuary attendants, consulted in low voices as to where they might find a suitable instrument of their will. "Say!" exclaimed George Challenge in a subdued proud thin whine that surely carried to the Selectman's ears, as it did to Hester's equidistant ones. "Don't Alenum Rust have the very thing on that buckboard he keeps paintin' every year? Seems to me the stock is light and the lash good and short." "That sounds like just the ticket," Judge Pitkin rumblingly concurred. Hester saw the vast mouth stir in Anak Welch's troubled face, but she could not hear the words that emerged—if, indeed, any did. Coit was sent off on a motorcycle to get Rust's whip. Cars, mostly containing womenfolk, kept driving up, and Hester could imagine what a cheery tintinnabulation of phone calls must be hurrying round the town. Soon Hester even saw Aunty Dorcas, given a lift to the common by a kind-hearted friend, moving with her eyes shrewdly narrowed among the whispers that flew on praying-mantis wings from head to head—Aunty Dorcas, oh! so afraid of a sparrow on her sill, but not of this; afraid neither of death nor of this, hardy old lady. Mrs. Tuller, teacher of innocent children, believer in counter-irritants, kept shaking her huge head with what seemed to be regret—regret, was it, of her disastrous hysterical charge among the woodchucks, or of the necessity (pressed by other folks, mind you!) of punishing Matthew Avered for what she had seen with her own naked eyes? George Challenge, no weasel to be napping now, was going around on his parenthetical legs canvassing opinion for future reference in political conclave. Friedrich Tuller of the crystal spangles, after his one brief protest down by the enclosure, had by now busied himself with conformity, and was, at one moment when Hester glimpsed him, standing on the whipping platform sucking a forefinger and making the face of one stricken, for, in helpfully removing thumbtacks from the notices on the bulletin board, he had apparently sprung a fingernail from its quick. Pale Pliny Forward, intent upon science, tried to start a discussion with the Selectman on what had gone wrong with the drive, but the Selectman seemed deaf as a wedge of cheese.

Hester fought her silence all along. She wanted to speak up ... but it would do no good, she kept telling herself. The village of Tunxis would simply vent one big unanimous guffaw at such interested testimony as hers would be. There was no chance of changing the course of things. There was something inexorable at work here, something on old iron rails that could not be turned aside; so she told herself. Besides (what a confused and mean comfort!), why was the Selectman so passive? Was he really somehow guilty of something? Why did he stare that way? Why didn't he fight? Coit had become a kind of hero now. His was the prize errand; he was astride his snorting two-wheeled machine, fetching the whip. He was a strong young man—maybe they would let him swing it, too. No! That would be too much! Hester swore to herself that if Coit were appointed to do the flogging, she would surely cry out.

Eben walked past, apparently moving for the sake of motion. He seemed to have been suddenly set back into a gawky adolescence; his face was even faintly blotched, as if about to succumb to a miserable acne.

"How can you stand by and let them do this?" Hester hissed at him.

"You're a fine one to talk," Eben said with a ferocity that was staggering. Hester felt that this must be a day of unburdenings.

"But your father didn't do a thing to me," she protested, appalled by Eben's fierce face. "I swear, Eben, he was just taking a speck out of my eye."

Eben looked tempted to believe; in need of belief; tempted and awfully torn. "Why didn't you fix up a better story?" he bitterly asked.

Rulof Pitkin returned, and several men worked at detaching the notice board from the whipping post. They threw each other occasional masculine morsels of advice and congratulation; the work went splendidly. A few drops of penetrating oil, a heave here and a counter-ho there, and soon the job was done. Four men carried the heavy bulletin board—Friedrich Tuller (what was it he'd said he'd come here looking for sixteen years before?) lugged at one corner in what appeared to be an ecstasy of accepted helpfulness, not foreign at all now, a real Tunxisman—and they leaned it carefully against the front wall of the Grange Hall. Then Coit was back, showing the whip to the elders, one by one; each nodded in sober admiration.

Hester's heart was on the run. She would just wait until Coit climbed up to the platform, then ... If she could but survive that long! She could hear the shushing of blood in her ears; her heart hurried toward toward toward toward toward toward ...

They were leading the Selectman to the platform; he had that faraway staring look in his eyes. He climbed the steps and stood there waiting. Judge Pitkin, standing on the ground in front of the platform, leaned forward and murmured to him, but the Selectman did not hear, so Judge Pitkin spoke louder; the Selectman leaned forward and Judge Pitkin mouthed something into his ear. The Selectman straightened up, turned facing the post, and removed his shirt. How softly white the skin of his strong back below the copper of his neck!

Anak Welch, holding the small coil of manila that

Manly Sessions had brought, climbed the steps and, while the Selectman agreeably held high his hands, the huge man, for whom this was no reach at all, lashed the wrists together and made them fast to the post. Roswell Coit stood at the foot of the stairs tapping the looped-back gad against his calf. Hester decided she was as ready as ever she would be.

Then Anak Welch went down the steps and took the whip out of Coit's hand and turned round, with an agonized expression on his face, the veins standing inflated on his wide forehead, and climbed back up again.

Anak Welch was going to do the work. Hester felt a surge of sickening relief. How could she protest now?

She looked around her, and saw the eyes of the natives bulging with delight, terror, and foul hope.

She ran.

She hid behind the trunk of a huge New England elm. Over the hushed heads on the green, Anak Welch's anguished voice came rolling: "I hope this'll be for the good of all of us, Matthew."

Hester did not hear any more because of the pressure on her ears of her vomiting.

■

AFTERWARDS everyone seemed to go out of his way to be nice to the Selectman, who, when he descended from the platform, still wore his faraway look; George Challenge told him he'd taken his castor oil like a man, and Anak Welch threw an arm around his shoulders. Hester, back among the crowd and watching again almost in spite of herself, had a peculiar feeling that these gestures were far from friendly; they seemed to represent some kind of clearing away of loathsome thoughts, some kind of hand-washing, and there was even, she thought, a hint of anger in them, as if to indicate that the Selectman should at least have whimpered under the wrath of the community.

"We'd better get down there and do away with the groundhogs before they start a-burrowing," the Selectman mildly said.

That quiet remark called for a picnic atmosphere among the townsfolk, who rushed to load themselves in the trucks and chattered and laughed and winked at each other. "Come on," Mrs. Tuller said to Hester, with a jovial, forgiving air, "let's go down and watch." Hester let herself be drawn along.

At the enclosure, Hester quickly saw that the thirst of Tunxis had not yet been slaked. Later, thinking back on what happened at the corral after the scourging, she guessed that the Selectman must have displayed an unbearably shaming nobility on the platform by the common, so that by the time the witnesses of that bearing had reached the woodchuck enclosure, they must have felt the choice of demolishing the man once and for all or feeling utterly ruined themselves.

"Who's going to help me kill these animals?" the Selectman asked, holding out before him and offering to a taker one of a pair of machetes he had brought. "We'll need about six people for a line," he said, "to corner 'em."

No one moved.

The Selectman looked around and evidently began to see what he was up against—but only began, dimly and unclearly, to see, for his locked mind was obviously on the work to be done. Still holding out the knife, pinching it by the blade so that someone could take the free handle, he glanced around at the faces near him and for some time seemed to expect a response, but no one moved, for the figures of the Tunxis people were frozen in a tableau of clenched wills.

At last the Selectman turned, with a slightly puzzled look, shrugging, and said over his shoulder, "If nobody'll waltz with me, I'll have to waltz alone." He dropped one of the brush knives beside the gate and, putting a foot up on one of its cross braces, vaulted into the enclosure, swinging the huge knife he had kept in his hand in a wide blue-flashing arc through the air as he jumped. He walked slowly toward the cluster of woodchucks at the center of the fenced-in square.

Coit was the first to laugh. From the beginning it was clear that the Selectman's situation was intolerable, and that he should never have let himself into it. He simply did not have the physical equipment to come upon these sly animals and destroy them all by himself. They were too many for him, too agile, and they had too much room to move about in. He seemed dazed and clumsy; they balked him and misled him and escaped him. He would make a stealthy, almost tiptoed approach, then would break into a sudden short rush and chop at—nothing. He became suddenly ludicrously angry, and when, at the end of one of his charges, he brought the machete whirling downward and again missed the scrambling animals and only split some sod, Coit laughed.

Then others did, too. There began to be a quiet little ripple of giggles after each frustrated rush, and then, as in his jerky, petulant dashes the Selectman grew red and wild-eyed, outright haws and roars began to be sprung.

The unhearing Selectman, culminating in his lonely onslaughts ten years of planning for this happy hour, evidently heard nothing, saw nothing, felt nothing but the need to destroy woodchucks.

Soon some of the Tunxis people had stitches under their ribs, and rocking, they gripped their waists to ease the pain of laughing.

Hester had bad trouble pushing down her own risibility, and once she caught a glimpse of Eben, letting up out of his mouth a little irrepressible laugh every so often; looking at him she was reminded of a pot lid occasionally jumping and releasing vapor and settling back again. Hester was far beyond protesting now, beyond even the sort of anger that engenders protest, as, clutched by some inner paralysis, she trembled on the silent edge of laughter.

The Selectman killed a woodchuck, caught it on the spine and cleft it in a ghastly, powerful, red-soaked whisk.

A few townspeople emitted a quiet "Aah!", but Coit led others in a laughing cheer; and when the Selectman missed his next stroke, the laughter was redoubled.

Soon the Selectman began to adjust his eye and his arm to the needs of his task, and he managed, not without many failing rushes, to kill another, and another, and others. A regular rhythm of laughter and mocking cheers was established. The Selectman seemed to hear none of that.

Mrs. Tuller, standing beside Hester in the audience outside the enclosure, paused in her laughing, wiped tears from her cheeks with the heels of her hands, and said, "Mercy me! Sometimes I wonder."

Coit, on the other side of Hester, gasped between laughs, "This is rich."

"What a fine person he is! Whenever there's nasty work to be done in Tunxis," Mrs. Tuller said, shaking with mirthful delight at her own heavy irony, "you

can depend on it, he'll be the one to do it for us."
She pointed at the Selectman and rode off again on
derision.

"Maybe," Coit said, fighting his bubbling laughter,
"maybe his heart's as warm as ever a flame,
ma'am—ho! ho! look!—but right now he's up to his
ass in blood."

"Roswell!" Mrs. Tuller said, sniggering as she
looked round at him. "You have the tongue of a serpent."

"You should've heard me when I was in the service," he said. "I'm nothin' but Casper Milquetoast
now." And as the Selectman killed an animal, " 'Ray!
'Ray!" Coit shouted.

Then in one of his unsuccessful clumsy sallies the
Selectman rushed close to the fence behind which the
main body of drivers stood in their hilarious condition. In this instance, a sharp burst of laughter
greeted the Selectman's failure, especially as he stumbled slightly, with a little besotted stagger, when he
made his futile lunge with the brush knife. Regaining
his balance he stood straight, not a dozen feet from
the fence, and, in a sudden lapse of his concentration
on the animals, he focused his eyes on the crowd,
took in the grimaces of his townspeople, heard their
pealing, and seemed for the first time to understand
something of what was happening to them and to
him. Hester saw the awful sting of recognition spread
across his face.

For a moment his lips trembled; it seemed as if his
face would crumple under the wrench of sudden overwhelming pain. Hester was positive, without having
seen, that no such expression had touched his face on
the platform in front of the Grange.

In a pathetic voice, a voice denuded of authority
and maturity, a voice without even the dignity of

penance done or of regret or of apology, he pleaded, "Won't somebody help me?"

The obdurate crowd was silent but for a few coasting murmurs of laughter, and no one moved; no one made a move to help.

A small pack of woodchucks seemed to be gathering not far from the Selectman, as if to rush at his legs, and someone cackled, "Watch out! Watch out for them groundhogs!"

The Selectman whirled. The pack moved toward him with rattling jaws. At first, instead of driving forward into the ridiculous posse, the Selectman backed away with a jarring timorousness; at last he made a half-hearted dash which scattered the animals.

The Selectman resumed his lorn work, and the townspeople tried again to laugh as merrily as they had before, but the lift had gone out of their effort. Still coursing erratically here and there, the Selectman seemed to have grown terribly tired, and he wore an expression of awful, incipient comprehension. He had destroyed perhaps thirteen or fourteen woodchucks, and now that he had no taste for it, he was learning craft in this unsavory contest and was having enough success so that it could be seen that with the help of half a dozen men to help condense the animals, the destruction would fairly quickly have been done with. He did not look at the crowd again. People began to drift away and go home.

■

WHILE EBEN WENT UPSTAIRS for the suitcases, Hester stood awkwardly with the Selectman and Mrs. Avered in the parlor. The Selectman was sitting in a straight chair, and Mrs. Avered stood protectively beside it. In the presence of his son and of Hester, the

Selectman had scrupulously and with hair-raising detachment told his wife everything that had happened to him—making it clear that he understood he had suffered all of it because of the failure of the drive. Hester had not been inclined to elaborate his understanding on that point, and Eben had merely glared at her. Mr. Avered had told the others that Anak Welch had suggested he ought to resign as First Selectman, and as to that, the Selectman had told his family he thought he would wait two or three days, let the tops fall off the waves, but he supposed he would have to go through with it. "You know, when Anak gets his mind set on an idea," he had said, with the haunting calmness of a man who has made several starts in the world, "you can't budge him with a team of workhorses. He's like a damnable stump of oak."

"We'll see," Mrs. Avered had said, evidently prepared to pick up and try to use whatever time might leave on her doorstep, "we'll see."

"One thing, though," the Selectman had said, with a brief and incongruous burst of intrepidity, "I'd awful much like to get some folks to go out there and do that drive over again. We know now how to manage it; we'd have that hollow cleaned out before you could say Jack-Be-Nimble."

"For God's sake, Father!" Eben had said with the vehemence that comes from shame. "Don't you know when you're licked?"

"I'd hazard a guess," the Selectman had said, his head tilted to one side, "that if you'd give me some time, give me a couple of years, you know how the years soften things and blur things . . ."

"No, no, Matthew," Mrs. Avered said, applying a palm to her husband's forehead and stroking it, as if to soothe an invalid, "leave the woodchucks be. Don't fret about going back in the hollow just yet. Leave them be awhile."

Hester felt weak, and there was a lingering bouquet of bile on her palate. Now, while Eben clattered upstairs, she experienced a sudden revulsion, and this revulsion produced in her mind a decision: She would not marry Eben Avered. At first she attributed this strangely comforting conclusion to a contempt she felt for Eben, based upon what she had taken in during the weekend, fruit of an accumulation of glimpses at an Eben she had never clearly seen before. Then slowly, with increasing discomfort, she began to wonder whether that feeling might not have been projected, whether the true target of her scorn might not be her own pitiful self; and fearfully she admitted the possibility that her decision about Eben was a decision to flee from the afternoon she had just experienced, to fly away from what she had learned about herself, to run away from the face of the son of the Selectman, to escape the Selectman's image, never to see the Selectman's face again and all its reminders, never to be visited again by the memory of her failure to loose the shouts that had lain beside her tongue ready for utterance that afternoon. And then, as her horror and disgust grew, she was rattled by a shudder very much like those she had suffered in the chill fog of the early morning before all this had happened, when she had been standing in the vague dawn not knowing really where she was; for she knew that even if she did not marry Eben, she would always henceforth be on the run, pursued by the Erinyes of the marmot drive.

"Why, child!" Mrs. Avered said. "You're white as the driven snow. Matthew! The girl's tired to death! Wouldn't you like a wee glass of winkum, my dear, to comfort you on the road?"

—

"No, thanks," Hester said. "I'll be all right in a minute."

Eben came down. He dropped the bags in the hall and joined the others in the parlor. Hester knew, looking at him, that she loved him as well as she could love anyone, and she felt a stab of compassion and perplexity and regret. She stepped toward the Selectman, who remained seated, and she wanted to say she was sorry if she'd—if she'd. . . . But what could she say? The Selectman did not know yet what had happened to him, or truly why, and only a few moments ago she had begun to be struck, for the first time, the first surely of many times, by the full force of what had happened to herself during the woodchuck drive. She said a flat goodbye. It had no love in it, and she was sorry. She shook Mrs. Avered's phlegmatic hand. As she went to the front door she saw that the wooden cogwheels out of the clock were still on the floor in the hall.

SPECIAL OFFER: If you enjoyed this book and would like to have our catalog of over 1,400 other Bantam titles, just send your name and address and 25¢ (to help defray postage and handling costs) to: Catalog Department, Bantam Books, Inc., 414 East Golf Rd., Des Plaines, Ill. 60016.

ABOUT THE AUTHOR

JOHN HERSEY was born in Tientsin, China, in 1914, and lived there until 1925, when his family returned to the United States. He was graduated from Yale in 1936 and attended Clare College, Cambridge University, for a year. He was private secretary to Sinclair Lewis during a subsequent summer and then worked as a journalist and war correspondent. His first novel, *A Bell for Adano*, won the Pulitzer Prize in 1945, and the next year he wrote *Hiroshima*, an account of the first atomic bombing. Since 1947 he has devoted his time mainly to fiction and has published *The Wall* (1950), *The Marmot Drive* (1953), *A Single Pebble* (1956), *The War Lover* (1959), *The Child Buyer* (1960), *White Lotus* (1965), *Too Far to Walk* (1966), and *Under the Eye of the Storm* (1967). *The Algiers Motel Incident*, an account of violence in the Detroit riot of 1967, was published in 1968. *Letter to the Alumni*, published in 1970, was the culmination of Mr. Hersey's five years as Master of Pierson College at Yale. Mr. Hersey spent the year 1970–71 as Writer-in-Residence at the American Academy in Rome. He now lives with his family in New Haven, Connecticut.

Great reading experiences

by

Pulitzer Prize winner

John Hersey

☐	THE MARMOT DRIVE	7468	$1.75
☐	HIROSHIMA	2827	$1.25
☐	A BELL FOR ADANO	2672	$1.25
☐	THE WALL	2569	$2.25
☐	THE CHILD BUYER	2318	$1.50
☐	WHITE LOTUS	2267	$1.95

Buy them at your local bookstore or use this handy coupon for ordering:

Bantam Books, Inc., Dept. JH, 414 East Golf Road, Des Plaines, III. 60016

Please send me the books I have checked above. I am enclosing $_____
(please add 35¢ to cover postage and handling). Send check or money order
—no cash or C.O.D.'s please.

Mr/Mrs/Miss_____

Address_____

City_____State/Zip_____

JH—6/76

Please allow three weeks for delivery. This offer expires 6/77.